The Foundling, the Heist, and the Volcano

The Azure Archipelago, Volume 2

K.R.R. Lockhaven

Published by Shadow Spark Publishing, 2023.

THE FOUNDLING, THE HEIST, AND THE VOLCANO

First edition. January 20, 2023.

Written by K.R.R. Lockhaven.

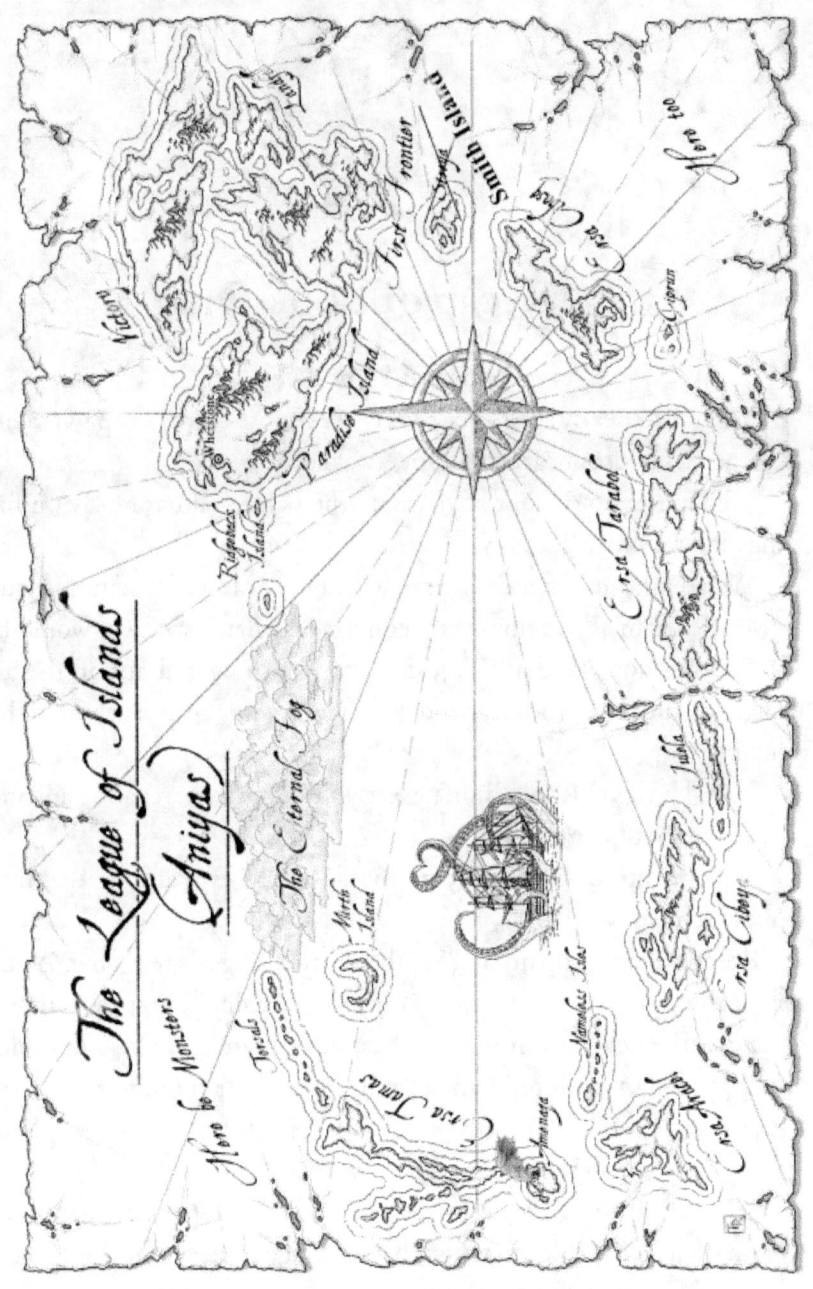

The League of Islands

Aniyas

Recap of Book One

Robin's Love Nest

Robin had nearly sunk into sweet, sweet post-coitus sleep when her partner, a handsome green parrot, awakened her.

"Tell me again of your adventure," the parrot said as he lay on his back, wings spread wide. "Please?"

"You're not just spending time with me because I'm semi-famous, now, are you?" Robin asked, not overly concerned what his answer would be.

"No. It's not like that. It's just that I like to hear about all the amazing things you did. I like the clear and concise way you recap everything that happened."

"Alright, then." Robin didn't exactly shy away from regaling anyone within earshot about her exploits.

"Thank you so much." The parrot closed his eyes and nestled into their makeshift nest.

Robin cleared her throat. "So, the whole thing started when Azure's dad joined this lame inaugural cruise thing with Reginald Pratt just after he was elected as the new governor of the League of Islands. Azure and I joined the cruise at the last minute in an attempt to save her tumultuous relationship with her father."

"Why was it so tumultuous?"

"He was all into Governor Pratt's 'Humans First' politics, and Azure couldn't stand that shit. Her mom had died at a protest that this Pratt asshole had organized in hopes to turn away refugee fauns from the Nameless Isles, where we lived.

"Anyway, we found out pretty quick that Governor Pratt was an even bigger prick than we had thought. There was obviously something nefarious going on, but we didn't know what it was quite yet.

"There were some murders on board, and Azure defended this talking skeleton, Elijah, and a gorgeous ciguapa woman named Brisa. She asked for a 'Trial at Sea,' and all of us ended up being marooned on this tiny island."

"Is this where the marauders come in?" he asked, eyes still closed.

"Alright, for one thing, let me tell the story. I was starting to get into a flow. And for another thing, you know damn well this is where the marauders come in, or has our little romp muddled your brain?"

"Little romp?"

Robin sighed. "I didn't mean anything by that. You were great. Fantastic, even." She knew males were easy to shut up. She just had to massage their fragile egos a bit.

"So, yes, the marauders, a group of pirates who would rather sing and have adventures than do any real pirating, swung by and picked us up.

"We learned we'd probably need some kind of Old Magic or some shit on Dragon Island, so we went there and awakened this idiot dragon named Zoth-Avarex. The dragon reluctantly agreed to help us rescue Azure's dad, but only because there was something in it for him."

"I still can't believe you met an actual dragon."

Robin took a deep, calming breath and continued.

"We tracked down the governor's ship, and Azure was captured. That was horrible. I'd never been so scared in my life.

"Governor Pratt awakened this horrible leviathan, and came damned close to ruling over the League of Islands. But, of course, we beat him, due in large part to me viciously pecking this guy's eye out. It was pretty badass, and also disgusting." Robin shuttered, remembering the taste of Paul Sancti's eyeball. "And that's about it." She shrugged, even though he couldn't see her.

"But that was almost too clear and concise," he said dreamily. "I was hoping for more."

"Well, you can hope in one foot, shit in the other, and see which one fills up first."

Robin wasn't sure if he heard her quip, because he didn't respond.

"Alright, a lot of other shit happened throughout our adventure. A kraken attacked the galleon we were on, and there was this curse of Dragon Island that we had to overcome, which involved falling meteors, giant tidal waves, and that kind of shit. Elijah, the skeleton, became a normal human again after a different curse was broken. Well, normal might not be the right word, because he's hot as shit, now. Did I tell you that he and Azure are engaged, now, too?"

Again, no response.

"I had some wonderful babies, who have all fledged and gone off on their own adventures. Oh, and Azure made up with her dad."

The parrot's breathing had become suspiciously deep and regular. Robin nudged him with a wing, and found him to be asleep.

Oh well. This would preclude any awkward goodbyes.

Robin took wing and made what Azure jokingly referred to as a *morning flight of shame* back to the *Adventure Ship*.

PART ONE
THE FOUNDLING

Homecoming

Azure sprinted to starboard, leaned over the rail, and threw up into the sea. She hoped no one aboard would notice.

Feeling much better already, she lay her head on the smooth rail, warmed pleasantly by the morning sun, and closed her eyes. She focused her attention, listening for any sounds that indicated she'd been seen by a member of the crew. After a handful of heartbeats, she felt confident she was in the clear. She pushed herself up, happy to not have to explain herself.

"Uh oh, Captain," came Blunderbuss's booming voice from the crow's nest above, making Azure cringe, "it's not a case of morning sickness, is it?"

Azure was absolutely sure it wasn't the thing he hinted at, because her fiancé Elijah held to frustratingly traditional values, and they had not been legally married, yet. She didn't begrudge him, though. He had spent a hundred years stuck in the form of a walking, talking skeleton. She didn't expect him to change his values overnight, although some nights she really wished he would.

"No, ya nosy bastard." She looked up at him, wiping her mouth with her coat sleeve. "Just overdid it with the rum last night." She tried her best stern look. "Now why don't you get your non-existent ass down here and make us some damn breakfast?"

"Aye, Captain." He chuckled to himself as he descended the rigging. "I'm sorry."

Azure shook her head as he passed into the galley.

Robin floated down from amongst the sails and alighted on Azure's shoulder.

"So, it's not morning sickness, then?" she said in a low voice.

"No, Robin. You know how stubborn Elijah has been. And we aren't even thinking about kids yet, anyway."

"Well, you never know." She shrugged her wings. "There's always a chance he'd give in and sneak a dinghy past the embargo. I mean, I don't know how he resists you. Your ass has never looked better if you ask me."

"Thanks, Robin." She smiled, shaking her head. "I really just drank too much last night. I guess I'm a little nervous about going home."

"Afraid your dad will be back to his old ways?" Robin cocked her head, knowingly.

"Yeah." Azure gazed out ahead, just able to see the white cliffs where The Red Dragon Inn sat, the Ring arcing up from it like a magical beacon guiding her home "It's just, we made so much progress. I don't want any of that to go away."

Robin nuzzled her ear, always able to say or do the perfect thing for Azure in her anxious moments.

It had been nearly a year since she had last seen her dad, and a lot had happened in that time. Robin's clutch of eggs had produced a brood of noisy hatchlings, all of which had fledged and flown away to seek their own lives and adventures. Mr. Cordingly, the old Sailing Master, had settled down on First Frontier with his wife and his new son, Brighton. The Marauder King's musical had been picked up by a prestigious theater troupe in Whetstone, and become an instant hit. There weren't too many places left in the League of Islands where you couldn't hear someone whistling or singing one of the songs from the play, especially Nargol and Orok's raunchy little ditty.

Nargol and Orok's daughter, baby Morgak—or was it toddler Morgak, now? —was a delight to have on the ship. Apparently, orcs matured much faster than humans, as little Morgak wasn't so little anymore, and she spoke like an eight-year-old as far as Azure could tell. It was a joy and an honor to be so close to her as she grew up. Every time the little orc called her Aunty Azure, she couldn't keep a smile from her face.

When the Marauder King left the Adventure Ship to run the play he wrote, the remaining crew held a vote. Much to her surprise, and due in large part to Mr. Threepbrush campaigning for her, Azure was unanimously elected as the new Captain. Mr. Threepbrush was elected as the new Quartermaster, and Syl was promoted to Sailing Master.

Azure still wasn't used to the idea that she was actually the Captain of a ship. She didn't think she'd ever be used to it. The honor was overwhelming, and she was extremely thankful, but imposter syndrome had plagued her ever since that day. Everyone else on the crew, aside from Robin, knew volumes more about sailing than she did. They had so much more invaluable experience on the sea than her.

Still...they had elected her. She must have been worthy in some way, at least a bit.

As a thank you, she had purchased a rosewood wand for every one of the crew members, and was teaching them how to use magic, with varying levels of success.

"Shall we make for the dock, Captain?" Syl's warm voice—heavily accented—followed the familiar click-clack of his hooves on the deck.

"Er...yes. Set a course for the docks...please." Azure's face flushed as she gave the ridiculous instructions.

"Aye, aye." Syl flashed her a playful grin devoid of any judgement.

As the ship slowed to a stop at the bay's only dock, Azure took in the humble sights of Barren, her hometown. Seemingly nothing had changed. The place still possessed a sleepy charm, the untroubled serenity that rested on the surface of most small towns. Unfortunately, Azure knew that looks were deceiving. The undercurrent of bigotry, she was sure, was still alive and well, here.

"You ready?" Azure felt the strong hand of her fiancé on her shoulder.

"As ready as I'll ever be."

Elijah kissed her on the forehead. "You want me to stay on the ship? I mean, I'll probably say something stupid in front of your dad and embarrass both of us." His confidence had come a long way since the days when he was a reanimated skeleton, but he still had a lot of work yet to do.

"Of course not. And you're not the one I'm worried about saying something stupid."

"Well, I'm going to bring him this big sea bass I caught just in case." Elijah held up a large, fresh fish with his other hand. Azure instinctively sniffed the hand on her shoulder but luckily found it to be clean.

Hand in hand, they disembarked, Robin flying close behind. Most of the crew stayed aboard for general repairs, while a small contingent went into town for supplies.

As Azure climbed the steady incline between the dock and the inn, she noticed her thumb was rubbing her forefinger raw. She shook her head and rolled her eyes, feeling silly about her anxiety level. Everything would likely be fine, and all of this worry would be for nothing. Actually, all worry was for nothing. Things either happened, or they didn't, and worrying about them never changed a single thing. Brisa had given her that little nugget of wisdom. But it was much easier to know it was true than to feel its truth at times like this.

Out ahead, a large puddle had formed in the middle of the road. Along the right side of the puddle, a small girl was fishing from it with a makeshift reel. Nostalgia warmed Azure's chest. This tableau had been burned into her mind nearly her entire life. She had seen this on multiple occasions before. She had been that little girl.

There was a legend among the children of Barren, going back to before Azure's time, that catching a puddle fish would bring unbelievably good luck. Azure had found out in her teens that it was a ploy used by parents to keep their kids busy, but close. She had spent countless hours at puddles like that, hoping for the luck and the prestige that would have come from catching the town's first puddle fish.

Azure looked down at the fish in Elijah's hand, and a fully-formed idea swam to the surface.

"Elijah, do you think I could have that fish instead?" She gave him her cutest look.

"Uh...yeah. Of course."

"Robin," Azure said, "could you possibly fly out ahead and distract that little girl from further up the road?"

"Sure." Robin zoomed away. Azure loved how her friend was always so ready to help or get into something, no questions asked.

Azure took the fish and hid it behind her back while Robin began talking to the kid. After asking Elijah to stay put, Azure crept forward.

"What are you doing?" Robin asked the little girl.

"Just trying to catch a puddle fish," she replied. "Mama says it's good luck."

"Oh, well, do you want to see me do a loop-de-loop?"

The girl giggled. "Sure."

Azure reached out, snagged the girl's line, and carefully pulled the hook from the murky water.

"Hey," the girl said, "aren't you that bird that talked to me before?"

"Uh..." Robin hesitated mid loop-de-loop. "Do you talk to a lot of birds?"

Azure pushed the hook through the side of the fish's mouth and slowly lowered it back into the water. Then she hurried back to Elijah.

"No. I've only ever talked to one bird. One night when this lady was cry—"

"I think I just saw your line move," Robin interrupted.

"You did?" The girl was incredulous.

"Yeah."

Excitedly, the girl reeled the line. "It feels different!" she exclaimed. "Heavier!"

As the long-dead fish crested the surface, the girl gave a shout that was equal parts triumph and disbelief.

"Wow," said Robin. "Nice fish."

"Thank you." The little girl placed it gently on the dirt road and looked around, eyes wide.

Azure and Elijah continued to walk toward her as if they'd never broken stride.

"I caught a puddle fish!" she called to them.

"Nice," Azure called back, giving an enthusiastic thumbs-up.

As she approached, Azure noticed it was the same girl—with the berry juice smudge on her cheek— the little girl who had helped Azure come to the conclusion that she should go after her father the night he joined Pratt's voyage. The girl was a bit taller now, but still had that same beautiful smile, bright as a sunbeam.

"If anyone doubts you, tell them to come and ask us at the inn. We saw it happen as we were walking up the road."

The girl nodded to Azure, eyes filled with wonder and shock. Then she grabbed the line in one hand, the rod in the other, and took off toward the dock, shouting the names of every kid in town as she went.

The warmth in Azure's chest intensified.

"Nice work, Robin," Azure said as her friend landed on her shoulder. "I'm sorry I spoiled your gift, Elijah. But my dad probably would have seen it as a shameless bribe anyway."

Elijah smiled, and they continued to the inn.

The Red Dragon Inn

At the door of the inn, Azure took in a sharp breath through her nose and blew it out in a noisy rush. She pushed the door open to find her dad sitting at a far table with his back to her. The table was strewn with loose papers.

The inn radiated comfort. The pleasantly musty scent, mixed with hints of ale and flowers, the tarnished sconces above every table, the cracking walls, adorned with Azure's best childhood artwork.

When the door creaked—that same familiar creak—Azure's dad whipped around, wiping at his face with his sleeve.

"Az!" He ran the sleeve of his other arm across his eyes as nonchalantly as possible as he hurried toward her.

The two of them embraced without a word while Elijah stood in the open doorway with Robin perched on his shoulder.

"Dad...Elijah and I have something to tell you," she said after they had stepped back from each other.

"That is, sir. If it's okay with you...John. Er...sir." Elijah all but groveled as he let the door close behind him.

Azure noticed the red in her dad's eyes but decided to address it later. "We're getting married," she said. The words were still strange to her. She was sure she wanted to marry Elijah but had never dreamed things would happen so quickly.

There was an awkward silence as John looked Elijah up and down.

Azure held her breath.

Her mind drifted back to the moment she knew she wanted to be with Elijah. She was standing at the starboard rail, just breathing, eyes aimed up, unfocused toward the horizon where the Ring touched down. She noticed his scent first, a pleasant blend of his natural redolence and the old-style soap that only he liked to use. Her pulse rate accelerated just enough to be noticeable. After a sharp inhale, Azure turned to see that Elijah had sidled up near her and rested his forearms on the rail before staring out to sea as well. He glanced her way, flashed a smile, then looked back to the sparkling sea. There they stood, not a word spoken between them, as ocean swells gently rocked the ship. She felt so many things in those moments; peace, comfort, familiarity, excitement. Her pulse sustained its pace, and she wanted nothing more than to slide over and duck under his arm. When he looked at her again with his chipped-tooth, perfect smile and warm, kind eyes, she just knew.

"Well...congratulations!" John's boisterous voice shook her from her reverie. He looked torn between hugging Azure again and shaking Elijah's hand. He ended up doing both, wrapping one arm around his daughter and gripping the hand of his future son-in-law.

Azure breathed a sigh of relief. Then, finding her face way too close to her father's armpit, she squirmed out from between the two men.

The handshake went on for an uncomfortable amount of time. When it finally broke, everyone stood and looked to each other in silence.

"You know, I kinda miss having Thunder Paws around," Robin said, her tone just a bit wistful. "He was a dumb son of a bitch, but I think I actually miss him." She shrugged her wings.

"Yeah," John replied. "I do, too." His gaze dropped down to the floor for a moment, before shooting back up. "Oh! I was going through some of your mom's old stuff," he pointed at the paper-strewn table, "and doing some deep cleaning around this place, and I found something." His face lit up with a giddy expectation.

A jolt of tingling energy started in Azure's chest and diffused into her fingertips.

"What is it?"

John hurried over to the table, grasped something in his hand, and hid it behind his back.

"I know this was really special to you, for a really long time."

Azure's entire body buzzed in anticipation. This couldn't possibly be what she hoped it might be, could it?

"I know we thought it had been lost forever," her dad continued. "But I found it underneath the bottom drawer of your old desk. It had fallen through a split in the wood. I'd have never found it if I didn't take the drawer completely out, which wasn't easy."

Azure's heart thumped.

"It's broken, a bit, but still mostly intact." He began to move his hand out from behind his back. "I still remember the day she gave this to you..."

He slowly stretched out the fingers of his closed hand, revealing a small metal ship's wheel attached to a simple leather string.

Tears welled up in Azure's eyes as a flood of memories washed over her. In her mind, she could see her mom's face as she handed the necklace to her, looking up at her with eyes as blurry then as they were now. She could hear her mom's voice, soothing and sweet.

"Never mind what he said," Azure's mom had told her in private. "You'll find as you grow up that men can be completely clueless sometimes." She had flashed her a warm smile that made Azure feel like a member of an exclusive group. "You can be anything you want to be, Az. Don't ever let anyone tell you otherwise."

As Azure rubbed the ship's wheel where one of the handles had broken off, she thought back to that day. While fishing from Barren's dock, Azure had told her father that she wanted to be a ship's captain when she grew up. He had chuckled, tousled her hair, and told her it would never happen. "I'm sorry, Az," he had said when he noticed her starting to tear up, "but it's just not a job for a young woman. I don't intend to be mean, but I want you to be realistic about these matters. There are so many other things that you could do with your life. I don't think you should waste your time on impossible dreams." He had given her a look that showed her he really cared, but his message had been devastating. Before that moment, nothing had seemed impossible.

Azure had lost the necklace sometime in her teens, sometime after her mom had allowed her mind to be poisoned by Reginald Pratt, and sometime after her mom had died at an anti-faun protest. The loss of the necklace was at least as devastating as the loss of innocence on the docks that day. But now it was back. Azure clutched the ship's wheel to her chest, then wiped away a few tears.

"She always believed in you," her dad said. "Even when…" He couldn't quite get the words out. "And look at you now."

"I'm the captain of a ship." There was no accusation in her voice.

Her dad's smile shone with pride and self-reproach. He reached out for an embrace but stopped short when a sizable black bird flashed in through the sea-facing window and alighted noisily on one of the tables.

"Shoo!" John called, flicking his hands at the bird. "Get out of here, ya stupid crow."

"I am most definitely not a common crow, and I will not be shooed away like some kind of pest!" the bird said, its voice haughty and regal. "My name is Sir Terry." He accentuated the word *sir*. "I belong to the noble race of ravens, the most dignified beings in this, or any other world." He raised his beak high in the air. "A crow is to a raven what lead is to gold. The two are simply not comparable."

"Okay. I'm sorry, sir." John said *sir* somewhat mockingly.

"I have come here from across the sea to bri—" When Sir Terry noticed Robin, he stopped, his beak dropping open. He shook off his shock fairly quickly, but it was still noticeable. "I am here to bring a message from Amenaza Island."

"To whom?" John asked.

"Captain Azure Brine." The raven bowed to Azure with impressive grace.

Azure stepped forward. "What's the message?"

Sir Terry gave Robin a quick glance. Robin dipped her head and fidgeted on Elijah's shoulder.

"I bring tidings from a human by the name of Wakeman Carlyle. He was a crew member aboard Captain Roberts' ship for upwards of twenty years."

A jolt ran down Azure's spine. "What does he want with me?"

"He wishes to offer you and your crew a potentially lucrative venture."

The raven paused, dramatically, while Azure stared into his shiny black eyes.

"You see, there is a treasure buried on Amenaza Island. A treasure that Mr. Carlyle buried there himself many years ago. He is extremely embarrassed about this turn of events, so your discretion is of the utmost importance whether or not you take this job, but he is presently unable to locate his buried treasure." Sir Terry cleared his throat. "If you are able to find this treasure, Mr. Carlyle is prepared to give you twenty percent of what's inside."

"How much does he figure is inside?" Azure asked.

"At least one hundred pieces of gold, probably more."

Robin whistled, and Azure's eyes widened. Twenty pieces of gold was a great haul. It was much more than they would get for transporting goods across the Mirror Sea.

Azure looked to Robin, who nodded enthusiastically, and Elijah, who shrugged.

"We'll do it."

"Wonderful." The raven bowed again. "I shall depart and tell Mr. Carlyle of your imminent arrival." Before he took wing, Sir Terry turned to Robin, head cocked to the side. "My lady, I would be remiss if I let this opportunity fly by without acting upon it." He paused; his impeccable grace marred only slightly by apparent nervousness. "Would you be so kind as to reveal your name to me?"

"My name is Robin." She gave an approximation of a curtsey.

"Robin...are you, by any chance, open to suitors?"

"I'm free as a bird," she said.

If ravens could smile, Sir Terry did so. "Well, then...upon your arrival at Amenaza Island, might you be inclined to accompany me for a night of dinner and fine wine?"

Robin shrugged her wings. "Sure. Sounds like a good time to me."

"Then I look forward to your arrival." He gave a final bow before taking off through the open window.

Captain's Log: Ascension 21st, 137

As I started going through the Marauder King's stuff (not because I was being nosy, but because he told me to). I noticed that he kept a regular Captain's Log. He would write in it most days. And it not only described the happenings of each day, but included MK's thoughts and feelings, as well. He has always worn his heart on his sleeve, but I think these logs were another means in which he could express himself in order to relieve the tension of being in charge.

I feel that tension very strongly. I feel so inadequate in this role, and yet, because I have such a strong and capable crew around me, I haven't let these feelings become overwhelming.

I still can't believe the marauders chose me to be their captain. There were so many people who were better suited for the job, and yet here I am. The cynical side of me can't help but think that they gave it to me because no one else wanted it. Mr. Threepbrush, in particular, was very vocal about me being the captain. He says it's due to my performance and quick thinking when we faced Captain Roberts, the most feared pirate in our islands, but I have my doubts. Not that I think it's some nefarious plot, but my self-image won't quite let me believe I've earned this position on merit alone.

Anyway, we've got a mission, now. One the Marauder King would be proud of. An actual treasure hunt! And the gods know we could use the money. Our transition into becoming a merchant ship has been slow going. We haven't yet built up our reputation as a reliable mode of transport for people's goods. I'm confident the contracts will pick up, but in the meantime, this treasure could be just the boost our empty coffers need.

On a more personal note, my dad took the engagement between me and Elijah quite well. I'm glad, but I have to admit a small part of me wanted more...drama, I guess. That sounds ridiculous, but this is all happening so damned fast. I love Elijah. I honestly don't have any complaints about him aside from being slightly annoyed with his outdated moral code regarding...certain things. But sometimes I stop and wonder where my life is going. It seems to barrel along on a trajectory I'm not always sure I chose. Before I met Elijah, when I pictured my future life, it was exactly the life I have, besides the betrothed part. It's not like I thought I'd have a man at every port or anything like that. But I had imagined myself being free from any commitment outside my ship and my crew. I want to reiterate that I love Elijah. I'm almost completely sure I want to marry him, but I'd be lying if I said I didn't have doubts.

Captain Roberts

Azure stepped out from her quarters to find her crew hard at work. The ship gained speed as it pulled away from her hometown, although the winds weren't ideal. Her eyes were drawn immediately to Elijah, who was climbing the rigging on the mizzenmast. She had the urge to go back into her quarters and burn what she had just written.

She didn't have time to give it a second thought, though, because the ship's bell clanged as if someone had attacked it with a war hammer.

"Roberts, Roberts, Roberts!" Orok cried.

Up in the crow's nest, Syl pointed to a spot along the western horizon. Mr. Threepbrush handed her a spyglass as she hurried to the port rail.

The first thing that appeared through the glass was a small ciguapa ship, but as she scanned further south, the unmistakable shape of Captain Roberts' ship came into view, and it was headed right for them.

A dozen thoughts seemed to compete for Azure's attention, the loudest of which told her to flee. They would almost certainly lose in a direct confrontation with Captain Roberts. And even though she had outsmarted him once, she knew that a battle on the open ocean was a horrible idea.

In the back of her mind, she had always been skeptical of the idea that Captain Roberts was afraid of the marauders. She knew this supposed fear stemmed from their friendship with a fire-breathing dragon, but she could never be totally sure that the captain would leave the marauders alone forever. And this, it seemed, was proof that her skepticism was well founded.

"What do you suggest?" she asked her quartermaster.

"I don't think we want a fight with him, Captain."

"I agree."

"But his ship is faster than ours. We can't hope to outrun him, either."

"I could summon Zoth-Avarex," she said, more of a question to herself than anything. The dragon had taught her an incantation that she could use to call him in an emergency. Although this definitely qualified as an emergency, there wasn't enough time for him to come all the way from Dragon Island in time to help.

"Do you think he'd make it in time?" Mr. Threepbrush said, as if reading her thoughts.

"No. Probably not."

She lowered the spyglass and closed her eyes in concentration.

"I know those islands behind us as well as anyone," she said. "Might we have enough time to get lost among them?" They were currently tacking into the wind, but the pirate ship's sails were full as it bore down on them from directly upwind.

"I think that's our best bet, Captain. Would you like me to turn around?"

"Yes. Thank you."

Mr. Threepbrush barked specific orders regarding the sails, then took the wheel. Azure did her best to absorb everything as it happened. She had come a long way in her knowledge of sailing maneuvers and rigging, but there was always more to learn.

Before long, the ship veered to starboard, and the Nameless Isles lay out ahead of them.

Behind them, Captain Roberts was gaining fast. So fast that Azure began to doubt they'd be able to lose him, even among the familiar islands.

"Use every inch of sail until we get close," she told Mr. Threepbrush. "We'll head east around the main island and try to lose him in the smaller ones." She pointed out ahead, eliciting a nod from her quartermaster.

The pirate ship continued to gain on them. It wouldn't be long before the *Adventure Ship* was in range of their chase guns.

As if on cue, a cloud of black smoke issued from the bow of the pirate ship. A fraction of a second later, the boom of the cannon could be heard, then a splash as the ball crashed into the sea, much too close for comfort.

To starboard, they were passing Azure's home island. Just ahead to port, the sheer cliffs of another island loomed up from the water.

"Can we round that island to port?" she said, pointing.

"Yes. But the question is, how tight do I have to make the turn?"

"Tight. There's another island that we can't see yet behind that one."

Mr. Threepbrush called out more orders, and the crew got to work. They began to spill wind, allowing the bottoms of the sails to flutter uselessly. The ship almost immediately began to lose speed.

"Do you think we'll make it?" he asked her, voice as trepidatious as she'd ever heard it.

Azure knew enough about the ship's capabilities to answer the question with a moderate degree of accuracy. At the current speed, she gave them about a fifty-fifty shot of rounding the first island without smashing into the rocks of the next. But if they remained within range of Captain Roberts' guns, their odds were much lower.

"I think it's our best shot."

Mr. Threepbrush gave her a solemn nod, showing a degree of trust that Azure wasn't sure she had earned.

"Nargol," he called. "Or any orc I can get. Come take the wheel!"

Orok was the first to answer the call, tentatively grasping the wheel as Mr. Threepbrush slipped out of the way.

"On my mark, I need you to turn to port as hard as you possibly can."

Orok nodded, his expression uneasy.

Mr. Threepbrush watched the shoreline of the island, gauging when they were clear to make their turn.

"Steady," he said, eyes focused on the water.

Orok stared down at him, muscles twitching in anticipation.

Along the shoreline was the alcove where Azure had her first kiss. It was the perfect place for it, with just enough lush vines hanging down to make a beautiful, even romantic, setting. She remembered her heart had been about ready to thump out of her chest, then, but it was beating even harder, now.

"Turn!" Mr. Threepbrush shouted.

Orok didn't waste a second. He threw the wheel to the left so hard it seemed as if it might shatter into splinters. Fortunately, it stayed intact as he continued to spin it like a child's top.

The ship rolled to the left, causing Azure to throw her hands out to keep her balance.

Another shot rang out from behind them. What would have been a direct hit a moment before, plunged harmlessly into the water.

Azure eyed the island as it came into view ahead of them. It was impossible to tell if the ship was going to make it past, or smash into the jagged rocks along its coast. She held her breath and clenched her jaw as the moment of truth approached. There was a dull scraping sound from the hull below. Azure's heart dropped as she pictured a hole being torn into the ship, but the scraping stopped as soon as it started.

Somehow, they had avoided the worst of the rocks. They were still afloat, and still moving forward.

"Stop turning!" Mr. Threepbrush shouted. "Back to starboard!"

The ship had made the turn but was now in danger of wrecking into the first island.

Orok roared as he corrected the ship's course with all his strength.

"Steady!"

The ship finally passed between the two islands, seemingly undamaged.

Several of the marauders cheered and praised Orok's name, but the mood was quickly dampened as Captain Roberts' ship began to make the same turn.

Unsure how they were able to do it, but without time to consider, Azure formulated another idea as the crew scrambled to put wind in sails again.

To the northeast was a narrow channel created by two tiny islands whose cliff faces stared each other down. It was a place the locals called the Dueling Cliffs, and was frequented by cliff-diving teenagers. But its other name was the Wind Tunnel, as a stiff wind always seemed to be coursing through it, even on calm days. Because of the shape and position of the islands, the wind always blew toward the southwest, so with their current course, they'd be sailing directly into the wind between the cliffs.

"Do you think we can fit between those cliffs?" Azure said.

Mr. Threepbrush studied them, then said, "It'll be tight, but I think we could make it. That is if the water is deep enough."

"It's deep enough," Azure said. "And there's no way Captain Roberts' ship would fit, right?"

"No. If we could get through there, he couldn't follow us."

A cannon ball smashed into the top corner of the stern, completely obliterating a small portion of the ship. Several marauders threw themselves to the deck with their hands covering their heads, but luckily, no one was injured, and the damage to the ship didn't hinder its ability to move.

"Let's go through, then!"

Azure's plan depended on Captain Roberts trying to go around the cliffs and meet the *Adventure Ship* on the other side. She hoped he would imagine a perfect opportunity for a broadside just beyond the channel.

Another shot whizzed by, this one just missing the ship and tumbling into the jungle of the island ahead.

As the marauders neared the start of the channel, Captain Roberts veered to port. Azure felt a wave of relief as her plan, the beginning anyway, was working.

"As soon as they're out of sight, I want to stop as fast as we possibly can."

Mr. Threepbrush nodded. His eyebrows were scrunched together just enough so Azure could tell he wasn't yet seeing the big picture, but he was willing to go with whatever she had in mind.

The Wind Tunnel lived up to its name. As soon as they sailed between the cliffs, the whistling wind pushed back on them.

Off to port, Captain Roberts' ship disappeared behind the island.

Mr. Threepbrush called out instructions, and the crew went to work like ants on a hill.

With a whoosh, the wind filled the sails in the opposite direction, creating a disorienting image above. The ship slowed dramatically, but still kept some forward momentum.

From what Azure could gather, it was a very delicate operation. The crew filled the sails with enough wind to slow the ship down, but not enough to cause any damage to the masts and yards.

"I need all marauders who aren't working the sails on me," Azure said as she sprinted to the bow.

A collection of about six people, led by Brisa, caught up to her at the rail.

"I need your magical energy," Azure said.

Without a word, Brisa reached out and grasped Azure's shoulder. The other marauders did the same. Azure was thankful that they had practiced the technique of combining their magical energy countless times, making the operation near flawless. Everyone around her closed their eyes as they concentrated. Azure felt their energy begin to buzz in her chest as she drew her wand and aimed it out ahead of the ship.

A likeness of the *Adventure Ship* began to materialize between the cliffs. Azure created the illusion piece by piece from memory, hoping the facsimile would look close enough to the real thing. She even remembered to take out the chunk the cannons had just blown away.

When finished, a very lifelike version of their ship floated just ahead of the real one.

With preternatural acceleration, the ghost ship lurched forward. Azure guided it between the cliffs and out the other side as if the Wind Tunnel had been blowing in the opposite direction.

In moments Captain Roberts' ship came into view, pursuing the illusion.

Azure nearly lost concentration as she pictured one of the pirates looking back and discovering the ruse, but not one of them did.

With the combined energy of her crew mates, Azure pushed the ghost ship eastward, out toward the open ocean. The pirate ship continued to follow while firing its chase guns at regular intervals.

As the two ships shrank away, Azure had another idea.

Out ahead, the *Adventure Ship* began to sink into the sea. It dove at a steady pace, submerging the hull up to the rails, then continuing down until all the sails had gone under.

When the ship had completely vanished, Azure broke the illusion and lowered her wand.

"Nice work," Brisa said, giving Azure's shoulder a firm squeeze.

"Thanks." Azure smiled, proud of herself for that one.

Captain Roberts' ship furled their sails, and through the spyglass, Azure saw him staring down into the water from the rail. His conjured gargoyle flew just above his head.

The *Adventure Ship* began to move backwards, and Mr. Threepbrush retook the wheel for the intricate process of backing out from between the cliffs. Azure kept the spyglass trained on Captain Roberts, hoping they wouldn't discover the ship as it backed away.

Now that she had more time to study it, Azure noticed a massive addition to the pirate ship. Mounted near the stern was some sort of giant weapon. It almost looked like a crossbow, but at least fifty times bigger. A giant crossbow bolt was loaded and aimed at the sky.

Was this the reason they were willing to come after the *Adventure Ship*, now? Did they think this crossbow was capable of taking down Zoth-Avarex? She considered the implications as she meandered back to the ship's wheel.

"When we're out of here," Mr. Threepbrush said, still reversing, "would you like us to head back to our original course?"

"Yes, please. And let's do our best to stay out of his view." She pointed toward Captain Roberts, whose ship was no longer visible.

"But, do you think this summons from Mr. Carlyle was a set-up? It seems strange that Roberts attacked as soon as we left for Amenaza Island."

Azure considered his words, upset with herself for not thinking about that already.

"I don't think they're related."

"Why not?"

"Why would Captain Roberts want to alert us to his coming? If he knew where we were, he could have caught us in port and had an easy go of us. Also, why would Mr. Carlyle tell us he used to be part of the pirate crew? If it was a set-up, I think he would leave that part out to not raise our suspicions."

"Aye. That makes sense."

It did, but Azure still had an uneasy feeling about this Amenaza Island business. They would have to keep their guard up.

Shaking off the unease, Azure faced the crew. "Is everyone alright?" she called.

When she heard a chorus of ayes and cheerful whoops, she said, "I'm glad to hear it." She shook her head and grinned. "Holy shit! That was unexpected. But you all rose to the occasion. Excellent work everyone!"

As the marauders cheered and rolled into a victory song, Elijah sidled up to Azure. "And you did great, too. Again." He flashed her a warm, knowing smile. "See, you deserve this position."

Her face flushed. For the span of a heartbeat, she thought about saying something along the lines of deserving some other positions, too, but she shooed the thought away. She had been friends with Robin for so long, she was starting to think like her.

"I don't mean to pry," Mr. Threepbrush said, "but I wholeheartedly agree."

Azure looked down at the deck.

"Thank you. Both of you."

Amenaza Island

The *Adventure Ship* pulled into the docks at Lavaview, the main port town on Amenaza Island. An ominous volcano loomed over the town, blocking out the morning sun and casting a shadow far out into the bay. Black smoke poured from its top, bending off to the right in the breeze.

Off to the east, seemingly way too close for safety was a spectacular lava fall. Glowing orange lava cascaded from the face of a cliff into the bay like a waterfall. When it hit the water's surface it sent billowing clouds of laze into the air, sometimes creating violent explosions that sent globs of half-formed rock spiraling off at all angles. The sight was both mesmerizing and terrifying.

"My people call that volcano Death Mountain," Brisa told Azure from the rail of the ship. "I'm fairly sure we'll find no Ciguapa living here. We've learned to avoid this island like a plague."

"Why?"

"The volcano is extremely active, and used to devastate the island every few years. But it had been somewhat dormant for twenty years now, or so I've been told."

Azure furrowed her brow, second-guessing her decision to undertake a job here. "Well, we'd better find that treasure quick and get the hell out of here, then."

A rough-looking man with a raven on his shoulder strode down the dock toward them, a woman holding a baby next to him. Azure, Robin, Brisa, and Mr. Threepbrush disembarked to meet him.

"Did you know Captain Roberts was going to attack us?" Azure called when they were still thirty yards apart, hand near her wand.

The man stopped moving. The innocent surprise and confusion on his face all but confirmed what she had suspected—that he hadn't set them up.

"No. I haven't seen him or my old crew for months."

Azure studied his eyes as well as she could. He seemed to be telling the truth.

"Well, they just ran us down off the coast of the Nameless Isles."

"That surprises me. Last I heard, the captain didn't want to have anything to do with you or your dragon."

"Do you promise on the lives of your family?" Mr. Threepbrush said, eliciting a shocked look from Azure.

"I do." He pulled his wife and baby in close to him. "I promise I had nothing to do with his attack."

They all stood and looked at each other across the dock.

"My dear, Robin," Sir Terry said, breaking the awkward silence, "shall we leave our friends to their negotiations and get an early start on our...time together? I could show you around this strange and interesting island."

Robin looked to Azure, as if for permission.

"Go ahead. We'll be fine." Azure flashed her a grin, satisfied with Mr. Carlyle's answers.

"Send a bolt in the air if you need anything." Robin took wing, and the two birds disappeared into the town.

"Let us hope that, despite our rocky start, we can become fast friends as well as they have," the man said. "As you know, my name is Wakeman Carlyle." He extended a calloused, dark-tanned hand as he approached. "And this is my wife, Hester, and our daughter, Anna."

"Azure Brine." As she shook his hand, she searched his face for any sign of ill will, unsure if she could see any. She gave his wife a polite nod and a smile, which she returned before shushing the baby.

"Aye, Captain Brine," Wakeman said. "I shan't be forgetting your face in this life. I was there to witness Captain Roberts' first and only defeat."

"It was my crew who won that day, but that was long ago."

"Not so long ago that my impression of you has faded." His smile seemed genuine, allowing Azure to relax her guard a touch. "Now, as Sir Terry has told you, I have a bit of an embarrassing situation I'd like your help with. I seem to have...misplaced a chest filled with most of what I earned while working on Captain Roberts' crew. I buried it back in my pirating days, but the island has changed since then. It has become overgrown, and my landmarks are no longer obvious." He lowered his eyes and shook his head. "The volcano has been more active than usual of late, and the islanders here say another big eruption is coming, maybe as soon as a few weeks from now. I'm afraid if the mountain really does go one of these days, I'll lose that treasure forever."

"They don't think the volcano could erupt sooner than that?" Azure looked to the smoking mountain with an uneasy feeling.

"No. The people here, you'll find, are pretty strange, but they do have an uncanny knowledge of how the volcano behaves. And they aren't even preparing for the virgin sacrifice ceremonies, yet, so we've got some time."

"Virgin sacrifice?"

"Aye. They believe it appeases the mountain. They believe it's alive, even god-like. I'm not sure why it would want human virgins, but that's their thing. Apparently, they've been able to forestall imminent eruptions in the past." Wakeman shrugged.

"Why did you leave Captain Roberts' crew?" Mr. Threepbrush asked, still not quite convinced.

"To tell you the truth, it was mostly that gargoyle of his. That creature gave me the all-overs." He shivered. "I think it brought out the worst in our captain, unfortunately. He was much more inclined to kill after conjuring it." Wakeman stared out to sea, seemingly lost in thought for a moment. "I don't know...piracy just kind of lost its appeal. I had enough money to settle down and try to start a family, so I decided to leave the pirate life for good." He looked down at the dock, again. "Well, I *had* enough money, anyway." He glanced at Hester, face red.

"Why leave the treasure here?"

"That's a great question, but one I don't have a great answer for. I think we just happened to be here when the idea struck me, to be honest."

"Why did you bury the treasure?" Azure asked.

Wakeman looked to her with an extremely confused expression. Even Mr. Threepbrush, who was usually over-the-top respectful, looked at her like she had just said the stupidest thing he'd ever heard.

"Uh...cause that's what one does with treasure." Wakeman couldn't keep the condescension from his voice.

"Aye, Captain," Mr. Threepbrush added, "what other choice did he have?"

Brisa smirked and subtly rolled her eyes.

Azure moved on. "So where can we find this buried treasure?"

"Well..." Wakeman pulled a well-worn scroll from his coat pocket, unrolled it, and handed it to Azure. "...that's the other embarrassing part." He rubbed the back of his neck. "I'm not completely sure what these clues mean."

"Did you not write the clues yourself?"

"Yeah...I wrote them. I just can't quite remember what I had meant by them."

Azure read the scroll aloud:

"Find the place ware rum grows frum trees.

See the smoke o'er the home of bees.

Make a line and marche out thirty.

Stop and get yer hands a'dirty."

Wakeman handed Azure a piece of parchment with a map drawn on it. The map was a crudely-drawn depiction of Amenaza Island with a red circle drawn near the northern coast.

"I know it's somewhere inside this circle." He pointed, blushing.

"Do you have any idea what you meant by, 'the place where rum grows on trees?'" Mr. Threepbrush asked while studying the map over Azure's shoulder.

"No. And therein lies the problem. This treasure was buried years ago, back when I was much fonder of strong drink and late nights. A few of my closest mates from the crew snuck away with me as the rest of the crew roistered about town and helped me with the treasure. Could be we found a rum-growing tree and drank its fruits, for all I remember of that night."

"But you do remember there were at least a hundred pieces of gold inside?"

"Aye. That part has stayed with me. Took me a long career at sea to scrape together that sum of gold, and I won't likely forget it until I'm sailing across the Ring." He pointed up without looking away from Mr. Threepbrush's face.

"Well, we'd better get started." Azure extended her hand, and Wakeman shook it, again.

"Thank you, Captain Brine. And good luck!"

Azure turned to Mr. Threepbrush. "Let's go round up the crew."

THE WILL-O'-THE-WISP flickered in the middle distance, barely visible through the too-damn-dense jungle. A crew of seven trudged toward it through the underbrush, hacking new paths with their cutlasses in the sweltering heat.

"Are we there yet?" Orok whined somewhere to Azure's right.

"I have no idea." Azure stopped to look at the map, again, still unable to discern anything resembling a landmark.

Just as she was about to slice away a hanging vine and forge ahead, something buzzed near her left ear. She turned to see a fuzzy bumble bee hovering way too close to her head.

After instinctually ducking away, a thought occurred. "The home of bees," she said. "The clues said something about the home of bees. Maybe we're getting close?"

A sharp sound, like a whoosh of air, filled Azure's left ear, and she immediately felt her equilibrium wane. In her slightly dizzy state, she saw a flash of black and yellow zip past, and the bee was gone.

"That was weird." Syl, the crew member closest to Azure, looked off into the jungle where the black and yellow blur had disappeared, obviously feeling a bit discombobulated, too.

Everyone stood in silence, panting. Most looked to Syl with vague expressions of confusion. Azure shook her head, finding that the dizziness was already fading.

"Well, let's keep at it." Azure cut the vine and willed herself forward. After several hard-won meters, she said, "Don't you guys have a song or something for an occasion like this?"

"As a matter of fact, we do." Mr. Threepbrush looked to the others, then began to sing. In the span of a few words, the others had joined in, only a hint of their usual vigor missing.

"LET'S DISTRACT OUR MINDS WITH A SONG.

LET'S SING ABOUT...BETTER TIMES THAN THIS.

MAYBE IF WE SING LOUD ENOUGH,

WE'LL FORGET THAT WE'RE KNEE-DEEP IN PISS."

"Remember the time," Mr. Threepbrush sang alone, "when Blunderbuss hooked himself a swordfish on his line? And just when he had called, 'I caught a fish with a sword!' the fish gave a tug, and pulled him overboard?"

"WAY HEY! SURE, WE REMEMBER THAT!" The crew sang together.

"Remember the time," Syl sang, "when we attended the Marauder King's play on opening night? And after the wonderful play was done, they gave *us* a standing o-va-tion?"

"WAY HEY! SURE, WE REMEMBER THAT!"

"Remember the time," Nargol sang, "when Mr. Cordingly shit the bed and—"

Her verse was cut short as the crew came out from the thick jungle into a clearing that was home to a small village.

Children played a game of tag amongst the rows of wooden houses, but every adult within view was turned to face the marauders, various makeshift weapons ready in their hands.

"Good day," a man in typical farmer's clothes holding a menacing hoe called, his expression wary.

"Good day," Azure returned. "My name is Captain Brine." Gods that still felt strange to say. "And this here is my crew. We mean you no ill will, and are only here in search of a treasure at the request of a Mr. Carlyle."

"Wakeman hired you, did he?"

"Yes, sir. He did."

The man stared suspiciously into Azure eyes. She held his gaze, doing her best to project confidence. Her hand found the ship's wheel that now hung around her neck. She rubbed one of the tiny handles with her thumb.

After several intense seconds, he broke his eye-lock with Azure and sized up the rest of the crew. Azure worried what his reaction to an orc, a ciguapa, and a faun might be, but he spent no more time looking at them than the other humans in the crew.

"Well all right, then." The man dropped the hoe and extended a hand. "I'm James, more or less the leader of this village. It's a pleasure to meet you."

The other adults went back to whatever they had been doing before the intrusion, and the kids continued their game.

Azure shook the man's hand. "It's a pleasure to meet you, too." She tried to hide a look of confusion. "So, you guys are the islanders, here? I—" She stopped herself short, unsure how to put her thoughts into words without being offensive.

"You thought we'd be some kind of uncivilized heathens?" James' smile was warm and un-accusatory.

"Uh..."

"Yeah, we know what kind of reputation we have outside of our little paradise. We know that most people in the Ring of Islands don't understand our ways. It's the virgin sacrifices that tend to throw people off, but if they'd seen what we've seen, they'd understand."

"Oh." Azure had no idea how to respond.

"Mordo is a vengeful god." He pointed to the column of black smoke in the sky. "Even now, his ire grows. It won't be long, now. Soon he will send the great red fire. Soon he will demand his offering."

Azure had even less of a clue how to respond than before.

"But where are my manners?" James continued. "First, we show you and yours unwarranted aggression, then I go right into my spiel about virgin sacrifices. I apologize if we're a bit on edge at the moment. It's just that there was a group that charged through here only yesterday, and they were much less polite than you lot. We thought it was another bunch of illegal trappers in search of tiddly dragons to sell as pets, but..." James wiped his brow with his sleeve. "But here I am, rambling again."

Azure fought the urge to ask about tiddly dragons, her attention piqued by the other matter. "What was the group doing?" she asked.

"They were looking for Wakeman's lost treasure, too. Only not at the request of the man himself, like you lot."

"Do you know who these people were?"

"Indeed, I do, ma'am. They work for that big casino on Mirth Island. I guess they figure that taking money through gambling isn't enough, so they've got their hands into everything else, too. Mordo, I'm sure you'll appreciate, is not pleased with this kind of thing."

Blunderbuss stepped forward and raised a hand like a child in class. "Uh, sir, what is a tiddly dragon?"

"Did you not encounter them on your way through the jungle?"

"Possibly?"

"They're the cutest little things. Only live here on Amenaza. Beloved of Mordo, they are." His eyes went skyward, as if looking for one. "The name tiddly dragon has a double meaning, really, because they're small, *and* they can make you feel a bit tiddly."

"Tiddly?" Azure asked, unfamiliar with that particular colloquialism.

"Like you've had a few too many." James mimicked taking a drink. "They can produce a sharp blast of air that disorients bees, which are their main food source. But if you get too close while they're feeding, you'll be feeling a bit tiddly, too."

"We saw a black and yellow blur in the woods," Syl said.

"Yep. That was one of 'em. They zoom around catching bees, as harmless as anything. But if you have to do much work around the hot springs it's a good idea to stuff something in your ears first." He barely paused for a breath. "Their coloration is quite beautiful if you ask me. But they're not orchidaceous at all, their color is aposematic in nature, you know, to scare off would-be predators and such. You'll get a chance to see 'em in the springs just past our village."

Azure loved the idea of tiddly dragons but needed to focus. She opened her mouth to speak, but James had already started again. "You know, they're much smarter than many give them credit for. They remember individual humans as well as any being I've encountered; better than most humans do. My daughter regularly feeds a small family of tiddly dragons who are fiercely loyal to her."

In the short pause that followed, Azure spoke up. "That's great. I hate to change the subject, but do you have any idea where Mr. Carlyle's treasure might be?" She figured it was worth a shot. With another crew out searching, they could use any advantage they could get. Twenty percent of that treasure could be a real boon to the marauders, and she didn't want to lose it.

"Unfortunately, we don't, or we could have pointed those arseholes from the casino off in the wrong direction." James shrugged. "Our little ones are forever off in search of the treasure, just for the adventure of it, but they've always come up empty handed. We don't have the foggiest where it is."

"Well I'm awfully sorry to be so hasty, but we should really get to finding that treasure before anyone else does. It was a pleasure to meet you, sir, and we thank you for the information."

"Happy to help a friend of Wakeman's. Good luck on your search, and may Mordo forestall your doom."

The crew nodded to James and the other villagers as they made their way through the village and back into the thick jungle.

"May Mordo forestall your doom?" Azure said to Brisa. "Pretty ominous way to say goodbye."

"I take it as it was meant. I think it's just their way of wishing you long life." Brisa shrugged. "It's nice when you look at it that way."

"Yeah, nice for everyone except the unlucky virgin who gets tossed in the volcano. I guess their doom won't be forestalled."

"That's true."

The jungle opened up again, more gradually this time, to reveal a series of bubbling pools surrounding a large black-rock mound. Upon closer examination, the mound had several pools naturally carved into its slope at random intervals all around. Water seemed to flow from the top of the mound, then cascade down, filling the pools with steaming water. The whole thing reminded Azure of something she had seen at the inn once when some rich patrons had stacked a pyramid of fancy glasses and filled them all by pouring expensive wine into the top glass.

The mound was alive with activity. Little glistening black and vivid yellow creatures dove, swam, and generally lounged around the countless pools. They looked like salamanders, except that they had leathery wings attached to their backs. Sometimes one of them would zip into the clearing from the jungle, pause in the air as if deciding which pool to enter, then dive headfirst into the boiling water. They looked exactly like cute little salamander dragons, and seemed completely impervious to heat.

"There's your tiddly dragons," Syl said, moving closer to crouch near one of the pools.

The creatures scattered, taking wing and bolting away with incredible speed.

"Sorry, little fellas." He stood and backed away. "I guess they're a little skittish."

"That's understandable if people are coming here to trap and sell them," Brisa said.

"Yeah. That's—"

"They're so warm!" Blunderbuss stood a good distance off between two different pools. He held a hand aloft, holding a piece of salted meat between his thumb and forefinger. Two tiddly dragons had landed on his arm and were nibbling at the meat. As the crew watched, another little salamander alighted on his head.

Syl shook his head, an incredulous expression on his face. "I'm supposed to be the one who's in touch with nature," he said with a smirk.

"Sorry, Syl." Blunderbuss petted one of the creatures on its head. "What can I say? I guess they like me."

"We'd better keep going," Azure said. She was quickly learning that being in charge often made her the chief fun killer. Keeping this crew on task was a challenge at times, but she was eager to find that treasure.

The Foundling

"I believe this is the center of Mr. Carlyle's circle," Mr. Threepbrush said, pointing at the map. "That little rocky ledge he drew looks a lot like the one we're standing on."

"All right," Azure called so everyone could hear. "We're going to fan out and form a line, with maybe...twenty feet between each of us. Then, as a unit, we can turn like the hand of a clock around this center point, making a circular grid. Remember, we're looking for a place where rum grows from trees, whatever that means."

"Can we go widdershins?" Syl asked.

"Sure. We'll go widdershins."

"What's widdershins?" Nargol asked.

"Counter clockwise."

"Isn't that bad luck?" Blunderbuss chipped in.

"No, it's good luck," Syl said.

"I could have sworn it—"

"Guys! Let's get going on this."

The crew began to line up, with Azure taking the spot closest to the center. When they were more or less ready, they began to walk in a big circle. Nargol had taken the spot at the end of the line, and Azure couldn't see her through the underbrush.

Everyone kept their eyes on the trees, looking for any indication of one that produced rum.

"Found it!" Nargol called from somewhere far off to the right.

Azure's heart leapt, but she quickly tempered her expectations. It couldn't have been that easy, could it?

The crew followed Nargol's voice, with Azure taking up the rear. When she arrived around the huddled group, she heard Mr. Threepbrush say, "Where? I don't see a thing."

"It's up above the bottom branches," Nargol said. "A human wouldn't have spotted it, but my head crested the first layer of the canopy. You want to see it, Captain?"

"Sure."

Nargol scooped Azure up as if she were a child and thrust her up through the bottommost branches. There, wedged in the crook of a bough, was an empty bottle of rum. The bottle was covered in moss, and seemed to be home to some kind of creature Azure wasn't very keen to meet.

"See it?" Nargol asked from below.

"Yeah. Just a minute." Azure craned her neck to look out through the branches in the rough direction of the volcano. When she located the smoke, she scanned the area for something bee-related. It didn't take long to find an old hive in the next tree over. "See the smoke over the home of bees," she said to herself.

"Huh?"

"You can let me down, please."

As Nargol set her back down on solid ground, Azure held a hand out, forming a virtual line between the rum bottle and the bee hive. "Make a line and march out thirty." She began to pace toward the hive, and toward the smoke. After counting thirty paces, she stopped and looked down.

Her heart sank.

The ground she was standing on was soft and freshly churned. The vegetation had all been cleared away, very recently.

Someone had beaten them to it.

Syl sighed. "That crew from the casino got to it first."

"Bastards," Blunderbuss said. "They stole it from Mr. Carlyle is what they did."

Now Azure sighed. She knew they were right, but had them dig anyway, just to be sure. When the dig turned up nothing, she racked her brain, but there was nothing left to be done. She'd have to go back to Wakeman, and his family, and tell him she had failed.

"Well," she said in her captain voice, "no use in hanging around in this sticky-ass jungle. Let's get back to the ship. I know about a merchant contract out of Ersa Aracel. It's not much, but it will be a whole lot better than nothing."

Dejected, the others followed as she headed back toward Lavaview. No one spoke as they trudged along. The only sounds were swords chopping through the underbrush and the occasional groan.

A wavering whistle sounded from the left. Azure turned to see an extremely agitated capybara staring right at her. Behind it was a small group of cappies, forming a rough semi-circle in front of a particularly large tree trunk. Behind them was a swathe of bright purple cloth and...

Azure took a step closer, to the great consternation of all the capybaras. They all grunted, or almost barked at her, jumping up and down with only their front legs coming off the ground.

Although she had never seen capybaras act like this, Azure dared another step forward, trying to confirm what she thought she had seen.

As she stood up on her toes, she could see that behind the protective wall of capybaras was, a child. A little girl of about five or six. She wore a strange purple dress decorated with strange creatures, the like Azure had never seen before. Her skin and hair reminded Azure of herself as a little girl. Her eyes were wet and fearful.

"Hello," Azure said, her voice a few octaves higher than normal. "My name is Azure, what's yours?"

The little girl's eyes met Azure's, a glimmer of hope behind the tears. She said something in a strange language. Azure looked to the crew, but got only shrugs.

"Do you speak the common tongue?"

Again, the girl said something unrecognizable.

Azure's eyebrows scrunched together. She had never met a human that didn't speak the common tongue. Was it possible that the little girl wasn't human? Azure checked her ears, having only the vaguest of ideas from storybooks about elves back on the Continent, but they seemed normal to her. Maybe this island was weirder than she had thought? Maybe they had created an entirely new language, here? James from the village had spoken common better than most, but with all that virgin sacrifice stuff, who knew?

The girl recoiled, clutching something in her hands.

Azure, now cognizant of how her face looked, affected her most welcoming smile. Gently, she waved the little girl forward, being careful to not make any sudden movements.

"I know you don't understand me, but I promise, I only want to help you. Can I take you back to the village?" She pointed in the general direction of the village they'd encountered. "I can get you back, but I need you to come out from there."

The girl repeated a word that sounded like, "Om," and held up the object in her hands.

Azure took a tentative step forward. When the girl didn't recoil, she took another step. Then another. The capybaras were not happy, but parted at Azure's approach. She slowly reached out her hand and took the object the girl had offered. It was a rectangular object made from materials Azure had never seen. It was roughly the size of a deck of cards, but a little bigger and flatter. One side of it was covered in glass.

Azure's finger pressed down on one of the ridges along the side of the object, and an incredibly life-like painting of three people standing in front of a strange and impossibly tall structure suddenly appeared in the glass. Azure gasped and dropped the object on the ground.

The little girl jumped up, scrambled through the underbrush, and picked the object back up, cleaning it with the hem of her dress. She said several more unrecognizable words, followed by the, "Om."

"I'm so sorry, Little One, but I don't know what you're talking about." She motioned for the girl to follow and turned to leave. "But if you come with us, we can take you back to your village."

Azure could see the wheel's turning in the girl's head. The little girl's eyes shot back and forth from Azure to the capybaras. Eventually, something must have clicked in her mind, because she rushed to Azure's side and clung to her hand.

A feeling unlike any she had ever experienced permeated Azure's chest. The beginnings of tears formed in her eyes, but she blinked them away and shook her head.

"I've got you, Little One. You're safe with me until we get back to your parents."

Azure pushed past the strange rush of emotion and, holding the little girl's hand, started back toward the village.

The crew had smartly backed away when Azure had first encountered the girl, but now they came into view, huddled together along the path they had cut.

Azure crouched down, and the girl moved closer to her. "These are my friends." She smiled and pointed. "They won't hurt you, either."

The little girl clung tight as they passed, keeping her eyes averted from the smiling and hesitantly waving crew.

The journey was slow. They took the trail they had made back through the buried treasure site, back through the tiddly dragon baths, and back into the village. Again, James met them as they entered. The children had moved on to a game with a coconut and some baskets.

"Any luck?" James called.

"We found this little girl in the jungle," Azure said, skipping any pleasantries. "Does she belong to anyone here?"

James looked her over. His gaze caused her to squeeze Azure's leg and turn away.

"I'm sorry, but I don't recognize her at all."

"Well, is there a chance she's from this village? Or maybe another one close by?"

"No, ma'am. As a village leader, I know every Amenazan on this island, and I've never seen this girl before."

"Shit." Azure stroked the girl's long black hair.

"Please don't use profanity here, ma'am. Mordo does not approve."

Azure ignored him and turned to see her crew lingering twenty yards behind.

"So, none of you are able to understand her?" she asked them.

Every one of them shook their heads.

Azure closed her eyes. What did she need to do, here? Who could this child belong to? And where the hell were they? If James could be believed—and there really wasn't any reason not to believe him—she didn't belong to anyone on Amenaza Island. That left only the group of people from the casino, but how could they have left a child behind? It didn't make any sense. If they could only talk to her...

"Zoth-Avarex," she said to herself. Maybe he could help? She had seen his magic do incredible things. There seemed to be a chance he could use it to understand the little girl.

After goodbyes with James, Azure led the foundling and her crew away from the village. When they were a good distance away, she stopped.

Reluctantly, she pulled out her wand and aimed it in the sky.

Channeling all her concentration and energy, she shook her head, squeezed her eyes shut, and said, "I need a hero."

Zoth-Avarex

This was happiness.

An entire island covered in priceless treasure, and no one able to find him or take it away.

Zoth-Avarex rolled up from his back, taking two great claw-fulls of gold coins as he stood and let them slip through his fingers, making wonderful tinkling sounds as they clattered back down against the treasure floor.

Nope, it didn't get much better than this. For the first time in his life, the dragon was content.

"Why was I never content before?" he said to himself, his voice more gravelly than usual due to lack of use. "I mean, I had a massive hoard before."

Zoth-Avarex contemplated his self-imposed question. The reasons were many, maybe. The chief of those reasons was his safety. He no longer needed to worry about...anyone taking him away from his beautiful hoard. He dared not give that *anyone* a name, fearful that they would somehow hear him across realms.

Another reason was tougher to admit, a foreign and relatively new concept: friendship. As strange as it was to say it, he had friends, now. The goofball Marauders, their new captain, even that shit-talking little Robin were beings that he...cared about. The thought made him shiver.

"Thinking is dumb." He shook his head and buried himself in treasure, leaving only his head sticking out. He pushed a claw up through and snapped an open-topped barrel of dark beer appeared, and he took a long pull.

From the corner of his eye, he saw a red glow through the Eternal Fog above.

"What the..?"

He rolled his eyes and sighed.

"I'm finishing my damn beer first," he said to no one.

He took a sip and tried to ignore the red glow. Then, after another dramatic sigh, he chugged the rest of the beer, jumped up out of the treasure, and flew straight up, above the layer of fog. Off to the southwest was a giant, fiery red dragon, as big as an island. The dragon was made of sparkly red embers, like fireworks. The sight would have been surreal and overwhelming to a human brain, but Zoth-Avarex had invented the spell to create it. This is how he taught Azure to get a hold of him if she ever needed him. He just wished he could have seen her face as she spoke the words he'd used for the spell.

"I hope they're all right," he said as he flapped his great wings, heading in their direction.

Such an un-dragonly thing to say.

Oh well.

The firework dragon circled slowly above a column of black smoke. He couldn't remember the name of the island, but knew they must have been on that one with the active volcano.

The flight didn't take long. When Zoth-Avarex wanted to get somewhere quick, he was fast as hell. His massive wings caught the air like galleon sails and pushed it back with the force of a thousand horses.

As he approached, a thin red line of light—visible only to him—came into view. It descended down from the glowing dragon, pinpointing Azure's location. She was in a thick jungle somewhat close to the volcano. Tucking his wings, he dove down to see what was going on.

AZURE HAD NOT BEEN ready for the colossal monstrosity that shot out from her wand. Zoth-Avarex had told her the spell would send him some kind of signal; he hadn't told her that a dragon made of red sparks, bigger than her entire home island, would emerge from her wand and circle the skies like a portent of doom. When she did it, she had looked around, embarrassed, hoping no one from Amenaza Island had seen her. The little girl had clung to her leg even tighter than before, burying her face in Azure's thigh.

Now, waiting and watching the skies for Zoth-Avarex, Azure wondered what the islanders were going to think about the giant glowing dragon. She hoped it wasn't going to lead to any extra virgin sacrifices.

A dark speck in the sky was quickly growing bigger. In the span of one breath, it was close enough to identify. In the next breath, Zoth-Avarex had landed, crushing a copse of smaller trees to Azure's right. Luckily, the little girl didn't look up, although her nails dug into the back of Azure's leg.

"Everything good?" the dragon said, voice booming. His concern seemed genuine.

"Yeah, we're all fine. But keep your voice down." She pointed down to the clinging girl. "We have a bit of a problem we could use some help with."

"This better be good. I was having a wonderful time on Dragon Island." He said this reluctantly, like an actor reading a script, unsure about his lines.

"We found a little human girl, but she speaks a strange language, and we can't figure out where she belongs."

"Is that it?"

"Yeah."

"All right." The dragon waved a claw and muttered a few unintelligible words. "There, that should work."

The little girl looked up at Azure, a confused look on her face.

"Hello," Azure said. "Can you...understand me now?"

The girl nodded.

"Good. My name is Azure. What's yours?"

"Oriana..." Her voice wasn't much more than a whisper.

"That's a pretty name."

The girl gave a hint of a smile for the first time. It was one of the most beautiful things Azure had ever seen.

"Do you know where your parents are?"

Oriana hesitated, then nodded, again.

"Are they on this island?"

She shook her head.

"Which island are you from?"

"Not an island," the little girl said. "Earth."

From her periphery, Azure noticed Zoth-Avarex jump at the mention of that word.

"I haven't heard of that." Azure wondered for a fleeting moment if it could be a place on the Continent. "Where is it?"

"Mama and Daddy had a...knife. When that..." Oriana re-buried her face in Azure's thigh, unable to continue.

"You're okay. I won't let anybody hurt you, Little One."

The little girl looked back up, and through force of will, continued. "Mama cut a hole in the air with the knife. She said it went to a different world. She said I had to go through first..."

"Where is your mama, now?"

"I don't know. I fell in the jungle, in the mud. I tried to get up and see, but I couldn't see anything. Then the hole Mama cut was gone." She squeezed Azure's leg, looking up with watery eyes that begged for reassurance.

Zoth-Avarex fidgeted.

"Does any of this make sense to you?" Azure asked the dragon.

"Well, sure. A portal-cutting knife is a trope throughout the multiverse. There are countless other worlds. I mean..."

"But this *Earth*. Have you heard of it?"

"Well, yeah. But there are countless versions of Earth. I would never be able to tell which one she was from unless she had that knife with her."

Oriana hazarded a glance in the direction of the dragon's booming voice, then buried her face even harder.

"It's all right, Oriana. I know he's big and scary and ugly, but that dragon is actually my friend. He's here to help."

At first, Oriana didn't move, but eventually, she looked back up at Azure. "You have a dragon for a friend?" Her eyes were incredulous but also shone with a glimmer of absolute wonder.

"Yes, and I have other friends here, too." She pointed to her crew. "A lot of them don't look like us, but they're all my very very good friends."

The little girl didn't turn to see, but her grip loosened a bit.

"So, she would need that knife to get home?" Azure said to the dragon.

As he nodded, Oriana said, "The loud men took it."

"Loud men? So, you had the knife here?"

"Yeah. I found it in the mud."

"But someone took it?"

"I heard some voices after I was out in the jungle all night. They were loud and scary, so I hid under a giant leaf. I came back out when they left, but the golden knife was gone."

"Did you see what they looked like?"

"Not really. But I did see something on their clothes." Oriana knelt and grabbed a twig, then began to draw in a patch of wet dirt with it. Her drawing was crude, but it reminded Azure of something—she just couldn't remember what.

"It's the symbol on the flag flying from the top of the Fortress," Mr. Threepbrush said, peeking over Azure's shoulder.

"The Fortress?"

"The towering casino on Mirth Island."

"Shit. It must have been those guys from the casino, then. They took Wakeman's treasure, then took Oriana's air-cutting knife."

"Well we'll just have to get it back from them," said Syl.

"How could we do that? They're a huge...operation. And I don't think they're going to just give it back."

"We could try."

"Yeah..." Azure looked to the dragon. "Maybe you *could* figure out which...uh...Earth she's from? Could you try?"

Zoth-Avarex sighed, his eyes darting away and back. "I suppose I could give it a shot, but I'm telling you, it'll be damn-near impossible."

Azure stroked the little girl's hair. "Oriana, my friend the dragon needs to ask you a few questions to help you get back home to your parents. Can you answer him?"

Oriana nodded without looking back.

"Okay," Zoth-Avarex said, voice mellowed. "Does your Earth have magic?"

"Yes."

"Does everyone, er, do all adults know how to use magic?"

"No. I don't think so."

"Are there dragons flying around?"

"No." That question elicited the tiniest of smiles.

"Are there...unicorns? Like the ones on your dress?"

"No." The smile widened.

"Is there a dark wizard who rules the entire planet?"

"I don't know." Her eyebrows scrunched together.

"Have humans come in contact with aliens yet?"

"I don't know."

The dragon shrugged. "It's too hard to narrow down. I don't know what to tell you."

"Well thank you for trying." Azure narrowed her eyes as she looked at him, wondering what could be making him so nervous. Dismissing it, she crouched to Oriana's level. "I want you to know one very important thing," she said, sustaining eye contact. "We will find a way to get you home; I promise."

"Promise?"

"Yes. Me, my crew, and the dragon will get you home safe, alright?"

"Mm hm." Oriana threw her little arms around Azure's neck.

Azure patted her gently on her back. She wanted to wrap her arms around Oriana and pull her in tighter, but resisted the unfamiliar urge. For a handful of heartbeats, they remained in the embrace. Then Oriana took a step back, releasing Azure fully for the first time since she had clung on.

"We might have to take a trip on a...pirate ship." Azure was unsure if the little girl would understand that concept. When her eyes lit up, Azure knew she understood. "Is that okay with you?"

"Yeah." The worry was all-but vanished from her face.

"Well, let's go, then." Azure took her hand and led her toward town.

As they passed Zoth-Avarex, the little girl gaped up at him.

"Ugly, huh?" He shook his head at Azure.

"Sorry." She shrugged, one hand in the air and a wry smirk on her lips.

"So, are you done with me, then?" The dragon eyed the sky, seemingly eager to leave.

"You don't want to help us get the knife back?"

"I just don't know how I could help with that." He rubbed the spikes on the back of his neck. "I mean, I could destroy that casino and take it back if you want me to, but..."

"No. I guess we'll have to be a bit more subtle than that. I'm going to go there and explain what happened. Hopefully, they'll give it back to us once they know what's going on."

"Yeah. Of course, they will." Zoth-Avarex had a tough time maintaining eye contact. "If, er, when they do, just cut a hole in the sky while saying *Earth*. A portal should open right up."

"Okay.... I guess we don't need you anymore if you want to go. Thank you for your help. I don't know what we would have done without you."

"No problem. Just...uh...signal me again if you need anything."

The crew, including little Oriana, waved to the dragon as he flew up out of the jungle and over the smoking volcano.

To the Casino

Before they got back to Lavaview, Robin came diving down out of the sky like Ringfall.

"What the fuck was that?" she said as she landed hard on Azure's shoulder.

"What?"

"*What*? Are you serious? The giant flaming monstrosity that encircled this entire island!"

"Oh, that."

Sir Terry, out of breath, flew in behind Robin and landed on a nearby branch.

"Yeah, that." Robin hopped in an agitated circle.

"It was the signal spell your buddy Zoth-Avarex taught me. We needed his magical expertise on something."

"On what?"

Azure nodded down to the little girl at her side. "Robin, meet Oriana. Oriana, this is another friend of mine, Robin."

"A talking bird?" The little girl's mouth dropped open.

"Yeah, yeah. Look at the funny little talking bird. Don't you dare ask me to say something stupid like, 'Polly want a cracker.'" Robin glared down at the girl, then looked back to Azure. "So, what did you need numbnuts for? I just saw him leaving back towards his treasure pile."

"He helped us with a spell so that we could understand Oriana, here. She came through some sort of portal from another world, I guess."

"What does that have to do with us?"

"Well, she's a little girl, and she was all alone in the jungle. It's kind of a long story, but I'll tell you all about it once we set sail for Mirth Island."

"Mirth? What about the treasure, here?"

"It's gone. A crew from the casino on Mirth Island took it."

Robin looked to Sir Terry and back. "So, we're leaving?"

"Yeah. We have to." Azure glanced at the raven. "But you can catch up to us later if you want."

"Nah." Robin had lowered her voice to a whisper. "This guy's about as prudish as Elijah. He's a great tour guide, and he's nice and all, but he just doesn't do it for me."

As Azure and crew began to walk again, Robin flew over to Sir Terry.

"Sorry," Robin said. "But I gotta go."

"T'is a shame," said the raven. "But I treasured every moment spent with you, dear Robin, and look longingly forward to the day you return here. If luck shines upon me, that day does come to pass, and you are inclined to pick up from where we are now leaving, you are welcome to call on me any time, day or night, calm or storm." He finished his little speech with a deep bow.

"Thank you for the tour," Robin said, curtsying. "If I do get back this way, I think I'll take you up on that." Robin flew back to Azure's shoulder.

"I thought you said he didn't do it for you?" Azure whispered.

"Well, maybe I was too hasty. He does know how to make a bird feel special." She glanced back at the raven, who stood with chest and head held high. "I mean, he does look pretty damned good, too."

Azure chuckled. "Sorry, Robin. But I kind of hope to never come back here again. That smoking volcano unnerves me."

"Yeah. I hear you on that." They both looked up at the smoke. "So, what's the deal with the kid?"

Azure filled Robin in as they made their way back to the *Adventure Ship*. She noticed that her avian friend couldn't keep her eyes off Azure's hand, which encompassed Oriana's.

Once back in Lavaview, they found the previously sleepy town now chaotic. Many people were directing loud, passionate laments at the sky and volcano, while others ran from place to place in apparent panic. A pang of guilt filled Azure's chest. She found herself concealing her wand with her arm, fearful that somehow, one of them would make the connection between her and the fiery dragon that had appeared over their island.

On the dock, they ran into Wakeman, alone this time. Again, Azure had to explain what had happened in the jungle, hoping he would take it well. It turned out he wasn't far from panic himself.

"I was starting to get as paranoid as the islanders, here. I thought the fire dragon they talk about was actually here to collect a virgin, or worse."

"Nope. Just a glorified firework."

"Well, that's a relief." Wakeman rubbed the back of his neck and stared at the dock.

He went on to say that if they could get his treasure back from the casino, he would bump their cut up to thirty percent. Azure told him they would do everything they could to recover it.

After thoroughly scanning the horizon for Captain Roberts, the *Adventure Ship* was back out at sea, a mild southeasterly wind filling its sails.

Oriana had not left Azure's side as she talked to the crew and gave them their orders. Once pointed in the right direction, Azure sat down cross-legged on the deck.

"So how old are you, Oriana?" She pushed some hair that had covered half of the girl's face behind her ear.

"Seven."

Azure found herself unsure of what to say. She wasn't used to talking to kids, let alone a kid from a completely different world. Thinking back to her own childhood, she tried to imagine what a seven-year-old would want to talk about.

"Do you have any brothers or sisters?" Azure had always wished she wasn't an only child.

"No."

"Any pets?"

"No. My parents won't let me." She hung her head.

"What is that...thing you were holding earlier?" Azure mentally kicked herself for not asking the dragon about that thing when he was still around.

"A phone." She fished it out of a pocket sewn into her dress. "But it doesn't work here." She touched the glass and held it up for Azure to see.

"This is me and my parents at the Space Needle." She touched the glass again, and the strange painting was replaced by a dozen multi-colored squares.

"Is that magic?" Azure asked.

Oriana's smile was ephemeral. "No. It's just a phone."

Azure had a hundred questions, but Oriana shot one back at her before she could get one out. "What's that?" She pointed straight up.

"That's the Ring. Is there not one in your world?"

"No."

During their conversation, Azure noticed that Elijah was more or less lurking nearby. He must have decided that now was the right time to approach. He moved slowly, as if he was trying not to startle Oriana. Azure was impressed with the consideration he showed. She wasn't sure, but she didn't think most men would intuit that such tact might be necessary. Certainly, her father wouldn't have. He would have charged in and wondered why the little girl wouldn't just cheer up. He would have meant well, but would have scared the shit out of her.

"Hey, you two," Elijah said, voice higher than usual. "Do you mind if I sit with you?"

Oriana looked to Azure. "He's my husband. Well, almost, anyway."

The little girl nodded to Elijah. He nodded back, kissed Azure on the forehead, and took a seat on the deck.

"My name is Elijah."

"I'm Oriana."

"Oh, I love that name. Do you want to see an amazing trick?" He held up a copper coin.

Oriana's eyes darted from Elijah, to Azure, and back. She shrugged.

Elijah held the coin in his left hand, then reached over with his right to pluck it away between his thumb and forefinger. The coin was now meant to be in his right, but Azure could see from her angle that it was cleverly hidden behind his left hand. He held his empty right hand up to Azure's mouth and said, "Could you give my hand a magic kiss, please?"

When she played along, Elijah opened his empty hand with a flourish, revealing that the coin was gone. Oriana looked to the other hand, but he showed her that it wasn't there either.

"Now, Azure. Did I touch your head at any time during that trick?"

"No."

"Well then how is the copper on your head, now?"

"It's not."

"Isn't it?"

Azure tilted her head forward, and a copper coin fell off, making a tiny metallic thud on the deck.

"What?" Azure didn't need to fake her surprise. She had never seen Elijah do something like that before.

The corner of Oriana's mouth quirked up. "Was that real magic?"

"Oh, no. Just a little trick I learned a long time ago."

"But there must be real magic, here," she stated, matter-of-factly. "There are dragons and talking birds, and purple people." She was really starting to open up.

"You're right," Azure said. "There is real magic, here." She took out her wand. "Would you like to see another trick?"

When the girl nodded, Azure stood, pointed her wand at Elijah, and asked, "Do you mind?"

He shook his head and was instantly lifted into the air. He floated about five feet off of the deck, making silly faces to ensure Oriana he was okay. Then, with a subtle flick of Azure's wrist, Elijah was turned upside-down. A copper coin fell from his coat pocket and rolled to a stop just in front of Oriana, who now wore a genuine, beautiful half-smile.

With a few more wrist flicks, Azure set her fiancé back down on his feet. The magical energy she expended had barely made her break a sweat.

As Azure and Elijah both sat back down, Oriana's smile faded. She seemed to be trying to hold back tears, trying her best to show them a brave face, although her pain was obvious. When Azure reached out to rub her back, a few tears made it through, running down her cheeks to collect on her chin.

Azure didn't speak, sensing that questions would be counterproductive. Instead, she simply rubbed the little girl's back and tried to show that she cared.

Out of the corner of her eye, she noticed several crew members, led by Mr. Threepbrush, forming together about ten feet away, near the main mast.

"Sorry," Oriana said, wiping her tears with her forearm. "I just thought of Daddy doing cartwheels..." She took a deep breath in through her nose and let it out through her mouth. "Back before he started working too much."

"You don't need to be sorry, Little Treasure." The nickname had come out without any conscious thought. "And we—" She stopped herself short, unsure of what to say. She had already promised to get her back to her parents, and she intended to keep that promise, but she had no idea if it was going to be possible.

Oriana used the hem of her dress to wipe her eyes.

"What do your parents do for work?" Elijah asked.

"They both work at some magic place. At the travel department, I think. Mama invented something that made people want to interview her and stuff."

"Do you know what she invented?"

Oriana's eyes rolled skyward as she considered the question. "Not really. But it had something to do with tracking people...across realms, whatever that means."

"Huh." Azure didn't really understand what *across realms* meant.

Tentatively, Mr. Threepbrush approached the little group. "Hello." He waved, keeping his distance. "I'm Mr. Threepbrush."

Oriana gave a half-hearted wave.

"I have two quick questions for you. Do people from your world think that farts are funny?"

"Yes." The little girl giggled, wiping away the remaining tear residue from her face.

"Oh, good. Are you familiar with the concept of princesses?"

"Yes."

"Perfect!" Mr. Threepbrush held up a finger. "We've got a song for you, then."

The crew members who had assembled behind him took a few steps forward.

Mr. Threepbrush began to sing, his voice off key, but not horrible.

There once was a princess, so proper and so fair.
She wore the finest dresses, and had the finest hair.
She carried herself with elegance and grace,

A look of serious dignity was always on her face.
But the princess had another life she didn't talk about.
She kept it to herself, when in public she was out.
Yes, the princess had a secret hidden deep within her heart...
When no one was around, the princess loved to fart!

OH, THE PRINCESS LOVED TO FART, OH THE PRINCESS LOVED TO FART.

SHE LOVED BUTT EXPLOSIONS, WITH ALL HER ROYAL HEART.

OH, THE PRINCESS LOVED TO FART, OH THE PRINCESS LOVED TO FART.

WHEN NO ONE WAS AROUND, THE PRINCESS LOVED TO FART.

"But who doesn't? Right?" Mr. Threepbrush gave an exaggerated shrug.
Everybody loves to fart, when they're all alone.
And the stinky air is not so bad, when it is your own.
The pressure release feels oh so good...
That's why everybody farts, and everybody should!

OH, THE PRINCESS LOVED TO FART, OH THE PRINCESS LOVED TO FART.

SHE LOVED TO BLAST HER BUTT CHEEKS APART!

OH, THE PRINCESS LOVED TO FART, OH THE PRINCESS LOVED TO FART.

WHEN NO ONE WAS AROUND, THE PRINCESS LOVED TO FART.

As the crew ended the song with a flourish, Mr. Threepbrush turned sideways and bent over. Blunderbuss, who was ducking down strategically behind him, honked a horn that was filled with flour, creating a puffy cloud that appeared to have issued from the bent-over man.

Throughout the song, Azure had toyed with the ship's wheel around her neck while watching Oriana, hoping that Mr. Threepbrush's gambit would pay off. She watched widened, reddened, unsure eyes begin to relax, to shine; the straight line of her mouth begin to curve, steeper and steeper, until her lips parted, revealing a missing tooth in the front that Azure hadn't noticed before.

As the crew applauded themselves and backed away, Azure mouthed, "Thank you," making eye contact with each member who had come to sing and comfort little Oriana.

THE CREW WAS TIRED, and no one seemed to be in a singing mood as night fell. Instead, most of the marauders separated into small groups around makeshift tables to play Dragon's Hoard.

Oriana had relaxed more and more as she spent time amongst the always-kind marauders. She was enamored with Brisa, and the Ring above. Both so beautiful she couldn't keep her eyes off them. Azure completely understood.

"Would you like to learn how to play Dragon's Hoard?" Azure asked Oriana.

The little girl nodded and smiled.

Azure scrounged up an old deck and a handful of tiny seashells from the captain's quarters. She brought them back out onto the deck and sat in a small circle with Elijah and Oriana. Elijah leaned over and kissed Azure's temple. Oriana's eyes widened as if this kind of show of affection wasn't something she was used to seeing. Robin fluttered down from the sails and landed on Azure's shoulder. Azure put roughly equal piles of seashells in front of Elijah, Oriana, and herself.

"Alright." Azure began to lay down cards face up on the timbers. "These are dragon parts." She pointed to several cards. "Here's an arm, a leg, a body, a tail, and a head. And these..." She riffled through the remaining cards until she found what she was looking for. "...are fire and water cards."

Oriana nodded.

"The point of the game is to build as much of a full dragon as you can, with all four limbs and a tail. If you have a fire card, and your dragon is whole, you get double the points. Does that make sense?"

"Yes."

"But if you have a water card in your hand, your dragon is worthless."

"Like Zoth-Avarex," Robin said.

Azure shook her head. "Everyone starts out with eight cards, which cost eight seashells, which we'll each put into the middle, in the dragon's hoard."

Azure gathered all the cards, shuffled them, then passed eight out to each player.

"When it's your turn, you can take a new card from the pile, and then you'll pass any card you want face down to the left." She indicated to Oriana which way that was since she looked slightly confused. "So, go ahead and go first."

Oriana drew a card, and a wide grin materialized on her face. She looked at her cards through narrowed eyes, then placed a different card between her and Azure.

"Alright, now if I think you've passed me a water card, I can say, 'Water,' and turn the card over if I want to. If it is water, I get to pick a card from your hand, but if it isn't, you get to take one from my hand." Now Azure narrowed her eyes and pretended to study Oriana's face. "So, did you pass me a water." She flashed a playful smile.

"No." Oriana shook her head, drawing out the word.

"Alright, I guess I'll believe you." Azure added the card to her hand. "I could have taken a card from the pile, but I want to take what you passed to me." Azure looked at her hand. "And now I'll pass a card face down toward Elijah."

Elijah made a show of deciding between Azure's discard and the pile, ultimately drawing a new card. He tossed a seashell into the pot. "Every time we get a new card, we have to put another coin, er, shell into the dragon's hoard."

"And after everyone gets a chance to play twice, anyone can shout, 'Battle,' and challenge the table to see who has the most complete dragon," Azure said.

"Heads and bodies are worth three points, a tail is worth two, and each limb is worth one."

Oriana nodded, again. Azure was impressed by how much the little girl concentrated, seemingly soaking it all in.

After they had gone around four times, during which Azure had passed her best cards to the little girl, Oriana shouted, "Battle!"

They each presented their cards. Azure's dragon was worth zero, since she had the dreaded water card in her hand, Elijah's was worth eight points, and Oriana's dragon was worth twelve.

"You win the hoard!" Azure patted her on the shoulder.

Oriana grinned as she dragged the hoard into her shell pile.

"You didn't exactly make it difficult," Robin said, shaking her head.

"Hey, she's just good at this," Azure replied. "A natural."

Robin harrumphed and flew away.

Azure rolled her eyes and dealt out another hand. "We keep playing until one player has all the shells."

It only took three hands for Oriana to collect all the seashells. She did her best to hide her bubbling pride, but it still shone through.

"Good game." Both Azure and Elijah shook her hand and bowed their heads to her.

"Now..." Azure yawned. "I think we should get some sleep."

"How about a bedtime story?" Elijah asked.

Oriana nodded and yawned at the same time.

Story Time

"**I** have a good one," Elijah said, "but why don't you go first, Az?"

Azure doubted his story was any good. He had an uncountable number of wonderful qualities; storytelling was not one of them.

"I could tell you one my parents used to tell me," she said to Oriana, who had lain down with her head on Azure's thigh.

"That sounds good."

"Alright." Azure tried to conjure one of their old stories to mind. When one of them popped into her head, she said, "This one is called *The Jaguar*."

Oriana's eyes widened.

"Do you have jaguars in your world?"

She nodded.

"Oh, good. So..." Azure cleared her throat. "In times gone by, there was a woman who lived alone in a quaint little house on the beach.

"One day, in the jungle behind her house, she heard a cry of great pain and misery.

"The old woman, thinking she could help whoever, or whatever, was making that sad noise, wrapped herself in a shawl and hurried into the jungle.

"After following the wretched sounds through several twists and turns, she found a jaguar stuck in a primitive trap on the bank of a small creek.

"'Help me,' said the jaguar, sounding scared and weak."

"Can jaguars talk in this world?" Oriana asked.

"No," Azure said. "Only in stories. None of our animals can talk. The only ones who can have been conjured from other worlds, like Robin."

"Oh."

"So, the old woman said, 'But if I help you, how do I know you won't eat me as soon as you get the chance?'

"'I wouldn't dream of it,' said the jaguar. 'Now please, can you just help me.'

"The old woman looked into the jaguar's sad eyes and she was moved. She made her way down the bank and pulled back on a lever that opened the trap that held the jaguar's leg.

"Then—" Azure stopped herself, thinking about what came next. In the story, the jaguar pounced on the old lady, and when she asked why he would trick her like that, the vicious jaguar said, 'Stupid old lady, you knew I was a jaguar all along,' before it ate her.

Did her parents really used to tell this story to her? Azure thought back, and yes, the memories were clear. They used to act it out and make it a fun thing, but she hadn't contemplated how horrible it was until just now.

"Then what?" Oriana said.

"Then...the jaguar led the old woman to a...lost city of gold, where she became very rich, and lived joyfully from then to never."

"Really? That's it?"

"Yeah." Azure shrugged. She supposed she probably shouldn't have been thinking ill of Elijah's stories, as her's wasn't exactly compelling.

"That's not the ending I've heard," Elijah said. "The one—"

Azure shot him a look that stopped him mid-sentence. "But I don't remember what it was." He turned to Oriana with a goofy grin. "Do you want to hear about Jacques, the Gallant Goat?"

"Sure." Oriana mirrored his grin.

"Great! Well, in times gone by, there was a goat, a gallant goat, named Jacques. Jacques was very handsome, and had the strongest, curviest horns you've ever seen. All of the girl goats were just wild over him, but he only gave his heart to one of them, a beautiful young princess goat named Mirabelle.

"One day, the evil Troll King came and stole Mirabelle away. He locked her up in a tall, smelly tower in the Troll Kingdom, across the raging Troll River.

"Jacques immediately set out on a mission to get his beloved Mirabelle back, but at the bridge over Troll River, he met a troll who lived under the bridge. The troll crawled up and said, 'Whoever would cross this bridge must best me in challenges three. You shall pick the first challenge, and I will pick the second, then you can pick our final challenge. If you beat me in all three, you may pass over the bridge in peace.'

"'That sounds fair,' said Jacques. 'For our first, I challenge you to a dance-off.'

"'Who shall be our judge?'

"Jacques called to a young couple walking down the path hand in hand.

"'Can you judge a dance competition between me and this troll?' Jacques asked.

"'But of course,' the young woman replied. 'We love to take strolls along the Troll River for that very reason. We were hoping to get called to judge something, and a dance competition is just the occasion to brighten our afternoon.'

"'Thank you,' said Jacques. 'You may go first.' He began to drum a beat with his hooves.

"The troll started to wiggle..."

Azure's eyes slowly closed as she drifted off to sleep.

Captain's Log: Ascension 23rd, 137

We have a foundling aboard. At least that's what Blunderbuss calls her. The little girl's name is Oriana, and we found her stranded and alone in the jungles of Amenaza Island.

I am now ostensibly in charge of her, and that is terrifying! I don't know the first thing about kids, and I have no idea how to talk to her. I can only hope we can get this whole thing figured out soon so she can get back to her parents.

I find it strange that I haven't thought about the fact that there are other worlds much in my life. I mean, I've known ever since I conjured Robin, but I've never felt an uneasiness about them until now. That someone from another world can cut some kind of magic hole and enter into our world is scary to me. And it makes me feel infinitesimally small to know that so many other worlds exist out there.

The concept makes me think of conjuring in general. Even though I've had a great experience with it, I can't help but think it's a practice that needs to be stopped. It's absolutely unfair to the beings who are conjured. I think about Thunder Paws, and all the time he spent away from his home. He was so kind and loyal to my dad, but he didn't choose to be in our world. I couldn't imagine just vanishing and reappearing in an alien world someday. It would be horrible. I shudder to even think about it, but that might be a real possibility.

I don't know if these log entries are helping or hurting me with my nerves! I'm freaking myself out at the moment when I need to focus on getting Oriana's portal-cutter knife and getting her home. And, hopefully, Wakeman's treasure, too! Our coffers are absolutely empty at the moment. It won't be long before the marauders really start feeling that. Blunderbuss is a wonderful cook, but he can only do so much with the dwindling options in our galley. That treasure would <u>really</u> help right now.

Another thing that has my nerves on edge is Captain Roberts. His attack on us wasn't a great sign of things to come. I imagine that his vendetta against us, against me, was likely further fueled by our escape. I'm kicking myself right now for not telling Zoth-Avarex about the giant crossbow thing I saw on his ship. I don't think he'll be overly concerned about it, but he should at least know it exists.

We'll keep a lookout for Captain Roberts. We heard from a ciguapa ship captain that he was seen heading east. I'll hope that report is true, but we have more pressing matters to attend to, for now.

On a quick personal note, Elijah is so good with Oriana. Why does that scare me even more? It seems so damned counterintuitive. He is a wonderful person who loves me and is really good with kids. I should be counting my blessings, but I suppose it scares me because I feel like the winds of fate, so to speak (I can't help using sailing-based imagery these days), are pushing me toward something inevitable. I mean, I think I want kids someday, but that someday feels too close right now.

The Fortress

A layer of light fog blanketed the horizon, and the towering casino loomed up out of it, standing much higher than anything else on Mirth Island. After sailing through night, they had arrived around mid morning, the air still and warm.

"It looks like a floating castle," Oriana said. "Is it?"

"No, I'm afraid not." Blunderbuss handed her a small plate filled with bacon. "But wouldn't that be something?"

According to Elijah, Oriana had fallen asleep shortly after Azure had. He woke them both so they could head inside to bed. Azure had carried the little girl—head resting on her shoulder—to the captain's quarters and lay her down in the bed. After tucking her in, Azure lay at the foot of the bed and fell asleep to the gentle rocking of the Mirror Sea, thinking about Oriana's adorable smile during the crew's song, and worrying about what was going to happen with her.

Now, as they approached, the zip line coming from the casino's top became visible. Someone jumped from the tallest turret, hurtled down along the line, and disappeared into the fog.

"That's where they have the knife you need." Azure pointed.

Oriana nodded, crunching into a crispy slice of bacon.

"What happened to the goat, anyway?" Azure asked. "I think I fell asleep."

"You did." Oriana giggled. "I think the troll challenged Jacques to a rhyming poetry battle or something like that. Then I fell asleep, too."

Robin soared down from the rigging and landed on the rail near Azure. "Good morning, Az." She stretched her head back as far as she could, yawning.

"Good morning."

"So, we're almost there. It'll be nice to get this whole...thing over with." If her nod toward the little girl was intended to be subtle, it wasn't successful.

Azure shot her a scowl and gave a much-more-subtle head shake.

"Oriana, would you like to meet some more of my friends? They're not human, but they're very nice." Azure turned her back on Robin as she spoke.

"Yeah." She seemed equal parts excited and scared.

Robin gave another overdramatic, "Hmph," and flew back up to the sails.

They first encountered Brisa, standing with perfect posture and gazing out at the rising sun from the starboard rail.

"Brisa, I'd like you to meet Oriana."

"Hello, Oriana." Brisa turned and smiled. "It is so good to meet you. I figured I would let you come to me when you were ready, and I hpoed to get to meet you this morning."

"You're the prettiest person I've ever seen." The little girl stared up in awe.

"Thank you so much. But you do know there is much more to being a girl than being pretty."

"Yeah, I guess. Daddy says it's important to be quiet."

Brisa and Azure shared disapproving looks.

"Are there any people like me from your world?"

"No. There are a lot of people with different skin colors, but not purple."

"Interesting." Brisa lowered herself to one knee. "May the fire in your chest burn bright, Oriana."

"What does that mean?"

"It's something my people say to each other. We believe that we have a fire in our chests that can help us know when we are acting with kindness and honor. When our fires burn bright, we know we are on the right track. When they smolder and dim, we know that we have strayed from the right path."

"Oh." Oriana did her best to not look confused.

"Have you ever felt anything like that?" Brisa asked.

"I think so."

"That's great." Brisa flashed the warmest of smiles.

"It is?"

"Yeah. And if you want to, you can try to pay attention the next time that feeling arises. It's trying to tell you something. Something only you can figure out for yourself."

Oriana nodded, still obviously awestruck by Brisa. "It feels kinda warm right now." She looked down at her own chest.

"Wonderful."

"Well, it looks like we're just about there, and I wanted Oriana to meet a few more crew members." Azure hated to rush, but their remaining time with Oriana was possibly coming to a close, and she wanted to get these introductions in.

Brisa traced a line from her head to her heart and drew a circle around her chest. "We are well met, Oriana."

"Bye." The little girl could hardly pry her eyes away from Brisa.

The two ship's capybaras, Eleanor and Alistair Covington, waddled nearby. Azure introduced Oriana—who was thoroughly amused—to them. She taught the little girl to bow to them and to show the proper respect whenever they crossed her path.

Next, they found Syl, Nargol, and Orok furling the mainsail and getting ready to dock.

After introductions were made, Syl asked, "Is there anyone like us where you come from?"

"No," Oriana said. "There are just people. Well, there are animals, too. But the only ones that can talk are, uh, humans."

"How interesting," Syl said.

"I thought I'd be scared around you guys, but I'm not. You're nice."

"Well that's great," Nargol said. "You have nothing to be afraid of from us."

"Yeah," Orok added. "You're part of the crew now, and that means you're under our protection."

Oriana beamed up at them. "Sometimes there are mean kids at school. I wish I could take you to school with me."

As everyone chuckled, Morgak came up from belowdecks holding a small bunch of bananas. Her eyes lit up when she saw Oriana.

"Hello," Morgak said. "I was about to go feed the capybaras. Would you like to go with me?"

Oriana looked to Azure, as if for permission.

"You should go." Azure pointed across the deck to where the Covingtons were now lazing away the day. "It's always fun to watch them eat."

Oriana smiled and the two fast friends ran off together.

AZURE DECIDED THAT she and Elijah would take Oriana to the casino to inquire about her lost knife. By the time they had docked and readied for debarkation, it was early afternoon, and Mirth Island buzzed with activity.

After they debarked and blended into the crowd, Robin caught up and landed on Azure's shoulder.

"Can I come along?"

"Are you going to be nice?"

"Of course. I'm always nice, aren't I?" Robin's voice had only the slightest hint of sarcasm.

Oriana took Elijah's hand and pulled him forward to look at something on the boardwalk—she had sure warmed to him quickly. Azure took the brief moment of privacy to ask Robin about her recent attitude.

"What's your problem with Oriana?"

"I don't know." Robin looked down and away. "I mean, could she be any clingier?"

"She's a terrified kid in a strange new world."

"Yeah. I know." Robin met Azure's eyes. "It's just that she's taking up all of your time, and I'm being jealous. I know most people think I'm perfect; and they're not far off. But I *am* capable of an imperfect moment, as rare as that might be."

"Well you have nothing to be jealous about, you big baby. You know you'll always be my best friend."

"I'd better be." Robin cocked her head in a half-joking, half-I'm-definitely-not-joking manner.

"You will."

"But..." Robin hesitated as if she might stop, but eventually went on. "You're about to be married. So, the thought of kids might not be far off, you know? And once that happens, you won't have much time available for your best friend, no matter what you promise." She shook her tiny head, as if embarrassed by what she was saying. "Seeing you with Oriana is making me think about all that. You are so gods-damned perfect with her. You'll make such a good mom. And I want that for you if that's what you want. It's just..."

"Well, if it makes you feel any better, you're not the only one worrying about such things. There's a mini crisis going on up here," Azure pointed to her temple, "about that very topic. Seeing Elijah with Oriana," now she pointed out ahead, "is having the same effect on me. A part of me wants to run away from the whole thing."

"Commitment is scary as shit," Robin said. "It's a little easier for us birds. My clutch of eggs took relatively no time to hatch, and my kids have already fledged. But you humans...that's a lifetime obligation."

"Exactly. My whole pirate captain thing is just setting sail and it seems like those sails are going to be furled before I really get a chance to reach full speed."

"You're really leaning into the sailing metaphors."

"They're bad, aren't they?"

"Not bad, but probably better used sparingly." Robin cocked her head. "Anyway, I'm sorry for being jealous."

"Oh, that's alright. I'm glad it came up. Feels better to have talked about it." Azure stroked her friend's head.

"Azure, do you see it?" Oriana pointed down to a yellow flower that had pushed up through the planks of the boardwalk with an impressive blue butterfly perched on its petals.

"Ooh, that's pretty." As Azure caught up to them, the butterfly took wing and flitted about in the gentle breeze.

"Don't worry," Robin whispered. "I'm resisting the urge to snatch it out of the sky and eat it."

"Thank you for that." Azure shook her head and smiled.

"It's not easy, though. That thing looks delicious, and I'm starving."

"You're a true martyr."

The casino was even more impressive close up. Its intricate design and insane attention to detail weren't apparent from further away. Every stone seemed brand new and perfectly placed, every door handle, sconce, and adornment polished and sparkling. The casino looked exactly like what Azure used to picture in her mind when listening to stories about princess's castles on the Continent.

A statue out front depicted an armored knight holding a sword and shield. The shield was etched with the casino's symbol, which was also on the countless flags all around the grounds—a jewel-encrusted golden crown with two golden chalices crossed below it.

The zip-line—dizzyingly high from this angle—came down to the east, landing in a lush meadow surrounded by white-barked trees.

"Fancy," said Elijah.

"Haven't you been here before?" Azure asked.

"Nope. This wasn't here until about ten years ago, and I was a reanimated skeleton at that time. Not exactly preferred clientele at a fancy place like this."

"Oh." It was still strange to recall that Elijah had spent the better part of a century being a walking skeleton.

The front doors were opened for them by two men in expensive-looking dress shirts. "Welcome to the Fortress," they said in unison.

"Thank you," Azure said as they entered the casino.

"Funny how they welcome me, now," Elijah said, not bothering to lower his voice. "A few months ago, they would have turned me away, and nothing has changed aside from my outward appearance." He shook his head. "Not really funny at all."

"No. It's not." Azure didn't know what else to say.

The inside of the place was every bit as fancy as the outside. The entire first level of the castle appeared to be one giant room swathed in a rich red carpet with golden borders. Most of the room was filled with gaming tables, most of which Azure couldn't identify. A sign just inside the door read:

<u>ABSOLUTELY NO MAGIC ALLOWED</u>
Violators Will Be Punished to the Full Extent of the Law.
Any Wands Used in This Building Will Be Confiscated.
Ciguapa Must Wear Clothing That Covers All Tattoos.
Fauns Are Not Allowed to Whisper.

Orcs Are Not Allowed in Groups of More Than Two.

Beyond the sign, there was a two-stair descent onto the playing floor. At the bottom of the stairs, front and center, was a glass display case that ran from the floor to the tall ceiling. On the front of the glass case was another sign; this one read: *Artifacts from the Continent!* Inside, there were three items being displayed. One was an ancient, battered knight's helmet with a plaque in front of it that read: *Actual Helmet Worn by Griffin the Unrivaled.* Azure wondered if that could possibly be true. The next item was a loaded crossbow, which also looked ancient, but still extremely lethal. The last item, sitting on a red velvet pillow, was a shiny golden dagger, inlaid with emeralds. On either side of the case was an orc, each wearing a huge shirt with the symbol of the Fortress sewn into the right breast area.

Gripping Oriana's hand, Azure approached the case.

"Is that your knife?" she said to the little girl.

Oriana nodded; eyes trained on the closest orc.

"Excuse me," Azure said to the orc guards. "Could I speak to whoever is in charge around here?"

The orcs both seemed a bit taken aback that a human addressed them, but they didn't let it show for more than a moment. "The boss isn't here, today," one of them said. "But you can find the second in command over at the casino office." He pointed to a room along the right side of the casino floor.

"Okay. Thank you so much, guys." Azure reached up and patted the closest guard on the shoulder.

"Yeah...uh...no problem." They obviously weren't used to interacting with a human who was so comfortable around orcs.

As they made their way toward the office, Azure took in the sights, amazed by the amount of people inside. All the workers she could see, besides the two orc guards, were human. Most of the customers were human, too. But there was a ciguapa man—surrounded by human women— playing a game in the "High Rollers" area. A vast bar area with a stage lay out to the right.

The double doors of the casino office were wide open, so they walked inside. The room had a large wooden desk in the far corner with two chairs sitting in front of it. A tall, slender man with slicked-back hair and a manicured black beard sat behind the desk, writing with a feather quill. He wore a black shirt that laced up in the front. Next to the desk was a perch, on which stood a watchful Peregrine Falcon.

"Hello, sir," Azure said. "Could we have a moment of your time?"

"Certainly." The man's voice was grandiose, with a bit of a nasal whine. "My name is Mr. Bancroft. How can I help you?"

"My name is Azure, and this is Elijah, Oriana, and Robin. We're here to inquire about one of the pieces in your display case. The knife you've got there actually belongs to this little girl." She aimed a hand at Oriana.

The man suppressed a chuckle, then glanced at the falcon. "That is quite an unexpected claim. One that, unfortunately, I am not authorized to handle. The owner of The Fortress, Mr. Pierce, is out today, and won't be back until tomorrow. When he returns, you can take the matter up with him, although I can't imagine that he'll be willing to part with such a valuable item."

"He might once he has heard our story. That knife is very important to my friend here, and it's imperative that she get it back."

The falcon eyed Robin, snapping its beak shut. Robin turned around and shook her tail feathers at it.

"I must express my regrets that I cannot clear this matter up for you, now. In the mean time, I would love to offer you a free room in our hotel. You could pass the time playing any number of our fine games of chance."

"I appreciate the offer, but my ship is docked nearby, and I'd just as soon stay there with my crew."

"Then I shall expect you back tomorrow. The owner should be back by no later than six o'clock."

"I thank you for your time, Mr. Bancroft."

The man gave a deep, slow nod, then returned to his writing.

Azure's eyes were drawn to a small treasure chest on the desk with the word *Carlyle* carved into the wood. It was so much smaller than she expected, but it must have been Wakeman's lost chest. She wondered if it could really fit a hundred gold coins.

"Uh...one more thing," Azure said.

"Yes?"

"That treasure chest, there. That belongs to a client of mine, a Mr. Wakeman Carlyle. He has tasked me with getting that back for him."

"Well you're just full of demands, aren't you?"

"I—"

"But this one I feel I can handle myself. There is no chance Mr. Pierce is going to let you take this. He has already picked out a place for it in his room on the top floor. I'm sorry about your client, but I think you'll find that the law heavily favors the possessor, as you may have heard."

"Well maybe Mr. Pierce will surprise you."

"Perhaps. Doubtful, but I guess you never know." He began to write again.

During the conversation, Robin had puffed herself up, and was staring at the falcon.

"Little bird," the falcon said before Azure could turn to leave, its voice decidedly female. "If you shit on one of the customers, or really anywhere inside this place, you will feel the sting of my talons."

Robin blurted a short laugh. "If I shit in here, it'll be on your head."

The falcon stood up straighter, more aggressive, staring Robin down with shiny black eyes.

"You don't scare me," Robin continued. "I've outsmarted hawks that made you look like a sea-sick duck in comparison."

"You obviously underestimate my abilities."

"Don't preen yourself, you scraggly bitch."

"Okay, Faron," Mr. Bancroft said. "That's quite enough."

The falcon relaxed its posture but never took her eyes off of Robin. As Azure left the room, Robin returned the stare, unflinching.

Mirth Island Fun

"What an asshole," Robin said. "*Don't shit on anyone.*" Her voice was mocking and over exaggerated. "I have half a mind to splatter the roulette table out of spite."

"Please don't."

"Fine, but only for you, Az."

"Thank you."

Azure slapped the back of one of the orc guards as she passed. "Thanks for the help, fellas."

The guards looked at each other with confused expressions.

"Uh...you're welcome."

Outside, Azure knelt near the knight statue to talk to Oriana. "We have to wait for a whole day and night to get you back to your parents. I'm sorry about that, but would it make it better if we had a little fun? This place has all kinds of fun stuff to do."

"Like what?" Her eyes were hopeful.

"Like waterslides, and carnival games, and magical reality games, and something called a rollercoaster."

"Can we do all of those things?"

Azure grinned. "Only if we get started right away."

After reporting what had happened back to the crew, and telling them they had the rest of the day and a night to kill on Mirth—to much celebration—Azure, Elijah, and Oriana hit the family fun area. Robin said she was tired and wanted to take a bath and a nap on the ship. There was a hint of lingering jealousy in her voice, but Azure didn't push the issue.

Their first stop was the waterslides in a relatively small alcove on the far east side of the island. Oriana was hesitant to climb the tall ladders at first, but with Azure climbing just behind her, she was able to make it to the top. Once she had slid down the first time, she was hooked. They must have spent hours going up and down those slides. Eventually, Azure had to coax her away by promising a cookie.

After a stop at the cookie stand, they made their way to the carnival games. Elijah disappeared while Azure and Oriana were unsuccessfully tossing little rings around empty bottles, then came back with two little stuffed capybaras he had won by knocking over milk jugs. He gave one to each of the girls, beaming with triumphant pride.

Next was the rollercoaster. On close examination, Azure discovered that it was run by a series of magic wands built into the tracks. She had no idea how someone had done it, but the wands somehow pushed the coaster up to a peak, then let its weight do the rest.

"How are these wands working without anyone holding them?" She asked herself more than anybody.

"I don't know," Elijah replied. "I've never been much for magic, myself."

However they worked, they produced big reactions out of people. Delighted screams filled the pleasantly humid air every time the coaster made the plunge down from the peak.

When it was their turn to ride, they were seated in the front. Oriana squealed with delight for the entire ride, Azure held on for dear life, sure that the cars were going to barrel off of the track, and Elijah puked on some nearby ferns seconds after the ride was over.

As they were walking along the boardwalk, looking for something to calm Elijah's stomach, Oriana stopped and stared up at a sign connected to a small building. The sign was a wooden carving of a mermaid with a vibrant aquamarine tail, with the words *The Mermaid Experience* painted across her body.

"Do you want to try that?"

She gave a very serious nod.

Inside, they were greeted by a Ciguapa woman named Tralo, who explained how everything worked. Oriana was right at the age where it was tough to say how well she would take the total immersion of magical reality.

"The hardest part to get used to is breathing underwater," Tralo told them. "You won't actually be underwater, but you'll be completely convinced that you are. At first, your body will be resistant to letting you inhale. But I assure you, if you just breathe, and let your mind relax, you'll enjoy the rest of the experience much more."

Azure had doubts about herself, let alone a seven-year-old girl, but Oriana was too excited for them to turn back now. Elijah, who was still feeling queasy, decided to sit this one out.

Just like at the Pirate Experience, they were brought into a darkened room with silvery glowing lines across the ceiling, floor, and all four walls.

"You ready?" Tralo said after all the preparations had been made.

"Are you?" Azure asked Oriana.

"Yes." She looked a perfect mixture of excited and anxious.

"We're ready," Azure told Tralo as she took Oriana's hand.

"Okay. Remember to breathe, and to let your mind relax."

Azure could feel the water before anything became visible. It was slightly cooler than the air in the room had been—very invigorating and refreshing. She closed her eyes and gave the little girl's hand a squeeze.

When she opened her eyes a fantastic kelp forest lay out before her. They were floating about halfway between the surface—sparkling yellow and white in the sun—and the busy ocean floor. Tropical fish of all shapes, sizes, and colors swam about in every direction.

As she took all of this in, she realized she wasn't breathing. She tried to take a breath, but her body rejected the idea. She looked to Oriana, whose eyes were wide. As calmly as possible, she closed her eyes and forced herself to inhale. To her surprise, it turned out that breathing didn't feel any different.

"Close your eyes and take a breath," she told Oriana. Talking, it seemed, was the same in this underwater experience, too. She had expected an effervescent surge of bubbles when she tried to talk, but nothing like that happened.

Oriana did as she asked, then opened her eyes with a relieved smile.

Before Azure could say another word, a gorgeous mermaid approached them from out of the kelp forest, followed by another mermaid who had tentacles instead of a tail.

"Hey, Oriana and Azure," the mermaid said, her voice melodic. "My name is Kelde, and this is my friend, Silvia. Could you two help us out with something?"

Azure looked to Oriana, wanting her to lead.

"Yeah." Oriana's eyes were wider than before, her smile bigger than Azure had yet seen it.

"Oh, good. We need help finding Sunny, our pet sea turtle. It seems she got lost again somewhere in the kelp forest. Could you help us look for her?"

"Of course!" Oriana said, buying in to the experience with all her heart and mind.

"Oh, thank you so much," Kelde said.

In the short pause that followed, Oriana addressed Silvia. "Are you a different kind of mermaid?"

"No, I'm a cecaelia. My people are really good friends with the mermaids, though."

Azure had never heard of the cecaelia, and wondered if they were real, or just part of this illusion. If someone would have told her there were mermaids with eight tentacles coming down from their waists instead of tails, she would have found it slightly off-putting, but Silvia was gorgeous, and the tentacles didn't seem out of place at all.

"You guys go that way." Kelde pointed to their right. "You'll find the Octoracle over there on her coral throne. She might be able to help. We'll go the other way and we'll all meet back here in a little while. Sound good?"

Oriana gave a serious, determined nod.

Still holding Azure's hand, Oriana started swimming in the direction the mermaid had pointed. When Azure tried to follow, she realized for the first time that she had a tail instead of legs, and somehow it just worked. Swimming with a tail was surprisingly intuitive.

"Sunny," Oriana called as they darted between tall swaying stalks of kelp.

They passed all kinds of sea life as they searched. There were stingrays, eels, seahorses, crabs, anemones, and urchins. To their surprise, most could speak and greeted Azure and Oriana as they passed.

As they came through a particularly dense thicket, an impressive chair formed from living coral became visible in a clearing of sorts. But the chair was empty.

"I thought the Octoracle was supposed to be here," Azure said as they swam closer.

"Me too." Oriana turned in circles looking for any signs of life.

"I am here," said a deep, melodic female voice.

The middle of the coral chair began to change color, revealing a purplish octopus sitting on the seat. Her eyes, with horizontal slits for pupils, were alien and beautiful at the same time. They exuded intellect, warmth, and pre-science. All eight of her arms waved at the new arrivals.

"I sense you are in need of answers. What answers do you seek?"

"We need to help a mermaid and a cec...a lady with tentacles like you find their lost sea turtle," Oriana said.

"Aah." She scratched her head with three of her tentacles. "I can only leave you with this clue; let the unicorns of the sea be your guide." She started to change color, again, blending back into her coral throne. "Good luck!" she called as she became undetectable.

"The unicorns of the sea?" Oriana pinched her chin with her thumb and forefinger. "She probably meant a narwhal." Her eyes drifted toward the surface, then lit up with excitement. "Like that one!" She pointed to the dark silhouette of a narwhal, shadowy against the bright, sunlight-dappled surface.

Hand-in-hand, the two of them swam up. When they got to the narwhal, they found that it was just a statue, a perfect replica made of carved stone.

"Maybe we should go the way its horn is pointing," Oriana said.

Azure was blown away by her problem-solving abilities. She hadn't even thought of that, yet.

"I think you're right."

Oriana led the way through the thicker, leafier part of the kelp forest. Before long, they arrived at another narwhal statue. Again, they followed the direction of its horn, which brought them back down to the ocean floor. After the third narwhal, they ended up under a dome-like canopy of kelp. The darkened area was alive with the electric pinks and purples of a thousand jellyfish; a blanket of stars glowing and twinkling overhead. In the background, the sounds of whale song echoed across unknown distances, resonating in the water around them.

And there, on the sea floor, was a turtle, swimming upside down with a starfish on its belly.

Azure and Oriana dove down toward it.

"Sunny?" Oriana called.

"That's me." The sea turtle smiled up at them.

"Kelde and Silvia are looking for you."

"Oh. I was just playing with my friend Sea Star."

Oriana was beaming.

"Well, could you come with us to find them?" Azure said, having all but forgotten that this wasn't real. "They're awfully worried about you."

"Sure. Let's go."

After saying goodbye to Sea Star, the three of them hurried back to the agreed-upon meeting place where they found Kelde and Silvia waiting. When they saw Sunny, they were ecstatic.

"Sunny! You found her! Thank you so much!"

"You're welcome." Oriana's face had reddened, and she almost held back a prideful grin.

"Well," the mermaid said, "I'd love for you to stay here all day, but we have to get going. Thanks, again for helping us find Sunny. You did such a great job! Goodbye."

The kelp forest vanished. The feeling of water and weightlessness subsided. They were in a darkened room again, standing on legs in dry air.

Oriana looked around, slightly confused, but it didn't take long for her to re-establish her bearings. "That was the funnest thing I've ever done," she said.

"It was up there for me, too."

For a short, but glorious time, Azure had been a kid again. She gripped the ship's wheel around her neck and smiled.

The Play

O n the way back to the *Adventure Ship,* a man in the middle of the
boardwalk announced something loudly.

"Come and see the Mirth Island Players perform *The Daring Adventures
of the Ingenious Marauders,* put on by the good people at The Fortress. Only
a copper to get in, and that's a bargain at twice the price!"

"The marauders play?" Azure said, stopping to try and find where the
stage was.

There was a tall wooden wall just north of the boardwalk. A skinnier
wooden path went from the boardwalk through an opening in the wall. In
that opening, Azure could see a small part of a large stage, illuminated by
dozens of torches.

"You want to go, don't you?" Elijah said.

"I would like to," Azure replied. "I'm curious to see how they portray us,
aren't you?"

Elijah fidgeted. "I'm not sure if I am or not."

Azure mentally kicked herself for asking him that question. She knew
how uncomfortable it made him to see himself as a skeleton. When they had
watched the official play in Whetstone, Elijah had smiled and tried to seem
happy, but Azure could see through his facade.

Oriana looked up at both of them with eyes half-closed.

"Maybe I can take her back to the ship and put her to bed?" Elijah said,
now clearly trying to avoid the play.

"Is that alright, Oriana?"

The little girl gave them a sleepy nod.

"And you're sure it's alright with you?" Azure wrapped her arms around Elijah's neck.

"Oh yeah, no problem."

There was a hint of something lurking behind the carefree affectation, but Azure couldn't be sure what it was. She debated going back with them, but she felt unexplainably energized, and the play tugged at her with unseen strings.

"Thank you," she said, giving Elijah a kiss.

He smiled at her, then gave her a kiss on her forehead. "In case I'm asleep when you get back." Elijah had given her a forehead kiss every night since they started seeing each other romantically. He hadn't missed one night, and Azure loved their little ritual.

Azure watched Elijah and Oriana as they walked away. After about ten steps, Oriana looked up to him and said something. He bent forward and scooped her up by her armpits, letting her head rest on his shoulder. Azure continued to watch them until they vanished into the busy Mirth Island crowd, a faint warmness building in her chest.

After fishing a copper coin from her pocket, Azure turned and made her way through the fence along the wooden path. She handed the copper to a woman at a ticket booth, who gave Azure a playbill.

As she descended the wooden steps to the seats, the play began. She took a seat in the back row as quietly as possible.

Just like the official play in Whetstone, this one opened with the Marauder King meeting his first love, Calliope, on the beach, helping her rescue a stranded dolphin. Azure was impressed with the quality of the actors, props, and everything else. It wasn't much different than the original, as far as she could remember.

One of Azure's favorite scenes was the fight at Wench's over the woman the Marauder King fancied, Chastity. In real life, the Marauder King had unintentionally picked a fight with a man who he thought was receiving a little too much attention from Chastity. The marauders and the man's friends had a brief fight that was broken up by security. Chastity brought them their check, and they left after paying.

In the play, however, the fight was much more dramatic, the marauders the clear victors. The character playing Azure, who was extremely attractive, much to Azure's delight, had some great fighting stunts, and took out three men from the other crew.

When the fight was over, Chastity thanked the Marauder King and gave him a kiss on the cheek. She begged him to stay when he said he had to go. He told her that he must go, but that he would return to her when his noble expedition was at an end. Azure wished it would have turned out that way in reality. The Marauder King deserved love, but it had been hard to come by for the misunderstood marauder.

Most of his story was told through song, and all the lyrics were printed on the playbill, allowing Azure to read along as the cast sang. One of the silliest songs was about the time they met Zoth-Avarex on Dragon Island.

In the play, as Azure and Brisa opened an ancient treasure chest, a cloud of smoke poured out of it. Partially hidden by the smoke, a great papiermâché dragon was rolled onto the stage, its eyes glowing red. The Marauder King was positioned so that only he could see the dragon, and the rest of the crew was left to rely on the description of what he could see.

After the dragon said, "It feels good to finally get out of there!" the song began. Azure read along, smiling the entire time.

MARAUDER KING
A dragon!
THE CREW
A DRAGON?
MARAUDER KING
A fearsome beast from beneath the beach!
THE CREW
WAIT, A DRAGON?
THE MARAUDER KING
Yes, a dragon.
THE CREW
FOR OUR GUNS WE INTEND TO REACH!
MARAUDER KING
No! This dragon is blessed with speech,
And to you, crew, I must beseech.
Allow me to parlay with the dragon today
And a treaty we just may reach.

THE CREW
  HE INTENDS A CONFABULATION,
  WITH A REPTILIAN ABOMINATION?
MARAUDER KING
  Yes. And I must now insist,
  That you cease and desist
  Calling names to this dragon
  Before it gets pissed!
THE CREW
  CAUSE IF IT GETS PISSED
  IT COULD SCORCH US WITH FIRE,
  GRIND UP OUR BONES,
  OH! OUR FATE COULD BE DIRE!
  IT COULD—

"What the hell is going on, here?" the paper-mâché dragon said, interrupting the song.

Azure put a hand to her mouth to stop herself from blurting laughter. She hadn't realized how much she missed the Marauder King, but seeing this musical again brought back all the good memories of her time with him. He was relentlessly positive, an eternal goofball with a heart of gold.

The most impressive scene was a depiction of the time a ringfall meteor nearly destroyed the *Adventure Ship*. The stage crew did an amazing job, darkening the stage, raining sparks over it, then rolling out a giant fireball, lit from within somehow.

All of the actors on stage began to move very slowly, except for the Marauder King, who took a position under a ghostly light.

The slow-moving actors performed a three-part harmony in which they all drew out the word *ringfall* in ominous voices.

Again, Azure read along with the song.

MARAUDER KING
Deim's icy fingers are enveloping my heart.

Fobos has full control of my mind.
Mordo's presence permeates the fiery sky.
I fear that my crew Tanos soon will find.
For the fire in the sky, sometimes pretty,
Now has our fates locked in its grip.
A fireball of quite epic proportions,
Is barreling down upon our humble ship!

The paper-mâché dragon darted out from the other side of the stage and blocked the fireball before it could crash into the crew. The audience cheered as the light of the meteor fizzled out. Azure clapped and whistled as loud as she could.

After a while, though, Azure's eyelids began to feel heavy, her energy having found its limits. The play was a lot of fun, but she was exhausted, and she had a big, important day tomorrow. Ducking low, she crept out of the theater area, hoping no one would notice her leave.

Mr. Pierce

The next morning, Azure took Oriana to see Mr. Pierce. After giving it serious thought, she decided Elijah should stay behind. Maybe this Mr. Pierce would have more sympathy for just a woman and a kid, and be more likely to turn over Oriana's knife.

The same two orc guards stood on either side of the glass case inside. Azure waved to them, but they didn't seem to notice. Mr. Bancroft—with the ever-watchful falcon on his shoulder—was working in the middle of a huge island of gaming tables.

To the left, two large signs she hadn't noticed before were sat in front of a red-carpeted staircase going up. The first sign read:

NEW to the Fortress
5-Star Gentleman's Club
18 and Older

The second read:

Dancers Wanted:
Only Humans and Ciguapas Need Apply
Inquire Upstairs

Azure entered the casino office, where a tall, muscular man in an expensive-looking suit was now sitting at the desk. His head was shaved completely bald and he had a reddish mustache over his serious, thin-lipped mouth. He was bent over a stack of papers, writing with a feather quill.

"Excuse me," said Azure.

The man continued with his work for several seconds before looking up, somewhat annoyed. He didn't say a word.

"Hello, sir. I was wondering if I might have a moment of your time." Azure's face flushed, and her heart beat faster, flustered by the man's appearance and apparent indifference. Captain Azure Brine, vanquisher of Captain Roberts, flustered by a man in a fancy suit. She took a sharp breath in through her nose and refocused.

"Just a moment," Mr. Pierce said. "I'm very busy, here. The government never seems to stop delighting in telling me how I'm to do things at my own casino." He shook his head in disgust.

Azure pulled Oriana forward, and the two of them took seats in front of the desk.

"I—"

"First we have to let orcs on the island," Mr. Pierce interrupted. "Then we have to employ them, and now they want to give them the same hours and work conditions that human's have? Iloxe's balls! Where does it end?"

Azure hated this guy already. Any feelings of being flustered vanished. Now she just needed to remember to be as cordial as she could for Oriana's sake.

"The Mirth Island Council is, and has been, getting carried away. Always keen to be on the cutting edge of giving human's rights away." He shook his head, again. "Things wouldn't be this way if Governor Pratt had taken his rightful place, but now they got him locked away." Mr. Pierce clenched his jaw. "If it wasn't for the draw, and the money that it brought here, I'd find a new base of operations." He thrust his quill into an inkwell and leaned back in his chair. "Anyway, what can I do for you?"

"There's—"

"You know, I would have been on Governor Pratt's galleon, but I couldn't get away from my responsibilities at the casino. Governor Pratt invited me, personally, to join." He beamed with pride. "It's a shame most people on that galleon died, but I don't buy for a second the story about what happened that day. Governor Pratt was betrayed, simple as that."

Azure's eye twitched, her hands involuntarily formed fists. She barely managed to not respond in anger through force of will.

"Are you gonna tell me why you're here or not? I've got a ton of work to do. We're adding a whole new layer of fun, here. Our Gentleman's Club is officially opening in two days."

"Yes. One of the artifacts in your case up front belongs to this little girl." Azure cleared her throat. "This might be hard to believe, but she actually comes from another world, and that knife you have in your display case is hers, and it's the thing she needs to get back to her home world, back to her parents."

Mr. Pierce made a tent with his fingers, his face unreadable. He had barely even looked at them since they'd entered.

"So, you're saying that the possibly priceless artifact my team risked their lives on an island with an active volcano to find and add to our collection...belongs to a kid from some *other world*?" He said the last words with a snide voice and an eye-roll.

"Yes, and we can prove it. Just let us—"

A man in a casino uniform burst into the room with a panicked expression on his face.

"Someone just won a hundred gold at Thirty-Seven Gods. They're cashing out now, and say they're gonna leave!"

"Where is Mr. Bancroft?" Mr. Pierce was calm, although obviously annoyed.

"He's interrogating a possible cheat in the back room, sir."

"Okay, I have another question for you, then. Are you fucking stupid?"

"Uh...no, sir."

"So, you're not an incompetent idiot, then?"

"No."

"Then why aren't you doing everything in your power to keep them here instead of talking to me like a gods-damned fucking idiot?"

"I...uh...yes, sir." The flustered man turned and rushed away.

"Gods!" Mr. Pierce said in disgust. "It is so hard to find competent help. That is *exactly* what I pay him for. And yet he wants me to hold his hand through every little decision." He continued as if he were imparting wisdom that Azure couldn't wait to hear. "In this business, there is only one rule; keep the money flowing in. I mean, of course you want them to have little wins here and there, and even big wins from time to time, but the secret is to keep them playing. We'll get it all if they play long enough."

After a brief, awkward silence, Azure spoke up. "So, as I was saying, we could show you that the knife is what we say it is if you give us a chance to prove it."

"Do you know how many crazy stories like that I've heard in my time here? People will try absolutely anything to get a piece of what I've built."

"But it's not like that. I promise you, my only interest is getting this scared little girl home."

"It's still firmly in the category of *not my problem*. I'm trying to run a business, here, not a charity. If I gave into every person that came in here with a sob story, I'd be broke." He still refused to even make eye contact.

"This—"

"You continue talking as if I didn't just definitively tell you no. So maybe I should make it clearer. The answer is no. You may not have our priceless artifact, that is likely from the Continent. Now, if you'll excuse me, it sounds as if we have a cheating problem in the backroom. Probably a faun. Half of them are professional card-cheats, I swear."

Mr. Pierce pushed away from the table and hurried out onto the casino floor without even looking Azure or Oriana's way.

Azure hung her head in shame. She hadn't been strong enough. She could have done so much better, and she hadn't even asked about Mr. Carlyle's treasure.

Unable to look Oriana in the eye, Azure stared blankly at the little girl's shoes. They were so unlike any shoes Azure had ever seen before, made from a strange, white, alien material. Painted on the sides were the same creatures from her shirt, the majestic white horses with horns jutting out from their foreheads.

The shoes were just so...out of place, here. They were from a completely different world, one with different rules and clothes and culture. They didn't belong here, and neither did Oriana. She belonged with her parents, who no doubt wore similar shoes and knew everything about her.

Azure looked at her own shoes- not much more than a strap of leather with a crude, weather-worn buckle on top. The difference was striking.

Without another thought, Azure stood and marched out of the office.

"Mr. Pierce!" she shouted across the casino floor.

He stopped, about twenty feet away, and turned around.

"I'm not finished, here," she said.

Mr. Pierced laughed and shook his head. "Yes, you are." He turned and began to strut away.

A low growl filled Azure's throat. Her face was hot in an instant.

She lifted a foot, ripped off one of her leather shoes, ran a few steps forward, and chucked it at Mr. Pierce, striking him in the back of the neck.

"That's all you got?" He faced Azure, a cynical grin spread wide across his face. Two human casino guards rushed to flank him on either side.

Mr. Pierce pointed to the front doors. "Get the fuck out of my casino, and never come back." He picked up the shoe and tossed it back to her, making a show of sniffing his hand and grimacing.

Reluctantly, Azure scooped up the shoe, never taking her glare away from Mr. Pierce, who continued to avoid eye contact. She turned to find Oriana standing at the office door. Teeth grinding, she took the little girl's hand and stormed away.

BACK AT THE *Adventure Ship*, Azure explained to the crew what had transpired.

"Well, we're just gonna have to steal it, then," Robin stated when Azure was finished.

"Steal it? From that place?" Azure pointed back to the towering casino.

"Yeah. I mean, we've got a crew already. Haven't you ever heard of a heist?"

"A heist?"

Robin hopped excitedly on the ship's rail. "Yeah. A heist! But we'll need a foolproof plan..."

INTERLUDE: A Message from the Marauder King

Amidst the heist planning, Nova, the Marauder King's conjured bird, alighted on the bar of the *Adventure Ship* and untied a rolled piece of parchment from his leg.

"I bring a message from the Marauder King," he said to anyone within earshot.

"Thank you." Azure picked up the parchment from the bar.

Several marauders gathered around as she unrolled it and began to read.

Dearest Marauders,

It is with great pleasure that I write to you this evening. I hope that this letter finds you well, in fantastic health, and even better spirits. The smashing success of The Daring Adventures of the Ingenious Marauders, I'm thrilled to say, continues. After selling the theater out for no less than seven straight months, the troupe and I decided to take a much-deserved break. Now, it is my dearest wish that this next part doesn't upset any of you, but the entire cast took a trip to Mirth Island so I could finally make an earnest attempt at winning the heart of my dear Chastity! I'm sorry I did this without you, but in my defense, it was a spur-of-the-moment lark, and we set out to Mirth when we were all three sheets to the proverbial wind.

Anyway, upon our arrival at Mirth Island, we enacted my plan. I went into her place of business and asked her when she would have the time to take a short stroll with me. She was actually quite receptive, and told me she had a lunch break due to her at that very moment! To say my heart was a flutter would be a colossal understatement. It felt as if two wild animals were engaging in a life-and-death battle inside my ribcage, to be honest.

As Chastity and I exited the building, the orchestra from our show began to play, filling the street with sweet, subtle music. Thousands of orchid petals rained down upon us, tossed by strategically placed stage hands. As the music built to a crescendo, I professed my feelings to her.

"Chastity," I said, "I have long cared for you. The mere thought of your pretty smile heartens me, even in my lowest moments. The memory of your voice, your laugh, brightens the darkest days. I realize that we don't really know each other, but that is something I do not wish to abide any longer. I know that I am a few years older than you, and that I am not the handsomest, or strongest, or most debonair. I know I am scarred, and one limb short compared to most men. I know I'm a goofball, and I now embrace that whole-heartedly. But this is what I can offer you: I offer you my love, my support, and my understanding. I offer you a man who will treasure you the way you deserve to be treasured, in good times and in bad. I offer you nothing short of a life filled with love and adventure." At this point, a flower petal fell into my mouth, nearly choking me. I spit it out as gracefully as I could and continued. "Chastity, will you decide, here and now, to give me an honest chance? I only ask that you consider me as a worthy suitor. Will you allow me to prove my devotion to you?"

The music stopped as the final few petals floated to the ground.

"You know what?" she said, her voice as sweet as honey. "That actually sounds pretty good."

Oh, joy of joys!

So, to make a long story shorter, Chastity has moved into my place in Whetstone! We are doing fantastically well. I cannot wait to see all of you, and for you to get to know her like I do! Please please please, when you get the chance, come and visit!

Yours Forever,

MK

As Azure read, Robin landed near Nova, who began his strange mating dance along the bar.

"Save your energy," Robin said. "I mean, that dance is incredibly sexy, but I'm good right now."

Nova hung his head. "Okay, fine." He looked up at her. "How are the kids?"

"They all fledged a while back. Happy and healthy, every one of them" She sighed. "I miss them."

"It's good to see you."

"Yeah. It's good to see you, too."

Azure lost the rest of their conversation as she and the marauders began to plan a visit to Whetstone after the whole ordeal with Oriana was figured out.

PART TWO
THE HEIST

Groundwork- Blunderbuss

Blunderbuss's role was simple.

He was tasked with getting a fake Gaming Commission badge from *The Underworld Market: The #1 Source for All Your Illicit Needs,* which was located on the west side of Mirth Island. Having done some time as a low-level smuggler in the years before getting on with the marauders, he knew the owner of the shop well.

He meandered through the seedier side of the island while whistling the tune to "The Princess Loved to Fart." He was no stranger to this side of the island, but was no longer drawn to the seedy or illegal as much as he used to be. His time with the childlike Marauder King had all-but worn that mindset away.

Blunderbuss found that walking for any significant distance was tough after both of his unfortunate accidents. He stopped and stretched his hamstrings often, and felt uncomfortable tension in his calves. Luckily, both shots had left most of the muscle in his ass intact. Sitting was painful, but walking was usually fine. He figured he'd just have to get used to it, and vowed to get more regular exercise.

As he passed a row of street vendors selling obviously stolen goods, he noticed a flash of vibrant yellow to his right. There, on a rickety old table sat a wire mesh cage. Inside the cage were about two dozen lethargic tiddly dragons, each of them with a tiny muzzle tied around their mouth. None of them flew. Instead, they lay around the bottom of the cage barely moving.

Blunderbuss ground his teeth and dug his fingernails into his palms.

"How much?" he said to the man behind the cage, as even-toned as he could manage.

"Only a Silver each," the man said.

Shit. Blunderbuss didn't have near enough coin to buy the lot and set them free.

"Are you interested? I'll throw in a cage and a muzzle for free."

An idea formed in Blunderbuss's mind. It wasn't a particularly good idea, but it was all he had at the moment.

"No," he said. "I'm scared of those things."

"Scared of these?" The man laughed. "They may carry the name dragon, but they are far from dangerous, I assure you."

"You're laughing at my fears, sir?"

"Well...no. I just...want to let you know how safe they truly are. That's all."

"What are you afraid of?" Blunderbuss said, straight-faced.

"Me? I'm deathly afraid of giant centipedes, but that's for good reason. They have enough venom in one bite to kill an orc."

"Oh, did you hear that an illegal animal dealer just had one of those escape last night, here on Mirth?" Blunderbuss put everything he could into his performance, trying his best to look dead serious.

"Really?" The man looked both ways down the street.

"Yeah. They're trying to keep it quiet, so no one knows about it, yet. But I overheard the news when I was selling goods just north of here. How big are those things, anyway?"

"They can get up to twelve feet long, and thicker than a fat capybara." The man fidgeted with the locking mechanism of a cage, his eyes darting back and forth.

"Okay, I gotta get going," Blunderbuss said with a smile. "Good luck with your miserable tiddly dragons."

The man was preoccupied but managed a feeble wave. "Have a good day, sir."

The Underground Market was empty when Blunderbuss strolled inside. But a bell attached to the front door rang as he opened it, and a middle-aged man came stumbling out from a back room.

"Simon?" he said, incredulous. "You look like absolute shit!"

"Julius!" thundered Blunderbuss. "I hoped you had given up on life and resigned yourself to working here forever! And here you are, my hopes realized!"

"Ha!" Julius seemed to really enjoy the greeting. "How have you been, you old bastard?"

"I'm pretty damned good, to tell the truth. But the name's Blunderbuss, now."

"Blunderbuss? Why in thirty-seven hells would you call yourself that?"

Blunderbuss went on to explain the big events in his life since last he'd seen Julius; from joining the marauders, to getting his first ass cheek shot off, then the adventure with Azure, and getting the other ass cheek blown off. He turned around to show his old friend the results.

"Well, shit. And I thought a life in illicit goods was going to be exciting."

The two old friends regarded each other for a silent moment.

"So, what brings you in today, Blunderbuss?"

"I was hoping to find an authentic-looking, official badge from the Gaming Commission."

"Dang! Not messing around, are ya? That's a serious request on this island, my friend." Julius seemed more than a little bit nervous.

"I wouldn't ask, but my...mission is of the utmost importance. Involves getting a little girl home to her parents."

"I don't want to know too much. If you say you need it, then I trust that you need it." He clasped his hands together, deep in thought. "Okay. For you, I'll do it. You'll have to give me a minute, as contraband of that nature is hidden and locked away pretty tight." He spun around and disappeared into the back room.

Blunderbuss looked around the store while he waited, remembering the days he used to run with Julius, and all the fun they had. After at least ten minutes, Julius came back out and handed Blunderbuss a shiny silver badge. It was intricate and detailed and had *Gaming Commission* stamped onto its face.

"What do I owe you?" Blunderbuss asked.

"Nothing."

"You sure?"

"Yeah. For anyone else, it'd be some serious gold, but I reckon I still owe you for saving my life on the Torsals that day."

"That was so long ago."

"You were a good friend to me, Simon. This is the least I could do."

"Well thank you so much! Your contribution will not be forgotten."

"And it will not be spoken of, either. Ever. If the wrong people heard I was involved in whatever you're doing in any way, I could be in a world of shit."

"I won't say a word. You can trust me on that."

"I know I can."

"It was nice to see you, Julius."

"Great to see you, too, Si—er, Blunderbuss."

Their handshake turned into an awkward, one-armed embrace. Blunderbuss stashed the badge in his pocket and left the store.

On the way back to the *Adventure Ship*, he veered back toward the tiddly dragon seller. He stopped near a food cart and contemplated his poorly-laid plan while stretching his left calf muscle.

Azure had given him a wand and had been teaching him magic in their down times. He wasn't particularly good at it, but he thought he might be able to pull his idea off.

As subtly as possible, he pulled out his wand and began to focus his energy. He pictured a twelve-foot-long giant centipede in his mind. Having never seen one, the task was a bit difficult. But he had seen a normal-sized centipede, so he went with a bigger version of that.

The thing that began to materialize in front of him was horrific. It looked more like a child's drawing than anything occurring in the natural world, but it was realistic enough to induce life-long nightmares. Its fangs were wicked, curved, shiny black spikes as big as daggers. Its hundred legs were in constant motion, making its body writhe unnaturally.

Not wanting to look it in the face anymore, Blunderbuss used his mind to send the abomination toward the tiddly dragon seller. He found that if his concentration broke, the beast would begin to fade, so he poured every ounce of focus he had into making it seem real.

The row of street vendors burst into chaos. Screams of existential terror sounded from all directions. Tables were flipped over, spilling all variety of stolen goods onto the ground. People ran for their lives with no time to worry about who or what they crashed into.

The tiddly dragon seller froze, his face a mask of pure panic. The centipede lifted the front of its sickening body off the ground, its giant mandible on level with the man's head.

All color drained from the man's face, and he collapsed in a heap behind his table.

Blunderbuss—feeling pretty stupid and sorry for the havoc he had just caused—hurried to the tiddly dragon cage and picked it up by its handle. As the giant centipede illusion faded into nothingness, Blunderbuss did his best to blend in to the tumultuous crowd.

Groundwork- Robin

R obin's role was simple.
　　 She was tasked with flying into the casino—under the pretense of looking for Azure—in order to case the place.

When she flew in through the front doors as the doormen were opening them for someone else, she decided to play it like a normal, relatively stupid Undering bird instead of the extraordinary, borderline genius other-realm bird that she was. Dumb birds would often accidentally fly into buildings and get stuck. Eventually people would try to shoo her back outside, but by then she would have a good idea of the layout.

She made a direct line to the display case between the two orc guards and made it look as if she smashed against the glass, not knowing it was there. In reality, she pulled back just before striking it, and kicked out with her feet to make it sound more dramatic. Then, while she pretended to thrash about like a panicked idiot, she studied the case's lock mechanism.

"Careful, little birdie," one of the uniformed orcs said.

The other orc guard tried to catch Robin between his huge hands, but she darted away from his grasp at the last second.

From the case, she made her way to the right, to the bar area. The place was far from packed, but there was a scattering of humans at the bar, and in front of the stage, where a traditional calypso band played classic cover songs. Robin alighted on a currently-unused bongo drum on the stage to scope the line of sight to the display case. She took off as the steel drum player took a swipe at her with his rubber mallet.

Robin flew past the double doors of the casino office and into the main gaming area.

"Shit," she said to herself.

That asshole falcon, Faron, was perched in the middle of the table games area on Mr. Bancroft's shoulder. Robin made a hard right, hoping she hadn't been seen. She entered another vast room with a high ceiling and a dozen rows of stadium seating around a completely enclosed wire cage. On the far side of the room was a long counter with a sign above that read:

Gargoyle Fights
Place Your Bets Here

Robin landed on the side of the cage and looked back. Luckily, there was no sign of the falcon. Before she took wing again, Robin looked at the inside of the cage. The canvas floor of the ring inside was marked throughout with dried blood stains. Robin shivered and took off from out of the room, flying low to avoid detection.

At the back of the casino floor was another sign. This one read:

Hotel Rooms and Suites
Magical Lift

Robin had no idea what a magical lift was, and didn't really give a shit. She continued past the sign over to the high rollers area in the back-left part of the casino. No one was playing there at the moment, so Faron wasn't looking in that direction. Robin made her way toward the front of the casino and shot up a red-carpeted staircase into the gentleman's club. The only people up there were a few casino employees putting the finishing touches on a stage in the middle of the area. Robin noted that the club lay over the top of the front quarter of the casino floor. There were several private booths surrounding the main stage, with curtains to block out prying eyes.

An idea forming in her mind, Robin dove back down the stairs, made a left, and landed on one of the Dragon's Hoard tables to think. The crew was currently obsessed with the stupid game. It was widely popular in the Undering, and Mirth Island was the place where all the top players came to play. Robin felt like she grasped the game well enough to take most of the crew's money at it, but *A*, she couldn't really play cards without hands, and *B* she didn't have much need for money.

Again, Robin checked the sight-lines from here to the office, and to the display case. She thought about everything's location relative to the second floor.

"What are you doing back here, little bird?" came Faron's voice from behind her.

Robin jumped, and just barely kept control of her bowels. She turned, embarrassed that she had let the falcon get the drop on her.

"I'm looking for my human companion. Have you seen her?" Robin showed no outward signs of shock.

"I have not."

"Oh. I could have sworn she said she was coming here." Robin shrugged her wings. "Oh well. I guess I'll get going, then."

"Hold it!" Faster than Robin could have ever guessed, Faron leapt at her and pinned her to the table with a talon. "I want you to tell me what you're really doing in here."

"Like I said, I'm looking for my human. Do you treat all your customers like this?" Robin's voice remained calm, although rage and fear were flowing through her little body.

"Only the ones who are acting suspicious."

"Suspicious? What the hell do you think you have to fear from a gods-damned little bird, you self-important piece of shit?"

"I could never fear one such as you, but being suspicious is my job." Faron released Robin from her grip and took a step back. "Perhaps you aren't here for anything nefarious, or perhaps you're here to try and steal the knife you inquired about the other day."

"How the fuck am I going to be able to steal that thing?" Robin hoped she was playing this believably.

"You couldn't. But that doesn't mean you're not dumb enough to try."

"Well, this has been great, but I gotta get going. If you ever touch me again, I promise you'll regret it."

Faron gave a short, mocking chuckle. "I'm sure I will. But if I see you back in here, I'm going to assume the worst. And then we'll see who has regrets."

"Okay, you little toady. You'd better get back to your master, now. I'm going to go fly around outside and be free."

Faron's eyes narrowed in anger. Her beak clenched shut.

"And you might want to work on your talon strength, too. That was pretty weak if you ask me."

Robin flew away, heart racing, and already regretting her taunting of the falcon. Those talons of her's were definitely not weak in any way.

Groundwork- Brisa

Brisa's role was simple.

She was tasked with getting a job as a dancer in the Fortress's new gentleman's club. That part was simple, anyway. But all the counting and remembering steps wasn't going to be easy.

Wearing her skimpiest outfit—a white romper that was so tight it could have been mistaken for body paint—she approached the casino, already feeling a strong revulsion to the place.

"All ciguapa have to cover their tattoos," said a human at the front door. "House rules."

"I'm here to apply for a job as a dancer."

The man looked her up and down. "Oh. Well, I suppose if you go straight upstairs it'll be okay."

Brisa entered the casino, passed two orcs guarding a ceiling-high glass case, and ascended the stairs.

"You're hired!" an approximately thirty-year-old human said before she had even reached the top of the staircase.

Taken aback, Brisa didn't respond.

"I'm assuming you're here to apply for a position as a dancer?"

"Uh...yes," Brisa said as she approached the stage in the middle of the large room.

"Well, with a body like that, I'd be a damn fool not to hire you."

Suddenly self-conscious of the man's eyes, Brisa cursed herself for forgetting to march off and count her steps. With a subtle shake of her head, she steeled her resolve. She was not going to let some creepy guy throw her off her task.

"I guess I need to get a few formalities out of the way, first," the man said. "You can address me as Mr. Norman. Can I get your name?"

"Brisa."

"Perfect. Are you a registered citizen of the League of Islands?"

"Yes."

"You sure? Not gonna make me check your documents, are you?"

"I can produce them if necessary." Brisa was registered, and did have the papers back on the ship. She had held out for most of her life, but she had needed them to get the job on Pratt's ship in order to spy on him, so she registered herself back then.

"Oh, that won't be necessary. That ass is all the registration I need to hire you here."

Teus's mercy! This guy was a creep. Had her mission not been vital, there was no way she would have put up with his shit.

"Are you aware of what the job entails?"

"Yes."

"All of it? I mean, I'm sure you know you're going to be dropping your clothes in front of crowds, but are you aware of the...extras some of our clientele are going to expect?"

"I'm aware." She hadn't been, but she kept a straight face.

"Speaking of that, let me show you one of our private booths." He led her to one of the many curtained booths surrounding the stage. She remembered to count her steps this time. "This is where you'll make the real money."

Mr. Norman pulled back the curtain to reveal a small room of sorts with a plush, cushioned chair on one side. "You're a tall drink of rum, but do you think you could...operate in here?"

"I'm sure I could manage."

"That's what I like to hear. I gotta say, I'm seeing nothing but gold coins when I look at you. You're gonna be quite a draw."

"So, I have the job, then?"

"Well..." Mr. Norman tried to contain a lewd grin and failed. "Why don't you show me what you've got? You can pretend I'm a paying customer who has taken you to this booth. I want to see how you'll leave our customers coming back for more."

Brisa resisted the urge to punch him.

"You see what I've got." She held her hands out to the sides. "This isn't the only game in town, you know. There are plenty of places on the west side of Mirth that would stumble over themselves to hire me. So, I'll ask again. Do I have the job?" Brisa swallowed and kept her face as calm and assertive as possible, even though she was regretting such a bold gamble.

Mr. Norman looked both disappointed and taken aback.

"Well, shit. If the boss saw you walking out of here and heard I hadn't hired you, I'd probably be kicking rocks. He's not the biggest ciguapa fan, but he knows a money-making opportunity when he sees it." He sighed. "So, yeah. You've got the job."

"When can I start?"

"The club's grand opening is tomorrow. Be here an hour before sundown. You're gonna be front and center at the ribbon-cutting ceremony."

"I'll be here." Brisa exited the booth and counted her steps to the staircase.

"Wear the exact same thing you're wearing now," Mr. Norman called to her.

Brisa kept counting, not even acknowledging her new boss.

Groundwork- Nargol

Nargol's role was simple.

She and Orok were tasked with booking a singing gig in the casino's main bar. With the popularity of their song on absolute fire in the islands, they figured the casino would be dying to book them.

As they walked into the casino, they were greeted by two tough-looking orcs. Luckily, they didn't recognize the guards.

"Wow, are you guys a sight for sore eyes," Orok said in the Orc Tongue. "You don't get a chance to see too many orcs outside of the Torsals."

The two guards seemed as if they wanted to chat, but weren't allowed. "Welcome to the Fortress," they said together in the Human Tongue.

"I get it. You guys can't talk while on duty. So, I guess I'll just do the talking. My name is Orok, and this is my beautiful wife, Nargol. It's really good to meet you guys." Orok had switched to Human.

The guards' mouths dropped open; tusks fully exposed.

"*The* Nargol and Orok?" one of them said in a low voice.

"That's correct. We're here to try and book a little concert in your bar. Could you maybe point us in the direction of whoever's in charge here?"

The orc who had spoken looked around as if checking for anyone nearby. "Well it's an honor to meet you two. I'm Kogar, and this is Borug. To say we're huge fans would be an understatement." Through apparent force of will, he wiped the smile from his face and straightened back up into guard position. "The boss's office is that way." He pointed.

"Thanks, guys. That means a lot. We don't want to get you in trouble, so we'll get going, now. It really was great to meet you."

The guards couldn't keep their eyes off Nargol and Orok as they made their way past the bar to the casino floor office.

Mr. Pierce was big for a human, but still relatively small next to orcs.

"Whoa, whoa, whoa. You can't just come barging in here." He held up his palms and stood up from his desk.

Nargol and Orok stopped at the double-doored entrance to the office. "Is this where you book entertainment for your bar area?" Nargol said.

"Yes, it is. But we're not really interested in any orc bands at the moment." He sat back down and began to shuffle papers on his desk.

"But we're not just any orc band. I'm Nargol, and this is Orok."

Mr. Pierce looked up, dubious. "*The* Nargol and Orok? The ones who sing *I Knew You Were Special*?"

"Yes. And if you don't believe us, go ask your guards out front."

"And you want to sing in my bar, huh?"

"Yeah. We're doing a tour of the islands, and this would be our first show."

"Hmm." Mr. Pierce appeared torn.

"We've got some brand-new verses to our song." Orok shrugged.

"New verses?" Now he looked more intrigued.

"Yeah. Including an entire verse dedicated to Orok's ass. The crowd is gonna go wild for it."

For an awkward interval, Mr. Pierce sat and thought, rubbing his bald head with both hands.

"You're not gonna cause any trouble in here, are you?"

"Absolutely not. Just want to sing."

"Well..." Mr. Pierce began talking to himself. Nargol had to strain to hear him. "It's not exactly the clientele we want in here, but gold is gold. That song is the most popular song I've ever heard before. They would be quite a draw. I mean, numbers have been down. And we could do it in conjunction with the grand opening of the gentleman's club. It could be a really big night, if we could just keep some of the riffraff out...." He looked up at Nargol and Orok. "Fuck it. Let's do it. Can you play tomorrow night?"

"Tomorrow night is perfect."

"There aren't any other orcs in your band, are there? Orcs are only allowed in groups of two in the casino."

Nargol narrowed her eyes at him. "We'll have two humans playing instruments with us. That's it."

"Okay. That'll work. Be here and ready to start at sundown."

"How much are you going to pay us?" Nargol asked. "We're not doing this for free."

Mr. Pierce low-balled the shit out of them. In any other circumstance, they would have walked away out of principle. But there was a bigger picture, here. And this prick was going to pay one way or the other. So, after a short negotiation, the two orcs agreed to a price, to be paid upon their arrival the following night.

Final Preparations

The plan was a living thing, ever evolving based on new information.

A bigoted comment by Mr. Pierce helped form the original idea. A chance encounter by Blunderbuss on his way to get the gaming commission badge lit new ideas for a contingency plan. Robin's reconnaissance led to an updated task for Brisa. And the date of Nargol and Orok's show effectively set the date for the heist. They now had one day to finish preparations and be as ready as they could possibly be.

Azure had gone to Mirth Island's costume shop to find something that would allow her to pass as an official from the gaming commission. She already had her blonde wig, but it was going to be important to look as official as possible.

She had brought Elijah and Oriana to the costume shop to help her pick something out. While Azure changed into various outfits, Elijah and Oriana were strengthening their quickly-formed bond. They laughed and carried on as they tried on different, progressively sillier, costumes.

They reminded Azure of the time her mom had hand sewed capybara costumes for the whole family on Masking Day—the one day of the year where the Ring was at its highest point in the sky, and people would wear masks in order to hide from the gods so they wouldn't see them involved in minor mischiefs, like pranking and heavy drinking. Her dad had been mortified by the idea of wearing the costume at the beach party Barren held every year.

"I am not going out in public wearing that ridiculous thing," he had said, red-faced.

"But you make such a cute cappy!" Her mom had tried to keep the mood light.

Azure and her mom, already wearing their costumes, got down on hands and knees and crawled around like lazy capybaras. They nuzzled her dad's ankles and made squealing sounds.

"Come on, Daddy," Azure had said. "If all three of us go, we could win best costumes."

"You two can win best costumes without me."

"But it's better as a family, right?"

Her dad had sighed about as dramatically as someone could sigh.

"If you do it, I'll make it worth your while later," her mom said.

Azure remembered her saying that, and being confused by it. She wished she still didn't understand the implication.

Her dad perked up, then. "I'll wear it for the contest, but I'm not wearing it all night."

"A reasonable compromise." Azure's mom had flashed her the satisfied grin of a co-conspirator, still pretending to be a capybara. "Now give us some fruit!"

"Yeah, give us some fruit!" Azure repeated, giggling.

As Azure remembered that day, she thought about all the fun she and her mom used to have when Azure was little. They used to get into giggling fits, which were usually initiated by messing with her dad in some way or another. She was such a delight when she had been present with her daughter. And although the memories were bittersweet, Azure was thankful she had them. She wished they would completely drown out the other memories, the depressing memories from the last few months of her mother's life, when her mom had let fear and propaganda turn her into something much more hateful.

Shaking her head, Azure pulled herself out of the reverie and picked up a false nose from a shelf.

The woman who ran the costume shop was very helpful. Being as vague as possible, Azure had told her that she wanted to look like an official from Whetstone, here on important business. The woman chose a simple blue and black dress that was beautiful, but not too flashy. Azure wasn't happy about the need to wear a corset with the dress, but the shop-owner assured her it was necessary if she was going to pass as an important woman from Whet-stone.

By the time Azure had made her choice, Elijah was wearing a coconut bra and a grass skirt, and Oriana was doubled-over with laughter.

Azure paid for her supplies and said it was time to go.

Reluctantly, Elijah and Oriana took off their costumes and followed her out.

"Could you look after Oriana during the heist?" Azure asked him in a low voice as they left the costume shop.

"But I'd like to help." Elijah seemed hurt by the idea.

"You *would* be a great help. Oriana has really taken to you, though. It would ease her mind a great deal, I'm sure."

Elijah started to speak, but Azure held up a finger. "Just a minute." Azure approached a fruit vendor along the boardwalk and bought a basket of mixed fruit. She offered a banana to Oriana, who took it and smiled. "I'm sorry, go ahead," she said to Elijah.

"I was going to say, maybe I should be the one pretending to be from the gaming commission. I mean, this Mr. Pierce has seen you already, and your costume didn't exactly work on Pratt, if you remember."

"I saw him for a matter of minutes. And I'll be smarter about the disguise this time. He won't recognize me. I'm sure of it."

"There's still a chance. And if he does recognize you, he could grab you right there and do gods know what. There isn't a chance he'd recognize me."

"But, my love, I don't..." Azure didn't want to sound rude, or belittling, but she didn't think Elijah could pull off this type of role. His confidence was improving, but wasn't quite at a pretending-to-be-someone-else-during-a-casino-heist level just yet. "I have a picture in my mind of how all of this is going to go, and I need to be front and center in order to pull it off. My disguise will be better this time." A thought blinked into existence. "You can have the final say on whether or not my disguise is good enough. How about that?"

Elijah was hesitant. "It's true that you would do a better job than I would. I just worry about you in there, that's all."

"You don't have to worry. I'll have a bunch of marauders in there with me, and I'm not the one in the most danger anyway. Syl is going to be at the most risk. It's him that I worry about."

Elijah didn't respond, instead taking Azure's hand and giving it a squeeze.

BACK ON THE *Adventure Ship*, the marauders were perfecting their roles.

After dumping the fruit basket out for the ship's capybaras, Azure tried to push everything away for a moment, closing her eyes and concentrating on her immediate surroundings. The gentle creaking of cordage. The breeze through the sails. The shush of the sea. The warm sun on her face.

The melody of the farting princess song tried to force its way to the forefront, but Azure pushed it away and refocused on the sea.

The moment didn't last, as worries and anxieties refused to be held at bay. Was this ridiculous plan actually going to work? Or was Azure putting marauders in potentially life-threatening peril for a long shot? Were they prepared enough? Would they ever be?

She was starting to feel like tiddly dragons were fluttering around in her chest when Elijah sidled up beside her and put an arm around her shoulder.

"You doing alright?" He kissed her temple.

"I don't know."

He gave her shoulder a squeeze. "Well, I know you have some minor stuff going on right now, but I wanted to run something by you, about the wedding."

Azure chuckled under her breath.

"Way back in the days, when I was human the first time, people used to do something called *vows* at their weddings."

"Vows?"

"Yeah. The bride and the groom would both get a chance to say something to each other. It could be something they prepared, or something they felt in the moment. It was a great tradition, and I'm not sure how it faded away."

"Sounds good to me." Azure knew what he was doing. He was trying to calm her nerves by distracting her. And even though the tactic was so obvious, it was working. The tiddly dragons had ended their feeding frenzy in her chest and were laying down for afternoon naps.

"I've actually been working on mine already. Would you like to hear one little part of it?"

"Is that allowed?"

"Sure. Why not?"

"Alright, then."

Elijah cleared his throat. "I love you for countless reasons, but I'll try to count a few here today. I love you because you don't choose the easy thing, ever. You choose the right thing, every time. I love you because..." He stopped and smiled, squeezing her shoulder again. "You'll have to wait for the rest."

Azure leaned into him and rested her head on his shoulder. "That was nice," she said, "but I'm not sure what the right thing is this time."

"Is *not* helping Oriana an option?"

"No."

Elijah said no more.

After a pause, Azure said, "I love you because you always strive to be kind."

"I may do my best to be kind, but I still feel pretty worthless most of the time."

"You've got to get past that."

"I know." He shook his head. "It's just so strange being human again. For a hundred years, people looked at me like a second-class citizen at best. So, to be treated as an equal now seems...superficial."

"But that's not a problem with you. It's their problem."

"I know. But it shakes my faith in humanity when I think about it too much. And I'm still having a hard time feeling my own worth."

"I've heard it said that you can gauge your worth as a person by what a child or underprivileged person thinks of you. And if that wonderful, innocent little girl sees your worth, which she absolutely does, then I think you're doing something right."

Her words seemed to work, as Elijah seemed heartened. She supposed that, at their core, that's what relationships were all about; heartening each other.

The two of them gazed out at the offing together.

"I just wish I could get some sort of sign to let me know I'm making the right decision, here," Azure said. In her mind, she flippantly asked Saga, the King of the Gods, to send something that could let her know she was pointing in the right direction.

The Covingtons shuffled into view as they made their way to a shaded corner of the ship. They had already devoured all of the fruit Azure had brought for them.

"Hello, Eleanor. Hello, Alistair." Azure and Elijah both bowed.

Without ceremony, Alistair mounted Eleanor and began to awkwardly thrust his hips.

Azure turned away and blurted laughter. She threw a hand over her mouth, not wanting to ruin the cappies' moment. Elijah chuckled alongside her.

"Well, there's your sign," Elijah said between giggles.

"I think that's a different sign." Azure couldn't help but to think that time alone with Elijah in the captain's quarters could really help to let out some tension and quell her anxiety, but she knew he wasn't quite as ready as Alistair Covington was for such things.

"Don't they usually do...that in the water?" Elijah asked.

"I have no idea." The question made Azure wonder if they should build some kind of fresh water pool for the capybaras, though. Maybe when all of this was over.

After a few more laughs, Azure said, "I suppose we should go over the plan one last time, and maybe write some stuff down."

AZURE BEGAN THE MEETING in the Marauder King's joking style.

"Why are fish so smart?" she asked the group.

When no one replied, she said, "Because they swim in schools."

There was a sprinkling of nervous laughter.

Elijah had the best handwriting, so he had been tasked with writing up the final plan. After a few items were discussed, Azure presented the plan to the marauders. It read:

Places and Times

BRISA GENTLEMAN'S Club 1 Hour and 15 Minutes Before Sundown
  Azure Casino Office 1 Hour Before Sundown
  Nargol and Orok Casino Bar 50 Minutes Before Sundown
  Syl Dragon's Hoard Tables 40 Minutes Before Sundown
  Threepbrush and Robin Gentleman's Club 20 Minutes Before Sundown
  Blunderbuss Outside Sundown

"ANY QUESTIONS?" AZURE asked.

There weren't any. The crew had already gone over their parts and how to play them ad nauseam. They were as ready as they were ever going to be.

"Good." Azure looked to Oriana, strengthening her resolve. "Then let's do this."

The Heist- Azure

A zure waltzed out of the Captain's Quarters in her costume.
"Do you approve?" she said to Elijah.

Elijah didn't answer at first. His jaw was slack, his mouth had dropped open.

"Well?"

"You look..."

"You look sexy as hell!" Robin chimed in from some nearby rigging.

"Yeah...that," Elijah stuttered. "I mean, I like your real nose better, but whatever Brisa did to your eyes just..."

Brisa had applied struck matches to Azure's eyelids, rendering them a chalky black. She had attached the false nose Azure had found at the costume shop and blended it into her face perfectly. She had also applied a bright red stain to Azure's lips, and placed a fake mole just above them on the right side. Azure's shoes made her stand at least two inches taller, and she wore a way-too-snug corset and blonde wig on her head.

"But do you think the disguise will work?"

"Yeah. I think it will. I mean, I can barely recognize you if I'm being honest."

"Perfect."

Elijah moved forward and pinned the gaming commission badge to her dress. Then he took her into his arms, careful not to smudge the makeup.

"Be careful in there," he said in her ear.

"I will." She gave Elijah a long squeeze.

With considerable effort, Azure took a knee in front of Oriana. "Have fun with Elijah. We'll be right back, and then we can get you back home to your parents." She tousled the little girl's hair.

"You look weird...but pretty."

Azure laughed, finding it a painful undertaking in the corset. "Thanks."

Oriana threw her arms around Azure's neck.

Azure closed her eyes and held the embrace. When she reopened them, she noticed the sun's position in the western sky.

"I'd better get going, Little Treasure."

As she stood, Robin landed on her shoulder.

"On to adventure," Robin said, head cocked to the side.

"On to adventure." Azure nuzzled Robin with her cheek, then turned to the gathered Marauders. "Everybody ready?"

When she got serious, solemn nods of assent she put on a confident—and completely fake—smile.

"Let's go!"

AZURE MARCHED INTO the casino like a woman on a mission. She didn't even acknowledge the orc guards up front, blowing past them on her way to the casino office.

The double doors were closed, and a man stood in front of them.

"Is Mr. Pierce in?" she asked.

"Yes. But he doesn't want to be disturbed. There are a lot of big things happening today and he's very busy."

"Well I'm sure he'll want to see me." Azure pointed to the badge above her left breast. "Tell him Cassandra Cosgrove from the League of Islands Gaming Commission is here on urgent business." She was very fond of the name she'd come up with.

"Sure." The man knocked on the doors, then opened one and poked his head inside.

Azure's heart thrashed in her chest. How could she be naive enough to think that a costume would work this time? Mr. Pierce, although an asshole, wasn't stupid. He would see through the costume, as good as it was. She still had the same eyes, the same teeth.

But even as she panicked about being discovered, she was able to calm herself. Mr. Pierce wasn't someone who seemed to give much of a shit about the people around him. He probably hadn't given Azure a second thought since she had left his office, even after the shoe-throwing thing. Maybe if she was taller, skinnier, or prettier, he might have paid closer attention, but a pe-on like her, asking for charity, probably didn't make much of an impression on him. She'd have to hope this assessment was right, anyway. There was no turning back, now.

"He says to come in," the man said, opening the door for her.

Inside, Mr. Pierce looked up at her, a vague annoyance on his face. His eyes widened when he saw her, but he played it off well. She hoped like hell that meant she looked hot, and not that he immediately recognized her.

"Cassandra Cosgrove?" he said, acting as if her presence barely registered to him. "You new?"

"No. I'm with the Player Fraud Division in Whetstone." Azure spoke with a raspy voice that was lowered by an octave.

She took a seat without being asked.

"Huh. I never heard of you."

"Well you wouldn't have done, as I am concerned with the other side of the table, so to speak." Azure and Elijah had practiced possible scenarios for hours.

Mr. Pierce stood and bent over his desk to examine the badge on Azure's dress. She looked him in the face as he did so, doing her best to keep her features placid.

After several intense moments, Mr. Pierce sat back down, seemingly appeased.

"How can I help you? We got an unbelievably busy night tonight."

"Have you heard of the faun card player by the name of Dechi?"

"Dechi?"

"Yes. He plays Dragon's Hoard, and is gaining a reputation around the isles as one of the best players around."

"Can't say that I have."

"Well, he hasn't set his sights on the big time, yet. He's been cheating his way through every card room in the League, taking untold amounts of money. He hasn't come to Mirth, until tonight."

"Tonight?" Mr. Pierce's face was pained.

"Yes, we expect him here within the hour, and we're fully prepared to take him down for good."

"I'm too busy for this shit. Why don't you just arrest him as he tries to come in here?"

"He has proved...slippery. We don't have any charges that will stick to him. But we intend to correct that tonight. I intend to catch him in the act of cheating—because believe me, he will cheat—and take him down then."

Mr. Pierce's wheels were turning as he stared down at his desk. "If the Commission agrees to drop their investigation against me, I'll let you grab your guy tonight. Otherwise, I'm going to have to say no."

Azure cleared her throat. "We were expecting you might offer such an ultimatum, and we are fully prepared to drop our investigation. This time." She had no idea what he was talking about but was really starting to get into this character.

"Alright." Mr. Pierce grinned. "I mean, it's not like you guys had a case against me, anyway. This is not, in any way, an admission of guilt. I just don't have the time to deal with your phony investigation right now."

"Like I said—"

"I don't know what the Gaming Commission was even doing. Did they honestly think I had people with wands underneath every roulette table? It's a ridiculous accusation, to tell the truth."

Azure waited for him to speak, not wanting to be interrupted, again.

"It was just the one isolated incident, and everyone involved has been fired."

After another pause, Azure said, "There's no need to sell me on anything, Mr. Pierce. Like I said, we are prepared to drop our investigation if you're willing to help us out."

"How can I help you, then?"

"If you and I can catch him in the act together, it will be easier to get a conviction. I'll only need you to see him cheat. Which, again, shouldn't be long."

"Those fauns would cheat their mothers out of their last copper, I swear."

Azure clenched her jaw. They had chosen Syl to play the role of the card cheat based on Mr. Pierce's prejudices, so this played into their plan perfectly, but it still pissed her off to hear shit like that said aloud.

The man at the door poked his head in, again. "Sir, the orcs, Nargol and Orok, are here with their band."

"I'll be right there." Mr. Pierce looked to Azure. "I've got several things I need to deal with tonight. Let me go handle this, then I'll be right back."

As he left, Azure followed him, but stopped outside the office doors to wait. She hazarded a glance toward Nargol, Orok, and the band, who were heading for the bar with their equipment. But before he went to greet the orcs, he waved Mr. Bancroft over from the gaming area.

As the two of them talked, Faron, the falcon, stared at Azure, unblinking.

Azure did her best to hide her initial shock, then concentrated on acting normal. And like everyone who tries hard to act normal, she failed miserably. She looked down at her badge and rubbed it with a thumb, then looked up at the ceiling as if inspecting it for building code violations. Finally, her eyes came back to the bird, who hadn't moved a feather.

She only stopped staring Azure down when the two men ended their conversation. Mr. Bancroft said something to Faron, then pointed across the casino. Mr. Pierce strutted to the bar and began chatting with Nargol and Orok.

All the way across the casino floor, Brisa stood, tall and beautiful, with a small congregation of humans at the bottom of the staircase that led up to the gentleman's club. She looked as nervous as Azure felt.

The Heist- Nargol

Nargol, Orok, and two marauder musicians named Theodore and William entered the casino as a striking sunset began to paint the western sky.

The two orc guards up front were the same two as before—Kogar and Borug. The guards gave them excited, but reserved nods as they entered.

Brisa, who had gone inside minutes before, was at the bottom of the stairs to the left with a small group of humans. She looked as stiff and grace-less as Nargol had ever seen her.

The place was absolutely packed tonight. Every gaming table was full. Customers milled about excitedly throughout the vast building.

The band headed straight for the bar, where they were greeted by Mr. Pierce.

"It's an exciting night," he said, without looking them in the eyes. "Word of your show spread through this island like wildfire. We're doing the best business we have in a long time."

Nargol was about to say something when Mr. Pierce started talking again. "I mean, I don't really understand the draw. Your songs don't really compare to the old human classics if you ask me."

"We didn't."

A shadow fell over Mr. Pierce's face, but passed quickly. Nargol couldn't tell if her comment had angered or scared him, and she couldn't muster the ability to give a shit.

"This is my casino. The biggest, most impressive casino ever built. You wouldn't be able to comprehend the amount of money involved, here. I'm going to need you to respect it at all times."

Nargol bit her lip. If she said what she wanted to say, they would probably be kicked out. She glanced at Orok, hoping he would keep it in, as well, but he hadn't noticed because he was looking at Azure, who stood by the double doors of the casino office. As subtly as possible, Nargol stepped on her husband's foot, snapping him out of it.

"With a big crowd, we're probably going to need magical amplifiers for our music," she said. "Is that kind of thing allowed in this big, impressive place?"

"Don't worry about that. We've got our own magical amplification system." He pointed to two human-high stands with golden wands attached to their tops. "This whole half of the casino will hear your songs loud and clear."

Nargol nodded as she lifted Theodore's bongos up onto the stage. Orok took a chair from the floor and set it on the stage next to the bongos—a place for William to sit and play his fiddle.

"Well, we're pretty much ready to go."

"Oh. That was fast. You guys can wait in the room behind the bar," Mr. Pierce pointed, "until we get everyone seated. We don't want to cause a scene before it's time to start."

"We're starting at sundown, right?"

"Yes. More or less. Gotta see how tightly we can pack these people in."

"We'd like to start at sundown. It's the best time for orcs to perform." This was complete bullshit, but Nargol doubted that Mr. Pierce would pick up on it.

"Why?" He seemed frustrated with himself for engaging as soon as the question came out.

"It has to do with our circadian sexual rhythms," she said, unable to resist messing with this asshole. "Traditionally, sundown is the time for orc lovemaking, so our senses are at their peak at that time. But when we're not making sweet love, we're able to focus those senses on other endeavors, like music. If you get us going at sundown, it'll be a great concert, guaranteed."

"Oh." Mr. Pierce seemed to be fighting the urge to run away.

She winked at the uncomfortable human.

"Well, that's fine, then," he said, looking anywhere but at the orcs. "Sundown it is. Now, if you'll excuse me, I have other pressing matters to attend to." Without another glance, Mr. Pierce hurried back toward Azure.

The Heist- Azure

Mr. Pierce returned from the bar with a sour look on his face.

Panic gripped Azure as she wondered what had gone wrong already.

After scanning the immediate area, Mr. Pierce said, "Between you and me, orcs are pretty disgusting creatures," in a low voice.

Azure did her best to not let her revulsion toward the man show.

"We're not really allowed to talk about such things on the job," she said, straight faced.

"Yeah, I know. You're from Whetstone, where you're not allowed to tell it like it is anymore."

As his eyes wandered over the bustling crowd, his sour expression turned into a smile.

"This place is hopping tonight." The smile was purely avaricious, without a hint of warmth to be found. "So, you say this faun should be here soon?" The smile slowly faded away.

"Yes. Any minute now according to our reconnaissance."

"I have to attend a ribbon-cutting ceremony over at the gentleman's club in a few minutes, here." His eyes lit up with devious amusement. "Have you ever considered being a dancer?"

Azure's bright red lips were a thin straight line.

"Oh, I'm just joking with you. I know you have a real important job already." He couldn't have been more condescending.

Wanting to change the subject before she blew her cover, Azure recalled Wakeman's treasure.

"While we wait for Dechi to arrive, I have another matter I need to discuss with you."

"Yes?" Mr. Pierce didn't try to hide his annoyance.

"A complaint was made to our office from a Mr. Wakeman Carlyle. He claims that people associated with your casino have stolen a treasure that belonged to him."

"Ha!" Mr. Pierce shook his head. "Filed a complaint, eh?"

"Yes. He fi—"

"Wait until ol' Kelton hears that. It'll have him roaring."

"Kelton?"

"An ex-crewmate of Mr. Carlyle's. They served together on Captain Roberts' ship. It was Kelton who caught wind of a treasure on that gods-forsaken volcanic island."

"He works for you, then? This...ex-pirate?" Azure looked around, suddenly nervous that this Kelton would recognize her or one of the other marauders.

"Yeah, he works for me, now. He's out of town at the moment, so I'll have to tell him about this when he gets back."

Azure hoped she hadn't given anything away.

"So, you're admitting that your people took Mr. Carlyle's treasure?"

"Oh, sure. I have it in my room on the top floor." He pointed up. "But there is no way I'm giving it back."

Azure was stunned by the admission.

"He can go ahead and try to prove when and where I got the treasure from if he wants to. My lawyers will find it exceedingly simple to cast volcanos of doubt on his story." Mr. Pierce chuckled. "He buried it years ago, but can't remember where it is. For all he can prove it's still in the ground."

"And you really have it here?"

"Listen. If he wants it back, he can fight his way past my door security, and take it back himself. I'd love to see him try it." Mr. Pierce looked suddenly self-conscious. "But no.... I mean I have *a* treasure in my room. Not necessarily Mr. Carlyle's treasure. Like I said, for all anyone knows that treasure is still buried on Amenaza Island, and will soon be covered in molten lava from what I've been hearing."

Azure was about to say something when Syl walked in through the front doors.

He strolled in with an exaggerated swagger that immediately turned up the corner of Azure's mouth. He wore a fancy, wide-brimmed hat with a peacock feather jutting out to the back, and a frilled, dark green suit that would have given the dandiest of dandies second thoughts. Azure had no idea he was going to play his role so...loudly.

Syl made his way down the steps and back toward the Dragon's Hoard area with a confident swash in his walk, rolling a gold coin over the knuckles of his right hand.

"Is that him?" Mr. Pierce asked.

"Yes. Not exactly subtle, is he?"

"I'm gonna love to take this guy down."

"I am, too. But I have to reiterate, we both have to see him in the act of cheating. This is very important if we're going to get the kind of conviction that'll have him locked up, and out of your hair, for a very long time."

"Yeah, I get it." He sighed as if exasperated. "You know, it wouldn't kill you to loosen up a little. Smile! You'll look better for it, I promise."

Azure did not comply. "This faun is capable of taking a lot of money out of your pockets. I think maybe you should take this matter more seriously."

At this, he sobered. "Alright, alright. Gods! I will take it seriously, but I need to get over to the gentleman's club ribbon cutting, first. Let's go." He waved her forward as he started walking.

Azure found herself following him, unsure of what else to do.

At the bottom of the red-carpeted stairs was a group of mostly humans, with Brisa and another ciguapa woman, standing around a thick red ribbon strung between two golden stanchions. A man holding an oversized pair of scissors stood in front of the ribbon.

"Here he is!" the man called as Mr. Pierce approached. "The visionary behind our great new attraction!"

The group applauded; a few of them whistled.

Azure glanced at Brisa, but both of them were careful not to look too long. She seemed extremely uncomfortable.

The man handed the scissors to Mr. Pierce, who played it up to the crowd, snapping them in the air above his head.

"Speech!" someone shouted.

"Do you really want to hear me talk?" Mr. Pierce said. "Or would you rather feast your eyes on this?" His open palm turned up, and he moved his hand down the length of the closest scantily-clad woman.

There were more whistles, and some laughs, from the crowd.

"No, no, I do have a few short words to say. Mr. Norman does me great honor when he calls me a visionary, but I'm not exactly the first person to bring tits and ass to Mirth Island."

As the crowd laughed, Azure rolled her eyes, hating this guy a little more every time he opened his mouth.

"But...I do think we're doing it in a way that only *we* can. In the fine tradition of The Fortress, we will provide you with a tailor-made experience. The absolute finest tits and ass experience you'll find in the Undering. We've spared no expense to bring you the finest setting, and, more importantly, the finest women the League of Islands has to offer."

"We can see that!" someone called from the back of the gathered crowd, eliciting chuckles.

"So...welcome to The Gentleman's Club!" Mr. Pierce opened the scissors wide and snapped them shut, cutting the ribbon at its center.

There were more cheers. Brisa and the women were ushered up by Mr. Norman, and the men in the crowd rushed up after them.

When Azure turned away, Mr. Threepbrush entered the casino wearing a tricorn hat.

The Heist- Robin

"Are you sure there isn't a better way?" Robin asked, staring at Mr. Threepbrush's hat.

"I don't know. I could put you in my pocket, but I think that'd be even worse."

"No, I'm not going in a pocket. I just wish there was a bit more dignified mode of transportation for me. What about a nice big bag?"

"I think the idea is to try and be inconspicuous. How am I going to get into one of those booths holding a big bag without drawing at least a little unwanted attention?"

"I know, I know."

"Speaking of that, I think you should probably get in the hat, now," Mr. Threepbrush said as they neared the casino.

"When's the last time you washed your hair?" Robin asked.

"Captain Brine let me use her bath not more than a week ago."

"Alright, that's not too bad. This is still kind of humiliating, though."

"I'll go as quick as I can."

Robin sighed, then fluttered up to stand on Mr. Threepbrush's head. Carefully, he placed his hat over the top of her.

Everything went dark.

"That's not too tight, is it?" he asked, his voice muffled.

"No, it's fine. Get going."

Moving in the dark was disorienting. It was like flying with her eyes closed, but worse. A wave of nausea swept over Robin, and her stomach began to rumble.

"I'm passing that statue out front."

Robin shook her head and took a deep breath, trying to alleviate her motion sickness.

"Okay. I'm about to enter the casino."

"You can quit with the updates. You'll look like a damned madman talking to yourself."

Mr. Threepbrush nodded in apparent understanding.

"And don't nod!" she hissed.

"Welcome to the Fortress, sir," a voice said.

"Thank you."

There was a noticeable change as Robin's transport entered the casino. The air was a little cooler, and the hubbub of the crowd permeated the small space under the hat. The place was obviously packed.

Mr. Threepbrush must have stepped down a stair or two, much too roughly in Robin's opinion. She clenched her beak and fought the urge to vomit.

"Excuse me," Mr. Threepbrush said. "But I was wondering if you could point me in the direction of the Gentleman's Club."

"Right over there," an orc voice said, "Right up those stairs."

"Thank you for your help."

"Uh...you're...welcome." It sounded as if the orc had never been thanked for anything in his life.

The ground under Robin's feet began to move, again. She clutched Mr. Threepbrush's hair with her claws, apparently scratching his scalp, as he let out a tiny squeal.

"Sorry," Robin whispered, unsure if he could hear.

The sounds of hubbub built in intensity.

"Welcome to the Gentleman's Club, sir. You're just in time. But I'd hurry up before all the best ones are taken, though."

As Mr. Threepbrush ascended the stairs, Robin was her dizziest yet. This must have been how Elijah felt when he rode that rollercoaster thing. She held onto his hair tight and tried to focus on her breathing.

The sound of a band playing very danceable music filled the second floor, and the air smelled like way too much perfume.

The Heist- Nargol

The audience was much bigger than Nargol had anticipated. It must have numbered in the hundreds; made up of mostly humans, but with quite a few more orcs, ciguapa, and fauns than she would have expected, too.

Coming out from the back room, she had a little bit of stage fright.

Nargol gripped Orok's shoulder, wondering how he was holding up. His face was pale and his eyes wide. Apparently, he was doing worse than she was.

She flagged down a passing waiter and ordered a bottle of rum.

"I don't know if that's allowed," the frightened waiter said.

"Would you like me to delay this concert to go find Mr. Pierce so he can tell you what's allowed?" she said, feeling bad about intimidating him, but needing to wrap up this delay as it was damn-near sundown.

"No...ma'am. I'll bring it right away."

"Thank you very much." She flipped him a silver coin.

When the man returned with the bottle, Nargol took a long pull, then passed it to her husband.

"Thank you," he said sheepishly before taking a few chugs.

At the bar entrance, Azure stood with Mr. Pierce. He was talking to her, hands flailing, while Azure tried her best to seem engaged.

Mr. Threepbrush had entered the casino only moments before. He was already upstairs in the Gentleman's Club.

Nargol held out a hand, and Orok passed her the bottle. After another pull, she said, "You ready for this?"

"As ready as I'm going to get." Now he held out his hand for the bottle. "But let me get one more chug."

As her husband drank, Nargol said, "Remember, this is a concert for two," in a low voice. "We only have to worry about Kogar and Borug. The rest is superfluous." She waved a hand across the vast audience.

"Superfluous, huh? Nice word." He smiled his handsome smile, the edge seemingly taken off.

Nargol slapped him on the butt. "Just get up there and sing your ass off."

When they took the stage, the crowd roared their approval. Nargol glanced at the guards up front and found them watching with rapt attention.

"Hello," Nargol said into the wand on a stand. Her voice amplified at least tenfold. It filled the bar, and likely most of the casino floor. "Whoa! This thing is loud." Many in the audience laughed.

"This is the voice of one of your thirty-something gods," Orok said with a wavering voice into his wand stand. "Orcs are not that bad. They're actually pretty great once you get to know them."

The crowd went mostly silent.

Nargol looked at him and shook her head. He must have had an empty stomach for the rum to catch up to him so quickly. It wasn't that she didn't love what he'd said—she did—it just seemed like the crowd wasn't quite ready for something like that yet. He gave her a cheesy grin and mouthed, "Sorry."

"Thank you for coming out to The Fortress tonight!" Nargol shouted, eliciting a giant cheer. "I'm Nargol, this is Orok, and this is our band. William on fiddle, and Theodore on percussion. We'd like to sta—"

"I knew you were special!" someone called out from the audience.

"We'll get to that, I promise. But we can't go calling 'Hoard!' with only a head and a tail in our hand." She figured a Dragon's Hoard reference in a casino would go over better than it did. "First, we're gonna do an old classic as a reminder that you should tip your waitstaff well. They're out there working hard to get you nice and merry for our show." With a motion from Nargol, the band began to play. "Oh! Here's a little teaser, though. We've got some new verses to *I Knew You Were Special* that we're going to debut tonight!"

The loudest cheer yet filled the bar.

As the music came back around, Nargol began to sing.

There once was a pub down by the sea,
And the name of the pub was The Lone Palm Tree.

Spirits went up as the drinks went down.

Drink my friends let's drink.

SOON MAY THE BARMAN COME, TO BRING US ALE AND WINE AND RUM.

SOMETIME WHEN THE DRINKING IS DONE, WE'LL TIP HIM WELL AND GO.

As she sang, Nargol looked to the guards again. They were all in, moving with the music and showing their tusks in wide smiles.

The Heist- Azure

"I don't understand the appeal," Mr. Pierce said while watching the crowd go wild for Nargol and Orok's show. "But I'm a genius when it comes to booking the right kinds of things to get people in through these doors." He nodded as if agreeing with himself.

"We should go watch Dechi," Azure said as nonchalant as she could. The guards near the display case were beginning to step away from their post and Azure did not want Mr. Pierce to notice.

"I was just thinking we should go and catch that bastard."

"Great minds think alike, they say." She hated herself for saying that, but she had to ingratiate herself to him if this was going to go smoothly.

As the two of them approached the Dragon's Hoard area, they were intercepted by Mr. Bancroft and Faron.

"He's sitting at the high roller table," Mr. Bancroft said. "Didn't start with much money, but already building his stack."

"Have you noticed any cheating?" Mr. Pierce asked.

"Not yet."

While they talked, the falcon couldn't keep her eyes off of Azure.

"What is your name, again?" Faron asked Azure as if the other two weren't talking.

"Cassandra Cosgrove." There was the slightest hesitation Azure hoped the falcon hadn't noticed.

"What's your badge number?"

"Three one four one five," she said, straight faced and thankful she had memorized the number on the front of her phony badge.

Faron looked over the badge, eyes narrowed.

"What's your address in Whetstone?"

"Mind your own business, Faron," Mr. Bancroft scolded. "Why don't you focus those raptor eyes on the card cheat who is probably pulling a fire card from his sleeve this very minute."

Azure felt a surge of relief as the falcon looked away.

"I don't know why we just don't take him down, now," said Mr. Pierce, pacing.

"We have to catch him in the act."

"Why, though? We can just say we caught him cheating. Who's gonna believe him over me...or you?"

"Like I said before, this guy has slipped through our fingers too many times, already. I want this by the book, with a table full of corroborating witnesses to back up our story. He'll cheat. Just give him a chance."

Mr. Pierce took a moment to consider his options, letting his eyes wander around the casino. "I suppose everything is running smoothly. Could you be a doll and grab me a chair?" He pointed at a table with a couple of empty stools.

Azure didn't need anyone's chivalry, but she couldn't help but compare Mr. Pierce to the Marauder King. It was like they were polar opposites. Begrudgingly, she grabbed two stools by their backs and scooted them across the carpet.

Without thanking her, Mr. Pierce sat and leaned forward, watching Syl.

Azure took a seat next to him, strategically blocking his view of the display case.

"Tell me the truth," he said, without looking at her.

It wasn't clear if he was going to continue or not. Azure's muscles tensed, but she kept her face impassive.

"You've seen a lot of cheating around the islands. I know you're probably not supposed to say, but I'll keep it to myself." He paused, again, then flashed a conspiratorial grin. "Humans are just different from all the others, right?"

"What do you mean?" Azure knew damn well what he was getting at, but it was good to keep him distracted for as long as possible.

"The others seem to have something in their blood. They lie, they cheat, they steal. It's way worse with them. You see that, right?"

Azure considered her words carefully. She had to hold back if she wanted to keep him talking, but she couldn't bite her tongue completely.

"If you want the truth, that's not what I've found at all."

"That's what you're supposed to say."

"You said this was between me and you. I don't think I have to worry about you going and reporting me, do I?"

"Of course not."

"Then why would I lie?" She tried to show him an easy-going smile.

"Because you people from Whetstone have been brainwashed to think it's somehow shameful to be a human."

"I'm not ashamed to be a human. I mean, I didn't have much choice in the matter." Azure shrugged.

Mr. Pierce shook his head, then waved as if to dismiss her. "I don't know why I even bothered. Let's just catch this *faun* so you can be on your way."

The Heist- Robin

As soon as Mr. Threepbrush got upstairs, he was greeted by another man. Robin hoped her friend could make this quick, as she was sick of being tucked away in the dark under a hat.

"Welcome!" said the man, jostling Mr. Threepbrush with what was probably a strong handshake. "The name's Mr. Norman. What can I get for you?"

"Well..." Mr. Threepbrush's voice was shaky. "I want that one. In a...private booth."

Another jostle. "Oh, you want a ciguapa, huh? Ya dirty bastard! Ha!" The jostling became more violent. "No, I don't blame ya. They are something else to look at, aren't they? And for the right price, she's available for anything you could imagine in your wildest fantasies."

Robin lost any feeling of nausea as righteous anger took its place. She had the strong urge to peck out an eye.

"Let me go get her for you," Mr. Norman said. He came back after half a minute. "This is Brizza. She'd be more than happy to share a booth with you. There's a great one right here."

"No," Brisa said. "I think this customer would be happier in the next one over."

"Well all the booths are exactly the same, so..."

"Let's just say I'd be more comfortable in this other one. Call it a ciguapa quirk... Sir, wouldn't you prefer me to be as comfortable as possible during our...time together?"

"Uh...yes. I mean...of course." Mr. Threepbrush was a less able improvisor by far.

"Well the other booth it is, then," said Mr. Norman. "It's two silvers to rent out the booth, then you two can negotiate further behind closed curtains."

The marauders had chipped in to cover the cost of the booth. There was a tinkling of coins, then the man said, "Thank you."

Robin's stomach dropped again as Mr. Threepbrush began to move.

"Have fun in there," Mr. Norman said. "Don't do anything I wouldn't do"

A curtain closed, and Robin flailed as Mr. Threepbrush sat down.

Dim light broke on the horizon as the tricorn hat was lifted. Brisa waved to Robin from the other side of the darkened booth. Robin jumped from Mr. Threepbrush's head and landed on a small table.

"Could you have made that ride any rougher?" she said in a low voice.

"Sorry. It's kind of tough when you've got a set of carpentry tools concealed in your pants, though."

"Oh, I know. I'm just messing with you. That was fine. I mean, you almost got a little something on your head, but I managed to keep it in."

"Thank you for that."

"How are you doing, Brisa?" Robin asked.

"Fine. Mr. Norman is horrible, but he's nothing I can't handle."

"It looks like I was almost too late," Mr. Threepbrush said.

"There was another guy who tried to get me into a booth, but I feigned a stomach ache, and then I...passed gas, right in front of him." Robin had never seen Brisa look so embarrassed.

"You're just like the princess!" Robin said, a little too loudly.

After harsh looks from her two companions, Robin said, "Sorry," in a quieter voice.

"I feel bad for the other girls in this place," Mr. Threepbrush said.

"I wouldn't necessarily feel bad for them. Some of the girls I talked to seem to genuinely enjoy their work. Just because it's not my thing doesn't mean it can't be a valid job."

"Yeah. I see your point."

"Alright," Robin said. "This is a riveting philosophical conversation, but we're the only potential bottleneck in this plan. Let's get to work."

The Heist- Nargol

Their first song was a hit. Most people on the islands knew it, so the sing-along was fantastic. They followed it with an orc song they had translated to the Human Tongue. This was less popular with the crowd, but they enjoyed it well enough. The audience was definitely getting louder and drunker as the concert rolled on.

Orok had stopped drinking after taking the initial edge off. He now seemed to be enjoying himself on stage. Nargol had to admit that she was having fun, too, although she kept an eye trained on the guards and the case whenever possible.

Luckily, they were eating the concert up. They seemed to be inching further and further away from the display case. The band would just have to keep this energy going, and keep the guards engaged.

Across the casino, Azure was doing a good job of keeping the bosses busy. And Syl looked both ridiculous and amazing as he played Dragon's Hoard.

Her mind wandered back to the day the marauders had found Syl, orphaned and starving on an uninhabited stretch of beach. He had been so scared, so skittish around the marauders for months. But slowly, he opened up to them. As he learned the Common Tongue, he began to tell jokes, and kept the crew laughing. He was a prodigy when it came to learning music, too. He picked it up so damned fast Nargol had wondered whether he had been a master musician in his past life and some of that talent had seeped through into this one. It was such a contrast from that scared little kid to the faun he had grown to be. To see him swaggering through the casino with such confidence was a wonderful thing.

"Nargol," Orok said, patting her on the ass.

"Yeah?"

"You alright? You spaced out for a second, there."

"Yeah, I'm good. What do you want to do next?"

"Is it time for the big one yet?" Orok immediately answered himself. "No, not yet, right?"

"Not quite yet."

"Why don't we do the one the dragon taught us?"

"Good idea," Nargol said with a smile. She turned to the audience and stepped to her magical voice amplifier. "You probably won't believe this, but this next song is literally from a different world." She paused, hoping that would have gotten a better response. "It was taught to us by a dragon, who learned it somewhere far away from the Undering." Some of the crowd laughed. "Anyway, it's called 'Don't Stop Believin.'"

Zoth-Avarex had taught them this song one night on the *Adventure Ship*. Nargol had no idea what a lot of the words meant, or where South Detroit was, but she had to admit the song was great for parties.

The Heist- Azure

"We don't want to alert him to us watching," Azure said. "But maybe we should get a little closer." She stood and made her way around a Thirty-Seven Gods table, getting a better view of Syl as he played, but more importantly, turning them further away from the front of the casino.

"How does he cheat?" Faron asked. "What are we supposedly looking for?"

"He usually uses a partner. Always a human, and always different." Azure was glad she had thought of this beforehand. "The partner will signal him which cards he has discarded."

"How can that create much of an advantage?" The falcon wasn't going to let this go easily.

"Knowing which cards any given player has can be a huge advantage, but that's not all he does."

"What else?"

"He's also known to carry realistic replicas of fire cards on his person, and he's extremely smooth at slipping them into his hand."

Mr. Pierce flapped his lips. "You can't fake our cards. I don't care who you are."

"You'd be surprised by the quality of replicated stuff one can find out there." Azure had to concentrate hard to not look down at her gaming commission badge. Faron, however, glared directly at it.

"How is it," Faron said, "that you know all about how this guy cheats, yet you haven't been able to charge him with anything?"

Azure started to answer, but the falcon cut her off.

"And your only hope of taking him down just happens to be here, on this exact night?"

"I don't know what's so special about this night as opposed to any other. This is the night Dechi chose to play here. We couldn't help that."

The falcon began to speak, but Azure cut her off this time. "And we know about how he cheats from dozens of reports around the islands. He has been caught on multiple occasions but was able to flee the scene. And by the time the authorities had been contacted, he had fled their jurisdictions. That's why we, an inter-island agency, have taken over."

"But—"

"Are you going to let your pet interrogate me all night?" Azure said to Mr. Bancroft. "Or are we going to catch this guy cheating and move on with it?"

"Gods-damnit, Faron. I already told you once to shut your beak. Now leave the lady alone."

"Yes, sir." Faron stared daggers into Azure.

"So, we just watch for him to take a card from his sleeve," Mr. Bancroft said in an attempt to change the subject. "He can't be that smooth."

"That's the idea," Azure said.

Besides the suspicious falcon, this was going exactly according to plan.

She couldn't wait for it to be over.

The Heist- Robin

Robin peaked out from the curtain as Mr. Threepbrush began cutting. He had smuggled in a small saw that was formed into a circle with the teeth all pointing down. A t-shaped handle allowed him to push down while turning the saw in circles, creating an approximately three-inch diameter hole in the floor. It worked great, but it was still slow going.

"That Mr. Norman guy is pretty close," Robin whispered. "You might want to saw a little quieter."

Mr. Threepbrush nodded and slowed down, sawing in time with the music playing outside the booth.

The saw had gone about an inch into the floor. The progress was about what they had expected. Brisa had made an excellent assessment of the wood used in the flooring. It was Aniyas Pine, a common softwood building material known for its beautiful patterns. The crew had purchased a floorboard from the lumberyard on Mirth Island and timed Mr. Threepbrush as he cut through it with the rounded saw. The practice run quickly devolved into a gambling opportunity, as the marauders took bets on how long he would take to cut through it. Elijah ended up taking the pot with his guess of six minutes and fifteen seconds, only five seconds off from the actual time. But Elijah being Elijah, he put all the money into the crew's rum fund.

"Shit!" said Robin, fluttering into a top corner. "He's coming."

Mr. Threepbrush stashed the saw in his jacket, looked around in a panic, then lay on his back over the cut floor. Brisa stood over the top of him and began to dance to the music.

Robin's heart raced as she contemplated being discovered. She mentally prepared herself to peck out an eye if necessary.

"Knock knock," Mr. Norman said, seconds before thrusting his head in through the curtain. "Whoa! Good view from down there, eh?" He laughed to himself. "Sorry to bother you, sir. Just making sure Brizza here was keeping you happy."

"I was perfectly happy until you interrupted, if I'm being quite honest," Mr. Threepbrush said, an annoyed frown on his face.

"I'm sorry, sir. It seems Brizza knows what she's doing. I'll leave you to it, then."

"She's everything I've dreamed of and more. And luckily, I've got enough money to cover at least an hour in here. So yeah, we're good."

Mr. Norman nodded and closed the curtain as Mr. Threepbrush called, "I do not want to be interrupted again!"

Brisa helped Mr. Threepbrush to his feet.

"Nice work, you two," Robin said. "I didn't know you had that in you, Threepbrush."

"Me neither." He ducked his head bashfully, then took out his saw and got back to work.

The Heist- Nargol

The strange, otherworldly song did pretty well. It took a while for the audience to get into it, but by the end, they were rocking to the beat.

"Alright, alright," Orok said. "Now it's the part of the show where we take requests. Does anyone have a request?"

With one voice, the crowd roared, "I knew you were special!"

"What?" Orok said. "You want another old orc folk song?"

The audience became a cacophony of sound.

"We have this song about the sound of the wind as it blows through tall grass. It's a classic."

Many understood the joke and laughed, but many more were getting restless.

"Alright, don't get bent out of shape," Orok said. "We hear you. 'I Knew You Were Special' it is!"

After a deafening cheer, the crowd quieted down. They were absolutely enthralled as the song began, and laughed at all of the punchlines.

When it was time for the new part, Orok shouted, "Are you ready for the new verse?"

Another huge cheer filled the casino.

Dramatically, Nargol approached the wand stand. She let the music go through for a measure to build the suspense, then began.

When I met you, I knew you were special,
You were so nice and so kind,
You treated me just like a lady,
A lady who loves your behind.

Orok looked to the band and made a slashing motion across his throat. The music stopped as Orok shook his head. A quiet hubbub spread through the crowd.

"A lady who loves your behind?" he said to Nargol.

"What?"

"We promised these people a great new verse, and this is the best we could come up with?"

"Well..." Nargol looked to the crowd. "I do have a little something extra I've been working on." As the crowd cheered, Nargol looked to the bongo player and said, "Hit it."

Theodore began to strike a repetitive bass note on his drums.

Thump, thump, thump, thump.

Orok turned around and began shaking his butt to the beat, eliciting a roar from the crowd.

Thump, thump, thump, thump.

Nargol approached the wand stand and began to sing in a rhythmic, almost spoken-word style.

When I see that ass, I'm titillated and I'm fidgetin',
I don't know if you've seen it, but his backside's Callipygian.
I hate to see him leave, but I love to watch him go.
I love that big round ass more than he could ever know.
The left cheek is great, and the right cheek is better.
I once wrote Orok's ass a love letter.
It read, 'Dear Orok's Ass, how I adore thee,
The way you move when Orok walks delights me.
Are you my favorite thing on the Undering?'

She paused and smiled.

'Yeah, you might be.'

The crowd lost their collective mind as Theodore kept the *thump, thump, thump* going.

Nargol's smile stayed plastered to her face. She didn't think the new stuff was necessarily *that* good, but it had sure worked for this drunken audience, and that felt pretty sweet.

After reveling in the moment, while Orok still shook his butt to the beat, Nargol remembered the point of this whole operation. She glanced toward the display case, happy to find the guards had all but forgotten about it.

The Heist- Robin

S weat dripped from Mr. Threepbrush's forehead as he pressed and turned, pressed and turned the little saw. Brisa had taken her turn and had sunk the saw at least another inch into the floor. The floor of the casino was definitely thicker than the board they had used for practice. But when Mr. Threepbrush took back over, he didn't think there was far to go.

"Should be just about there." Mr. Threepbrush kept saying, wiping his brow and continuing to cut. "It feels like it's going to drop every time I turn the saw."

Robin continued to keep watch through a tiny opening in the curtain. Mr. Norman was making his rounds around the place but hadn't been back to bother them again.

There was a sudden jerky movement as Mr. Threepbrush's hand dropped to the floor with a bang.

"We're through," he said, probably a bit too loud.

"Oh, we're not through yet, baby," Brisa improvised. "We're just getting started."

Robin nodded her head in approval, then jumped down near the hole in the floor. She leaned forward, gazing cautiously down into it. Light beamed up at her from the casino floor. She could see the entire inside of the glass case from here; the portal-cutting knife was right there, about ten feet below.

A sudden wave of panic rolled over her. This whole plan was contingent on Robin unlocking the case from the inside. It would be humiliating, and possibly life threatening if she were to fail.

Her constant outward show of confidence was just that, a show. Privately, she was just as unsure of herself as the next bird—a secret she would only admit to Azure.

But it would be more than humiliation and danger. If Robin failed, Azure's plan would fail, and they wouldn't be able to get the kid back where she belonged. Azure would be heartbroken, and Robin had dedicated her life to making sure Azure's heart remained intact.

"You ready?" she said to Mr. Threepbrush, steeling her resolve.

"Hold on." He tucked the saw back into his pants and straightened his jacket.

Brisa checked him over to make sure it wasn't obvious.

He took a deep breath. "Okay. Let's do this."

Robin dove head-first into the hole, and Mr. Threepbrush replaced the small table over it.

The Heist- Azure

Azure's heart had leapt when the piece of floor fell down into the display case. She scanned the area around it, and fortunately, no one seemed to have noticed. When Robin fluttered down into the case, Azure's knees went weak. She took in a sharp inhale through her nose and turned away.

"What seems to be bothering you?" Faron asked.

"Nothing. This corset is on a little too tight, but that's it."

"What is your deal tonight, Faron?" Mr. Bancroft said. "You're supposed to be watching the faun, not Miss Cosgrove."

"Yes, sir." Faron gave Azure a long look before turning back to the card table.

"He's holding his cards too high," Mr. Pierce said. "Doesn't seem like a professional player to me."

"But look," Azure said. "He's got a full dragon already. This would be the perfect time for him to pull out a fire card. That hoard is massive. This is probably the moment he's been waiting for."

Azure knew he wasn't going to pull a card from his sleeve, but she wanted to focus their attention, as Robin was in the case and the heist was almost complete.

The orc guards were still enrapt in Nargol and Orok's show, although they had just finished their hit song, and Azure wasn't sure if they had planned for anything after that.

"He just called 'Hoard,'" said Mr. Pierce, shaking his head. "He won that giant hoard without sneaking a fire card." He looked to Azure. "I'm getting pretty impatient, here. I'm not going to spend this important night watching a gods-damned Faun pile up money. I know that for sure."

"I'm getting impatient, too," Faron said, her head on a swivel.

"I'll tell you what," Mr. Pierce said to Azure. "I'll give this little operation one more round. If he doesn't cheat by then, I'm done with it."

"That's fair." The words just came out, and Azure immediately wished she could take them back.

What if the round was short? What if that didn't allow Robin enough time to unlock the case? If the bosses weren't here watching Syl, they would head back toward the front of the casino. They would see the orc guards away from their post and send them back. Then the orcs would see Robin fluttering around in the case. All would be lost.

She considered giving Syl some kind of signal to draw out this round as long as he could, but she didn't know how to do that without being too obvious.

Eyes skyward, she asked the gods for just a little more time.

The Heist- Nargol

Someone in the audience began chanting for an encore. Before long the entire crowd chanted in unison.

"Encore! Encore!"

Nargol sneaked a look at the display case. She could see Robin working inside.

The guards were starting to drift back toward their post, although they were still watching and chanting with the crowd.

"Shit," she mouthed to her husband. The plan had been to peak as the heist was wrapping up, but they had gone a bit too fast.

Nargol dashed across the stage and pulled Orok away from his wand stand.

"What should we do?" Orok asked before she could. "Should we just give them what they want?"

"I think we should dangle an encore out in front of them. Keep them engaged for at least one or two more songs with the promise of ending with their favorite."

"That's a good idea. What song, then?"

"We could play a Marauder song?" Nargol said. "Maybe Marauder's Green?"

"Yeah. Or we could do the new one I've been working on."

Nargol thought for a moment. "This crowd might not like that one."

"I really don't give much of a shit if they like it." Orok shrugged. "I mean, it's got a lot of cussing in it, so I'm sure they'll go for that. At the very least, it will cause a stir."

Nargol considered the idea. She wasn't sure if the timing was right, on an immediate or big picture scale, but they needed to keep the guards' attention.

"Okay. Do Theodore and William know it?"

"No. I was thinking I'll do it acapella. I think it might work that way."

Nargol slapped Orok on the ass, projecting as much confidence as she could. "Do your thing, then!"

Orok stepped up to the wand stand.

"I promise we will do 'I Knew You Were Special' one more time to end the night. But first we're going to do a few others. Anyone interested in a new song?"

The crowd murmured, lukewarm to the idea.

"Alright. This one may not be quite as fun as the last, but it's important, so give it a chance."

The audience quieted down.

Orok took a deep breath, then began to sing, his gravelly voice resonating through the casino.

The Heist- Robin

Robin alighted on the handle of the dagger, then hopped over to the lock mechanism in the corner of the display case.

"Shit," she whispered to herself. The lock was more complicated than she had been able to see from the outside. She had hoped it was nothing more than a simple latch she could lift open with her beak, but it was a magical lock, which Syl had told her about one time.

The lock was formed by four brass squares that were formed together to make one larger square. To open it, someone with a magic wand who had seen the lock, and could visualize its opening would simply need to make the four squares move away from each other equally until they formed the corners of a bigger, vaguely outlined square. It was, as far as Robin knew, the very latest in magical lock technology.

So, sans magical abilities—besides being able to talk, which was apparently seen as magic in this world—Robin had to figure out how to push the four squares out into their corners. And seeing as how one corner was about two Robin-lengths from the next, this was going to be a problem.

She sneaked a look out of the case. The two orc guards were several steps away from their post, watching Nargol and Orok's show. She knew the band had just finished "I Knew You Were Special," which was supposed to be their big closer. But the crowd was cheering for more. Robin hoped they had more to give.

"Focus," she said to herself as she faced the lock. "They'll deal with their parts. I gotta open this gods-damned lock."

She jumped up on the brass squares and positioned herself with a claw on the top left and bottom right. She grabbed the top right square with her beak as best she could and started to push out with her head and both feet. The squares budged, but not much more than that. She was able to get the squares about one tenth of the the distance they needed to go. She did notice something that was possibly helpful, though. If one of the squares moved, apparently all of the squares moved. So, if she could manage to get one of them into its proper place, the others would get there, as well.

She looked around in the display case for anything that could help her. The only things in there were the portal dagger, an old knight's helmet, a loaded crossbow, and a broken crossbow bolt.

Her bird mind, small but mighty, worked hard for a solution.

She studied the crossbow. It had a loaded bolt, ready to fire. The string could be useful if she could get it off. It was under a shitload of tension, though. And how would she even do that anyway? She began to think about human weapons. When did they stop using crossbows and start using firearms? It was interesting to think how the humans had developed guns as a counterpoint to the magic that all other beings had back on the Continent.

"Shit!" she said aloud. She was letting her mind wander. That tended to happen sometimes when she was nervous or overwhelmed. "Focus, Robin."

Having no other obvious options, Robin grasped the broken bolt in her claws and flew up to the crossbow. She began to saw at the tensioned string with the head of the bolt. She wasn't very confident, but it turned out to be easier than she expected. The cutting action was awkward, but the string itself was old and brittle and cut more easily than she could have hoped. The head of the bolt was extremely sharp, too.

After about a dozen good slashes, the string released its tension with an ear-splitting *thwap*. The loaded bolt was sent flying, ricocheting off the glass on the side of the case where the guards stood.

Robin held her breath, knowing the guards were going to turn around and see her. But they didn't. Their eyes stayed glued to the stage in the bar.

A frizzled piece of string, about a foot and a half in length, lay on the floor of the display case. Robin picked it up in her beak.

The knight's helmet was the closest thing to the lock, so she flew up to it. With considerable effort, she managed to tie one end of the string around a slit in the visor. Then she took the other end to the lock. She pushed the squares away from each other just enough to fit the string between them. It took her three tries, but eventually she was able to thread the string around the top right square.

Grasping the end of the string in her beak, she flew back to the helmet and started to pull as best she could. The square moved in the right direction, but it still had a long way to go.

"Shit," Robin said, shaking her head.

The Heist- Nargol

Nargol took a few steps back and listened to Orok sing.
When you fell out from your mother,
You were what you were, couldn't choose to be another.
You could have been an orc, a human, or a bird.
Hating you for what you woke up as is so fucking absurd.
He stepped up the intensity as he rolled into the chorus.
Hating another race is the stupidest fucking thing,
Yet so many choose to do it in the Undering.
You fear what you don't know, you grow to hate what you fear.
So, let's go to the bar and get a fucking beer!

As Nargol watched her husband sing, she was filled with a warm pride in him. Being orc refugees on the islands wasn't easy, but here he was, bravely using his voice to try and make things better; not just for himself, but for everybody.

The audience had been quiet at first, but they were starting to get into it. Some of them tried to sing along as Orok repeated the chorus, again. The display case guards stood completely still, mesmerized by the song. Nargol felt a strong solidarity with them. It would have been hard for a human in the crowd to truly understand how courageous singing this song really was.

During the song, Theodore left his bongos and took the steps off the stage to talk with a waiter. As the song ended, he came back with two frothy beers in his hands. He handed one to Orok, then raised his glass as if for a toast.

"Who wants to raise their glass with us?" Orok said, lifting his into the air and sloshing half of it out.

More than half the audience raised their drinks, it might have been closer to three quarters of them.

"Here's to health and understanding for each and every one of you."

Orok and Theodore clinked their glasses together, then chugged their beers down, arm in arm.

The Heist- Azure

"Fuck this," said Mr. Pierce. "I'm not waiting for this round to end. What would Governor Pratt say if he saw me lurking around, begging for a gods-damned faun to cheat me at one of my own tables?" He held up a hand and a group of seven security people rushed to him. "You see the faun playing at table three? I want you to take him into custody for cheating."

"But you'll ruin our investigation," Azure said, holding up her hands. "We don't have a solid case against him, yet."

"I've got at least seven witnesses to his cheating right here. Right, boys?"

The security guards nodded their assent.

"Two more minutes!" Azure pleaded. "That's all I'm ask—"

"What are you waiting for?" Mr. Pierce said to the security people. "Get him!"

The security force surrounded Syl, then converged on him. He shot up and tried to escape, but they were too many, and they caught him with ease. He tried to resist, struggling to break free while stomping on as many feet as he could, but they held him fast.

"Well, you've ruined our whole operation," Azure said. "But I'll take him into my custody, anyway. Maybe I can salvage a charge or two. You'll need to hope and pray that the gaming commission doesn't see this as a breaking of our agreement."

"I don't think so," said Mr. Pierce. "That's not how we deal with cheats, here. Mr. Bancroft and I have our own way of dealing with cheating fauns in the back room."

"I'm an official from the League of Islands Gaming Commission!" Azure shouted, starting to panic. "You do not have the authority to take a prisoner from my custody."

"Are you, though?" Faron asked from Mr. Bancroft's shoulder.

"I...of course I am." Azure waggled her badge.

Faster than Azure would have thought possible, Faron leapt from Mr. Bancroft's shoulder and swooped toward her. Azure barely had time to cover her face with her hands before the falcon ripped the blonde wig off of her head and dropped it on a Dragon's Hoard table.

"What in thirty-seven hells is going on here?" Mr. Pierce asked, brow heavily creased.

"This is that girl who came in asking about the knife in your display case," Faron explained in an admonishing tone.

"What?" Mr. Pierce's scrunch-faced expression of confusion would have been funny in any other circumstance.

"I have no idea what you're talking about," Azure said. "I just like to wear blonde wigs. It's all the rage in Whetstone."

The falcon turned its head, looking directly at the display case. All eyes followed her lead.

And there, standing on the knight's helmet, was Robin, wrenching on a piece of string.

"Are you...actually trying to steal something from this casino?" Mr. Pierce said, working out what he could see aloud. "From me?"

"No. That's probably just a bird that got trapped in that case somehow."

"A bird just happened to find itself in a case that can repel a rifle shot, and is secured with the latest in magical locks?"

"Yes?"

"Get her," Mr. Pierce said to his men.

"Shit!" Azure said, heart bounding.

She thrust her hand into the top of her dress and pulled out the ship's whistle. It was time for the contingency plan. It was their only hope of escape, now.

But as she brought the whistle to her mouth, Mr. Pierce brought a fist down on her wrist, sending shocks of pain up and down her forearm. She dropped the whistle to the floor and Mr. Bancroft scooped it up.

Azure's head darted around like a trapped animal. The casino's security force had her surrounded, and without the whistle, all hope was lost.

The Heist- Robin

Across the casino, Robin had seen that asshole falcon take off Azure's wig. She had seen the casino security capture both Syl and Azure.

Mr. Threepbrush lurked nearby, looking confused about what he should do.

Robin had to get this case opened.

Thinking about her best friend in trouble, Robin reached down as far as she could on the string and secured it in her beak. Then she wrenched back on it with every bit of might she had in her little body. Her claws clenched tight to the helmet; she flexed her legs to create more pulling force. Grunting, with eyes closed tight, she pulled on the string like Azure's life depended on it.

There was a tiny click.

The door of the display case cracked open.

And Faron flew inside with the speed and deadly intent of a crossbow bolt.

The Heist- Nargol

Nargol noticed the commotion first.

The crowd was in a strange state. Many seemed to enjoy the last song, but others seemed agitated. Many called for them to sing "I Knew You Were Special," again.

Nargol narrowed her eyes, trying to figure out what was going on across the casino floor. She found Azure and Syl, both in the custody of casino security.

"Orok!" She pointed to the Dragon's Hoard tables. "Let's go!"

She sprinted stage right and leapt to an empty space on the floor. People screamed and scurried to get out of her way, but she had to help a few of them along.

Once free of the bar crowd, Nargol made a b-line straight for Azure and Syl. She wasn't sure what she was going to do, or why Azure hadn't blown the ship's whistle, but she had to do something. Things had apparently gone to shit in the blink of an eye.

Nargol glanced behind to see Orok pushing his way through the busy casino floor. There were shrieks all around as the two orcs rushed by.

As they approached, the security force squared up to face them. Each had a flintlock pistol in their belts, some of them fumbled at pulling them out and aiming them at the orcs. Most, if not all of them looked terrified.

"Please let our friends go," Nargol said, forceful but polite.

Mr. Pierce stepped forward. "These criminals are in our custody, now. They were caught trying to scam the casino and will be dealt with according-ly. This is none of your concern."

Azure began to speak, but a man forced his hand over her mouth. As Nargol started toward him, Azure stomped down hard on his foot. He bellowed in pain as Azure wriggled from his grasp.

"The whistle! He has it!" Azure pointed to Mr. Bancroft.

Nargol closed the distance to the man in a flash. Looming over him, she asked nicely for the whistle.

Mr. Bancroft searched for an escape route in a panic.

"Don't give it to them," Mr. Pierce ordered.

Several security guards aimed cocked pistols at Nargol.

"I will give you to the count of two," Nargol said in a slow, calm voice. She thought about little Morgak, and how she didn't want to leave her motherless at such a young age. Inside she was panicking, but she kept her composure. "One..."

Mr. Bancroft thrust the whistle out in his open palm.

Slowly, Nargol took the whistle, brought it to her lips, and blew. Its piercing squeal resonated around the casino, stopping damn-near everyone in their tracks.

As a sudden hush fell over the casino, Nargol reached into a pocket, pulled out some loose stuffing, and placed pieces of it in her ears. Orok, Azure, and Syl did the same.

The Heist- Azure

Blunderbuss—with stuffing coming out of both ears—burst in through the front doors of the casino holding a large wooden crate. With an awkward gait, face red with exertion, he made his way down the steps to the area where the gaming tables began, and set the crate on the ground.

As he turned to the side, a wire cage could be seen hanging from his back with a strap. Inside the cage was a writhing mass of black and yellow.

Blunderbuss took a knife from his belt and pried open the top of the crate. A massive swarm of bees poured out into the casino. Screams filled the air as people ran for cover.

Paying no mind to the bees, Blunderbuss methodically unslung the cage from his back and placed it gently on the floor. He was about to open it when one of the orc guards from the display case tackled him to the ground.

Azure could hear the air forced from his lungs over the screams of the casino patrons.

The Heist- Robin

Robin was thankful for the weight of the knight's helmet. As soon as Faron had entered the display case, Robin had zipped into the helmet through its open visor. When Faron tried to get to her, she inadvertently slammed the visor down, trapping Robin inside.

She wasn't exactly trapped. She could probably fit through the eye slit if she wanted to expose herself to a furious, murderous falcon in tight quarters, but Robin was happy to remain inside her safe prison until she could think of a better way out.

"Get out of there!" Faron demanded as she tried to lift the helmet's visor with her head.

"Eat shit," Robin taunted.

Outside the case, it sounded like all hell was breaking loose. Robin had heard the whistle, so she knew everything had gone to shit and Blunderbuss's plan—the last resort—had been enacted.

She needed to get to Azure, even if that meant risking her own life.

Through the eye slit, Robin watched as the falcon positioned herself between the helmet and the glass, then started to push. The helmet moved, starting to tilt to the side. It wasn't quite enough to tip it over, but it gave Robin a bigger opening along the bottom.

Eyeing the open door of the display case, Robin zipped out from the gap under the helmet and sped toward the opening. But the falcon was too quick, abandoning her efforts with the helmet and moving to block Robin's way with unreal speed.

"Shit!" Robin veered right, then flew up to the ceiling, hoping to go back up through the hole in the floor above.

Before she could cram herself into the hole, she felt Faron just behind her. Instinctively, she dodged to the left, narrowly avoiding a clutching talon.

Without thinking, Robin circled around and latched onto the falcon's back, digging her claws in as deep as she possibly could.

"Get off me!" Faron said while violently shaking her body in flight.

Robin was almost flung from her back but managed to hold onto the falcon's feathers.

Faron didn't hesitate. When the shaking failed to dislodge Robin from her back, she dropped down to the floor of the case, turned, and smashed Robin into the glass.

All the breath was pushed from Robin's lungs in one long painful wheeze. And before she could even attempt a breath in, she was smashed into the glass, again.

Faron took wing, flying about halfway up the height of the case, then careened into the glass, back first.

This one was too much for Robin to take. Her vision blurry, she let go of the feathers on Faron's back and plummeted to the floor, landing with a tiny thud.

The falcon looked down from above—a nightmare vision that was likely the last thing countless creatures had ever seen.

"Goodbye, Little Bird," the falcon said before diving down, talons outstretched.

Robin looked to her right and found the pointy end of the broken crossbow bolt laying next to her.

Still unable to breathe, Robin rolled and grasped the broken bolt with both feet. With a wheezing battle cry, she turned it up at the attacking falcon.

Robin braced for impact, but Faron halted her dive just in time to avoid Robin's weapon.

Furiously flapping her wings, the falcon hovered just out of reach of the bolt. She seemed to be waiting for an opening.

The falcon feinted left, causing Robin to swing the bolt across her body to fend off the nearest talon. Faron charged the other way, but Robin was quick to move the sharpened bolt between herself and the falcon.

"What, are you afraid of a *Little Bird*?" Robin said, figuring her only chance was to goad the bird of prey into a mistake. "I've seen chickens with better fighting instincts."

Faron growled in frustration before lunging down much closer than she had before.

Using every muscle in her body, Robin swung the bolt at the encroaching talon

A screech echoed through the case, and blood splashed down onto Robin's chest.

Faron landed less than a foot away, head curling underneath herself to assess her injury, which, as far as Robin could tell, was a deep cut to the meat of her right leg. Bright red blood gathered in a small pool beneath the falcon.

Robin dropped the bolt, rolled to her feet, then flew out of the display case before the falcon could look back up.

Once outside, the chaos and the buzzing of bees became much louder.

Blunderbuss struggled under the weight of one of the orc guards, and Threepbrush—stuffing in his ears, too—was trying to get to the opened case past the other guard.

Every flap of her wings brought searing pain, but Robin knew what she had to do. She flew over Blunderbuss and landed on the wire cage. She fidgeted with the simple lock until it sprang open.

As the door of the cage flung wide, the true chaos began.

Tiddly dragons flashed out in all directions, nearly knocking Robin to the floor, again. Their percussive blasts of air stunned bees and humans alike. As they went into a feeding frenzy throughout the casino floor, several dizzy people fell to the ground in heaps.

The orc holding Blunderbuss suddenly let go and rubbed his right ear, allowing Blunderbuss to jump up and get away.

The orc standing between Mr. Threepbrush and the case was seemingly disoriented by a tiddly dragon, as well. As he staggered on his feet, Mr. Threepbrush dodged past him, threw open the case, and grabbed the portal knife. Faron tried to take a bite at him as he did so, but he was able to just avoid her lunge and slam the door of the case shut before she could get out.

Knife in hand, Mr. Threepbrush reluctantly sprinted out through the front door. Azure had told him to leave everyone behind if he had to. Getting that knife to Oriana was the most important thing in her estimation.

Robin jumped up from the cage and, dodging through a throng of bees and hungry tiddly dragons, headed for her selfless friend.

She had almost made it to the first gaming table when a tiddly dragon's air blast knocked her from the sky. Her mind muddled, she made feeble attempts to right herself. As the world darkened, she crashed into a stack of chips at a Thirty-Seven Gods table, breathing, but barely holding on to consciousness.

The Heist- Nargol

Many of the security guards ducked and ran for cover as soon as the bees began to swarm the casino. Most of the guards who had stayed were rendered woozy by the tiddly dragons and their blasts of air.

As Nargol started forward, one of the guards fired his pistol at her, narrowly missing over her left shoulder. She barreled ahead and knocked the pistol from another man's hand before he could fire it. To her right, Orok lifted the man who had fired at her and tossed him onto a Dragon's Hoard table, scattering cards and chips everywhere. He raised his fist at another guard, who immediately cowered so hard that he fell to the floor.

"Let's go!" Nargol called, grabbing Azure by the arm and wrenching her away from the guard who held her.

Azure elbowed the man in the face for good measure, then followed Nargol toward the front. Orok and Syl were just behind.

They met little resistance on the way out. Another gun fired, but the ball struck a chandelier above, shattering shards of broken glass over the panicking people below.

The marauders continued to dodge through the crowd, jumping over people or pools of vomit when necessary.

When they were almost to the front, Nargol noticed Robin laying belly up in a pile of chips on one of the tables. She had a line of blood across her chest, but seemed to be alive and talking to herself. As quick and careful as possible, Nargol scooped up the bird in her hands.

"Sure, Sir Terry," Robin mumbled. "I'd love to..." She giggled; eyes closed. "Sure, sir. Shurshur..."

"Stop!" came an orc's voice from just ahead.

Nargol looked up to see Kogar and Borug standing in their path, palms upraised.

"I'm sorry," said Borug, only slightly woozy, "but we can't let you leave."

"You've got the biggest decision of your life, here," Nargol said, voice almost motherly. "You can choose to keep working for that Mr. Pierce asshole for the rest of your lives, or you can join us, right now."

"Join you?" Kogar said, massive eyebrows scrunching together. "You mean join the marauders?"

"Yes. But you better decide now. Because I promise you, we're getting out of here either way."

Kogar and Borug looked to each other, both of them shrugging at exactly the same time.

"Well come on, then." Kogar waved them forward as he ran to hold open the front door.

The Heist- Azure

As Nargol talked to the guards up front, Azure noticed that several of the guards with Mr. Pierce had gotten their shit together and were heading for the front of the casino.

Another shot shattered the display case not two feet to Azure's right. Apparently, it wasn't actually bulletproof.

Brisa rushed to the group from the stairs, and before Azure could acknowledge her, she traced one of her tattoos and muttered a word.

The world vanished in a cloud of thick fog. Azure could barely see Brisa, who was within arm's reach.

"Let's go," Brisa said, waving her in the right direction.

Azure began to follow but stopped as a thought popped into her head.

Wakeman's treasure.

She had all but promised to get the treasure back for him, and this whole thing had started because they had taken a job from him. Plus, the money was going to be even more important now that the marauders were outlaws.

Even though she knew it was stupid, with an escape to freedom so close, she decided to go back for the treasure, which Mr. Pierce had told her was on the top floor.

"Brisa," she called. "I have to go back for something."

"No. We need to go."

"Please, just trust me. Take everyone back to the ship and set sail. I'll be right there."

Reluctantly, Brisa nodded and disappeared into the fog.

Azure headed for the bar area, hoping to go around Mr. Pierce and any security people. Moving in the fog was slow, cautious work. Especially with people panicking worse now that visibility was gone. Many thought the casino was on fire, according to the disembodied voices around her.

Eventually, Azure found the stage and used it as a visual anchor to carry her through the bar faster.

She had gone about halfway through the bar when she was tackled from behind. Azure and her attacker crashed into a table, shattering a dozen partially-filled beer mugs as they hit the carpeted floor. A shard of glass cut a line of pain across her forehead.

"Got you!" came the voice of Mr. Pierce as he tightened his massive arms around her waist.

Azure wriggled and fought to release herself from his grip, but couldn't budge an inch.

Mr. Pierce got to his knees, intending to lift Azure off the ground like a rag doll. But as he moved, his hold on her loosened enough for her to turn her body toward him.

With one motion, Azure grabbed a beer mug that was still intact from the ground and brought it down as hard as she could on Mr. Pierce's face.

He wailed in pain and released her, clutching his ruptured nose in both hands.

Azure shot to her feet, then bashed him on the back of his head with the mug, crumpling him to the beer-soaked ground.

Without hesitation, Azure turned and hurried through the rest of the bar. Blood flowed into her eyes, but she took a cloth napkin from one of the tables, wiped the blood away, then pressed it to the wound.

By the time she passed the casino office, the fog was starting to clear a bit. Able to see about five feet in front of her, Azure jogged for the lift in the back.

When she arrived at it, the doors opened and two security people holding pistols burst out. Azure tensed up, ready to pounce on the nearest one, but they ran past her into the pandemonium.

Breathing a sigh of relief, Azure entered the lift. There were several buttons on the wall to the left, numbering from one to thirty-seven. Above the last number were the words *Mr. Pierce's Suite-Authorized Personnel Only!* Azure pressed the corresponding button, and the lift doors closed in front of her.

The ground moved under her feet. It was something that might have toppled her to the floor two years ago, but her life at sea had prepared her for such things, as strange as it was.

As the lift rose higher into the castle/hotel, Azure wondered how it worked. She knew there had to be a series of magic wands strategically placed, just like the rollercoaster, but she still didn't understand how they were able to function without a person to direct the magical energy. Maybe there were people somewhere nearby, somehow directing their magical energy. If that was true, she hoped they were well-paid employees rather than anyone being exploited by that asshole Mr. Pierce.

Before she had time to really contemplate it, the floor stopped moving, and the doors reopened. Azure hurried out into a small foyer with an ornate door on the other side. She tried the knob and found the door to be unlocked. She pushed it open and entered a huge, lavish room with windows all around. There was a massive fireplace in the middle of the room, with a chimney that led up into the tall ceiling. All around the fireplace were plush chairs, couches, and footrests, with many small decorated tables among them. Azure headed there first, circling the fireplace while searching every table with her eyes.

When she didn't find the treasure chest there, she rushed to the formal dining room off to the right, then the kitchen area behind that.

"Shit," she said to herself as she came back out into the main room.

There was an ornate sign above a door across the room that read: *The King of the Castle.* Azure rolled her eyes and ran to it.

Inside was a four-post bed decorated in luxurious dark red linens. Next to the bed, on a huge bed-side table, was Mr. Carlyle's stolen treasure. Azure grabbed it and searched the area for something to stuff it into. A large cloth bag embroidered with the crown and crossing goblets of the Fortress sat on a chair in the corner. It was filled with bottles of expensive-looking wine. Azure picked it up by the bottom and dumped the bottles out on the floor. She tossed the treasure chest into the bag and threw the bag's strap over her head and one arm. Then she ran back toward the lift. But just as she got to the door to Mr. Pierce's rooms, the doors of the lift opened. Mr. Pierce and two security guards were inside.

With a shriek that would have been embarrassing in a different situation, Azure spun and sprinted away. But Mr. Pierce's residence made up the entire floor. She was completely trapped up here, unless...

She darted for one of the many windows and threw it open. She could hear footfalls just behind her as she jumped out the window while twisting to catch the sill. Now facing the approaching guards, she had very little time. She looked down to find thick vines covering the outer wall. Thankful, she used them to scurry to her left, just avoiding the nearest guard's clutching hands.

She climbed up as fast as she could toward what seemed to be a platform just above Mr. Pierce's rooms. While climbing, she could have sworn she saw something pass quickly between her and the Ring in the night sky, but there was no time to consider it. Her hands were already tight and painful from climbing, and she had at least ten more feet to go. She tried her best to find footholds in the stone under the vines, but they were hard to come by. Azure grunted with the effort of each movement as she pulled herself up with just her arms. Eventually, out of breath, she made it over the railing that sur-rounded the platform.

Once on her feet again, she realized she was in the place where people would pay to ride the giant zip-line. The line was anchored to a sturdy pole near the center of the platform and went off to the west. There was a casino worker near the edge of the platform helping a middle-aged woman with the mechanism that Azure assumed would take her down to the ground safely.

Mr. Pierce shot up from a set of stairs, his face bloodied and balled up in anger.

"Get her!" he yelled to his guards, who wasted no time.

Azure headed for the zip-line. When she got there, she said, "So sorry," to the woman as she pushed her out of the way. She grasped the strange han-dles—connected to a wheel—that sat atop the line. And with no time to think of the dizzying heights, she jumped from the top of the Fortress, grip-ing the handles with everything she had.

While speeding through the night air with incredible intensity, Azure hazarded a glance back, thankful to have made a last-second escape. Mr. Pierce snatched a pistol from one of the security guards, aimed it at the zip line in front of him, and fired at point-blank range.

Azure became completely weightless as the line that held her snapped. She lost hold of the handles as she started to free fall, twisting and flailing.

This was it. A fall from hundreds of feet in the air would kill her, no doubt about that. Images zipped through her mind. Robin, Elijah, her parents, the marauders. She clenched her eyes shut, wondering if the gods were real, her last vision that of the glowing Ring above.

Her fall halted abruptly, and as far as she could tell, she was still alive.

She opened her eyes to find Zoth-Avarex looking down at her.

"That was a great catch, if I do say so myself," he said as he sped away. "I mean, that was an all-timer. Epic as shit, right?"

Azure said nothing, too stunned by everything that had just transpired.

"What's up with your nose?"

"It's fake," she said, staring at nothing.

"Oh, well if you're wondering why I'm here, I was just checking to make sure everyone was okay. I felt a twinge of regret for not helping you with this whole thing, so I was circling above, waiting to see if you were gonna need any help. Good thing, too!" The dragon smiled. "I hoped I might have to roast some people with dragon fire or something. Didn't expect to catch you out of the air like a gods-damned epic hero."

Still discombobulated, Azure's eyes started to drift closed.

"I get it," Zoth-Avarex said. "You can thank me later."

The dragon flew out over the docks and placed Azure down gently on the *Adventure Ship*.

"Captain's on board!" he called to the marauders working to raise the sails. "Here, let me give you a little boost.

Zoth-Avarex flew aft, around to the stern, and gave the ship a push toward the Mirror Sea.

Azure sat up on the deck, a dreamy smile on her face as she saw Elijah with Oriana and Morgak on either side of him.

INTERLUDE: Another Letter From MK

Mirth Island was still visible behind them when Nova landed back on the bar, another rolled parchment attached to his leg.

"Back so soon?" Robin asked as she alighted near him.

"Yeah." His voice was glum and dejected. He barely glanced at her as he untied the parchment from his leg. "Not very good news, this time."

"Is MK alright?" Azure said as she snatched the note from the bar, heart pounding.

"Yes. He's alright."

Relieved, but still anxious, Azure quickly unrolled the letter and began to read.

Dearest Marauders,

Hello to all. I hope everything is well and that you're having SAFE adventures! The reason for this letter is, unfortunately, not as joyous as the last. Chastity and I are still doing great, but it is another matter I write to you about today.

As I prepared backstage before one of our shows, I heard a louder and much more aggressive crowd than usual filling the theater. I peeked out from behind the curtain to see Captain Roberts and his crew, drunk as skunks, taking their places in the front row!

I was terrified, but the show must go on. We didn't get very far before they started heckling us. My actors were consummate professionals, but the rude treatment continued. At one point, Captain Roberts stood, looked me dead in the eyes, and asked where the Adventure Ship was. He said, "Where can I find Azure Brine? I have a score to settle with her."

I'm so sorry to be the bearer of troubling news, but I wanted you to be on the lookout for Captain Roberts, as it seems he still carries a grudge.

There is something else I think you should know, as well. Two days ago, there was an attempted jailbreak, done by several of Pratt's most fanatical followers. They were unsuccessful, but the fact that they even tried is troubling to me. I hope that nothing comes of this, but simply wanted you to be aware.

I look forward to seeing all of your faces again, hopefully much sooner than later! Be safe out there!

Yours Forever,

MK

"Shit," Azure said, scanning the horizon. She already knew that the captain had it out for her, but this note further confirmed that he didn't intend to stop until he'd had his revenge.

PART THREE
THE VOLCANO

A Quiet Night

O riana yawned, stretching her tiny fists up over her head.

The marauders had all congregated around the bar; the people who had been involved in the heist telling their stories to the ones who hadn't. The alcohol flowed and laughter filled the cool night air. Little Morgak had already fallen asleep on her mother's shoulder while she recounted the night's events. Azure wanted to join them, but she wanted to give Oriana the attention she deserved.

"I'll take her in and get her situated for bed," Azure said to Elijah. "You go ahead and join them. You'll want to hear the stories now, before they get too embellished."

"It doesn't sound like they'll need much embellishment." Elijah kissed Azure's forehead.

"No. They really don't. It was a crazy night, that's for sure." Azure moved her mouth closer to his ear. "I'll be back out to tell you all about it after I get Oriana down. Have an ale ready for me." She gave him a light pat on the butt.

Azure took Oriana's hand and led her to the Captain's Quarters. She helped the tired girl into bed, tucking her in like Azure's mom used to do for her.

"Do you want to hear a song that my mother used to sing to me when I was your age?" Azure asked, moving the hair from Oriana's eyes.

Oriana nodded, a faint smile on her lips.

"Okay, here it goes." Azure's mind wandered back to her room in Barren. Her mom's singing voice had been so beautiful, so comforting. Azure began to sing, hoping she could remember all the words, and trying her best to stay in tune:

The world outside is scary, you really should beware,
There are people who'd be cruel to you, and monsters everywhere.
There are monsters on the land, and monsters in the sea.
Monsters that will try to take you away from me.
But you.... are so safe here, don't worry about a thing,
And if you die before you wake, you'll end up on the Ring.
Here.... you're safe and warm, all cozy in your bed.
Here you don't have to fret about your wonderful little head.

What in thirty-seven hells? It had been a long time since she had thought about that song, and she didn't remember it being so dark. Azure had always looked back on those nights, wrapped up snug in too many blankets, with a warm fondness. The mental image of her mother above her was burned into her mind, a comforting picture she would always treasure.

But the song, though.

She hadn't remembered all the *us against them*, or *the world is evil and scary* stuff. With a worldview like that, it was no wonder Azure's mom was so easily turned to fear.

She looked back at those nights in a new light, now, wondering how an adult could sing a song like that to a child—the kind of song that could lead someone to hate what they didn't understand. It was just like the stories her parents used to tell her—fear the other, stick to your own.

And maybe her mom believed preparing her daughter for a life in a cruel world was the most important thing she could do, but Azure felt so much differently. She was sure her mom had meant well, but it was that kind of *them against us* mentality that had made her susceptible to Pratt's rhetoric, and ultimately led to her early death.

Dreading what was coming up in the next verse, Azure tried to improvise different lyrics:

Sure, the world is harsh sometimes, but it's also beautiful, too.
And the only proof I need of that, is this moment here with you.
There are so many kind people, doing so many kind things.
So, live your life with kindness, then watch for what it brings.

Azure was pretty proud of herself for coming up with that on the spot. Not perfect, but not horrible either.

When she stopped singing, though, she figured her momentary lyrical skill was likely lost on little Oriana, as the gentle rhythm of her breathing indicated she had already fallen asleep.

"Oh well." She tucked the blanket under Oriana's chin. "Goodnight, Little Treasure."

Before heading back out to the crew, Azure allowed her mind to wander as she lingered to make sure Oriana was asleep. Her thoughts were drawn to her mom, and the stark contrasts that made up her life. She could be so caring, and silly, and fun. They used to laugh together all the time. Azure's memories came in tiny snippets, but almost all of them were good. She could still hear her mom's laugh—a staccato with an undeniable musical quality—and see her smile.

But then there were her other aspects, many of which Azure didn't understand while her mom was still alive. She seemed to be a troubled woman, now that Azure was looking back at her. She had grown up with a strict religious family that mainly worshipped Iloxe, the god of vengeance, or justice, depending on the mood of the worshipper. Azure had only met her grandparents, who lived on one of the smaller Nameless Isles, a handful of times. Most, if not all, of those experiences were unpleasant. Her grandfather was fanatical in his belief of the gods. Every subject, even the personal and benign, could be twisted into impromptu sermons about Iloxe, and his divine purpose for humankind. She remembered being afraid of him. And even though her mom would have never admitted it, Azure sensed that her mom was afraid of him, too. Either that or desperate to earn his approval.

The dichotomy of her mom's personality was striking. At times she was sunny and full of joy, and at others, overcast and seething with anger. Azure supposed it was natural to have dramatic swings in mood, but it seemed more pronounced in her mom.

She wished her mom was still here. She wished they could have come to an understanding, like Azure had done with her dad. And even though Azure had grown, she knew they could still be silly with each other. She wished they could tease her dad together, and she could hear that wonderful laugh again.

Gazing at Oriana's serene face, Azure chased the thoughts away. No amount of wishing would bring her mom back, and thinking about it only served to darken her mood.

There was ale to drink, and stories to hear. Maybe she would even tell her version to everyone.

Her mood already brightening at the thought, Azure stood and sneaked away.

Back out on the deck, Robin was telling everyone about her fight with Faron. She, of course, had the entire crew both enrapt and cracking up. Elijah handed Azure a frothy ale and put his arm around her waist. Together, they listened to Robin's story.

Captain's Log: Ascension, 26th, 137

W ell, we're outlaws, now.
I don't know what that's going to mean for our futures, but it can't be good. I have a sinking feeling about our prospects as a merchant ship after we get Oriana back home. How are we going to get contracts to ship goods when the authorities are likely going to be looking for us at every port?

I've ruined our prospects of a sustainable future before we ever had the chance to really get going.

But what choice was there? We had to do something. We had to get that knife to get little Oriana home. And every single marauder made that decision along with me. But I still think of myself as a failure...

And that's not even mentioning the whole thing with Captain Roberts. I don't see how that can possibly end well. He seems intent on getting revenge against us, or me, more specifically. His ship is bigger, faster, and has more firepower than ours. His crew is better trained for battle, and he is terrifying. And it's not like I can just have Zoth-Avarex fly around with us all the time. I think he'll usually come when I call, but I can't rely on him, alone. And even then, Roberts has that giant crossbow on his ship, now. I have no idea if something like that could really take a dragon down, but I wouldn't want to put him in the position to find out.

I suppose I should take a page out of Brisa's book, and not obsess about the uncertainties of the future. All we have control of is the decisions we make now. We'll get Oriana back home, and then we'll take the next day as it comes.

I'm really going to miss her...

The Portal Knife

The next morning, Nargol and Orok presented the two orc guards from the casino to Azure.

"This is Kogar and Borug," Nargol said. "And this is Captain Azure Brine."

Azure shook their hands.

"They would like a chance to join the marauders."

"Well..." Azure found it strange that they were even asking her. Who was she to judge? If Nargol and Orok trusted them, then Azure trusted them, too. But she figured she should at least show a bit of authority, seeing as how she was the captain of the ship. "Have you read the Marauder's Code?"

"Yes, ma'am," both orcs said.

"And do you agree to live by that code while on this ship?"

"Yes, ma'am."

"And do you agree to call me Azure, or Captain Brine, instead of ma'am?" Azure gave them a warm smile.

"Yeah." Their smiles were tusky and great.

"Welcome to the marauders, then. I hope you like to sing. Do either of you have any particular skills?"

"We're really good in a fight," Kogar said, shrugging.

"I bet you are, but we try to avoid those as much as possible."

"I'm not bad at building things," said Borug.

"Perfect. You can report to Mr. Wain, the ship's carpenter." Azure pointed him out. "He was just asking me about getting him some able-bodied help."

The two newest marauders nodded, then hurried away to Mr. Wain.

"Thank you," Orok said.

"You know you don't need my permission for stuff like that. I trust your judgment, completely."

"Well you *are* the captain, and we voted you there for a reason. We trust your judgement, too."

Azure always felt the need to deflect praise. "We're almost to the Torsals." She pointed to the stretch of jagged islands laid out past the bow. "How long has it been since you've seen them?"

"Far too long, to tell you the truth. It will be good for Morgak to see others like her. She can't help but feel isolated at times. She seems to really long for other kids to play with, too. Oriana and her have been great together, but she's about to go home."

"Maybe after we send her home, we can spend some time here? The gods know we should probably lay low for a while and see how this whole stealing from a powerful casino thing works out." Azure flashed a nervous smile.

"That would be great."

Zoth-Avarex, who had shrunk down to orc-size and had been hanging out on the deck ever since the rescue, stepped forward.

"Can I see the dagger?" he asked Azure.

"Sure." She took it from her belt and handed it to him.

"Hmm." He studied the knife for at least a minute. "I haven't seen this one before."

"But it will work to get Oriana home, right?"

"Yeah. Like I told you before, just slash at the air and say *Earth*. It will open a portal back to her home world."

"Thank you."

"Alright, well I'm going to get going, then."

"Why? I thought you might want to be here in case we can't get it to work."

"Oh, it'll work great. You don't need me for that." Zoth-Avarex was acting weird, again; unable to make eye contact and relentlessly picking at a scale on his forearm. "And how do you think the people on the other side of the portal will react when they see a horrifying red dragon with their daughter? No, it's probably best if I'm not around."

"Okay, but I'm calling you back here if we need you." Azure still couldn't figure out what his deal was, but she didn't have the time to try and find out, as they were just about to make landfall on one of the Torsals.

"See ya." As the dragon took wing, he changed back to his normal dragon size.

THE *Adventure Ship* docked near a small village along a rocky coastline. Several orcs, including children, were fishing from the dock when they arrived. All of the orcs from the marauders disembarked first and talked to them in the Orc Tongue. Little Morgak was ecstatic when she saw the other orc kids, letting out an adorable squeal and rocking back and forth.

"This is Jukha, the chieftain of this village," Nargol said, holding out a hand to an orc that looked no different than any of the others, fishing pole in hand. "And this is Azure Brine, a dear friend, and captain of this ship."

Jukha handed the fishing pole to a nearby kid and took Azure's hand in a gentle greeting.

"Welcome to our..." He looked quizzically at Nargol.

"Village," Nargol said.

"Welcome to our village." Jukha was obviously new to the Common Tongue, but his words were clear and understandable.

"Thank you." Azure gave him an awkward half bow, not sure what the protocol for meeting a chieftain was.

"Please let us make...feast for all of you," Jukha said after being introduced to Elijah and Oriana.

Azure shot Nargol and Orok a glance. Their faces were excited and hopeful.

"That would be great, Jukha. Thank you very much." Azure held a hand toward Oriana. "I need to get this little girl back home, first. But I'll be right back."

Jukha nodded, although it was clear he didn't totally understand what Azure had said.

"I'm hungry," Oriana said, pulling on Azure's dress.

"But don't you want to get back home?"

"I do, but I wouldn't mind having a feast first, with Morgak."

Azure looked to Nargol, who shrugged as if to say, "Why not?"

"When would this feast happen?"

Nargol spoke to the chieftain in the Orc Tongue, then said, "He says they'll start preparing it right now."

"Alright, then. Maybe we can call it a goodbye feast for Oriana, too?"

"Perfect." Nargol and her husband were giddy.

Morgak took Oriana's hand and led her to a group of kids on the rocky shore.

"What will we be eating?" Elijah said.

Again, Nargol spoke to the chieftain, who replied in the Orc Tongue.

"He says we're having live spiders, a real delicacy."

Elijah paled, mouth agape. He was about to respond when Nargol guffawed into her hands.

"I'm sorry," she said. "I don't know what's gotten into me. I'm just feeling happy and silly right now."

"So, no spiders, then?"

"No, we're having fish and rice and crab puffs, seaweed salad, and fruit salad."

"The spiders are for dessert," Orok said with a wry smile.

THE FEAST WAS HELD in the village square, underneath a massive, open-air structure. A light rain had begun to fall, but they were dry and warm under the roof. Two extremely long tables stretched the length of the protected area. A pleasant din of activity resonated under the structure, making an almost musical impression when accompanied by the tapping of the rain.

The marauders were given seats closest to the food, and were the first people invited to serve themselves from the bountiful buffet line.

The food was prepared in ways Azure had never seen. It didn't exactly look appetizing, but it smelled delicious, so she took a little bit of everything.

Oriana was a bit more apprehensive, passing on the multiple types of fish dishes, but filling her plate with rice and fruit salad.

When everyone had gone through the line and been seated, Jukha addressed the group from between the tables. He spoke in the Orc Tongue, so Orok and Nargol divvied up translation duties between them.

"He's talking about how each new day is an opportunity to learn and grow," Orok whispered. "He says, 'Today, we have been presented with an opportunity to engage with people from the islands, and to show them our hospitality and our giving spirit. We don't have a lot of time in this life before we're returned to the River. It's important to seize moments when offered, and to create experiences that can enrich our lives every single day.' And stuff like that."

Jukha turned to the marauders. "Welcome to our village. Now let's eat and have a good time."

Dozens of young, possibly teenaged orcs appeared, carrying giant trays filled with mugs. They circled the tables, handing out a mug to anyone who wanted one.

Azure took a mug with a thank you, then peered inside. The liquid was golden, like an ale, but smelled unlike anything Azure had experienced.

"It's a mead, flavored with hot chili peppers." Orok grinned. "Try it."

Azure took a tentative sip, recoiling at the instant spiciness. Not wanting to be rude, she swallowed it, regretting that decision immediately. She looked around for another kind of drink, but there was nothing but the mugs of molten lava ale.

Orok bellowed laughter, then chugged his mug down in a single swig.

The heat in Azure's mouth only intensified, tingling and burning all the way down her throat. She shoveled fruit salad in to try and extinguish the heat, her eyes watering.

"It's not that bad, is it?" Elijah said, taking a gulp.

"I am *not* a fan of spicy stuff," Azure said, rubbing her tongue with a slice of mango.

Now everyone in the vicinity was laughing. The orcs from the village seemed to find it hilarious, although they tried their best to hide their amusement. Oriana covered her mouth with both hands to stifle her giggling.

Azure smiled and held up her mug, then stuck out her tongue and fanned it with her other hand. Her performance elicited open laughter from the villagers.

Jukha approached holding a mug. He set it down in front of Azure and said, "No spice," then mimicked her tongue-fanning act.

"Thank you," Azure said, taking a long drink. Much to her relief, this version of the mead was cool and sweet.

With the show over, everyone quieted as they dug into their food. As they ate, Jukha remained standing, and began to speak, again.

"He's telling a classic orc parable while we eat," Orok said with a mouthful of rice. "It's a tradition at our more formal meals."

Azure nodded while taking a bite of fish smothered in a kind of green paste. The taste, which was absolutely delicious, brought her back to her dining table in Barren, when her mom used to cook meals for the family every night. She used to make something that smelled and tasted a lot like this. It was one of Azure's favorites. They called it the *fishy dishy,* much to her dad's chagrin.

Azure recalled snippets of conversations they would have.

"What would you like to have for your birthday dinner?" her mom would ask.

"The fishy dishy!" Azure would shout.

"You wishy to have the fishy dishy?"

"Yes!"

Her dad would shake his head with just a hint of a smile on his lips. Azure knew he liked that her and her mom were silly together, but he would never join it.

When Azure brought herself back from the reverie, she realized that Orok had been translating Jukha's story to her.

"And the poor couple who had shown such hospitality was rewarded with a strong young bull," Orok said, apparently finishing his translation.

Jukha looked to Azure and said, "Did you...enjoy the story?"

Azure hoped her embarrassment wasn't showing through as she answered. "Yes, I liked it very much," she said, nodding vigorously.

Jukha said something in the Orc Tongue to Orok, then finally sat down to his plate.

"What'd he say?" Azure asked.

"He said it was obvious you weren't listening, and that he hates you, now." Orok kept a completely straight face.

"I..."

Against his efforts, a grin broke through Orok's stoic expression.

"I hate you, now!" Azure said, punching him in the arm.

"Sorry! I guess I'm feeling as silly as my wife. It's just so great to have these two worlds come together like this."

As the feast went on, the laughs continued. Despite the language barrier, the marauders got on with the villagers quite well. At one point, Syl ended up in a chugging contest with Jukha as everyone under the canopy cheered.

The sun dipped under the horizon, and many of the orcs said their good-byes and headed home. After thanking Jukha, Azure took Nargol aside and said, "I think we'll let you guys linger while we go off and try to send Oriana back."

"You're right, it's time." Nargol took Morgak's hand. "Morgak, do you want to say goodbye to Oriana?"

Morgak nodded, then waddled over to Oriana and gave her a near-smothering hug.

"It was so good to meet you, Morgak," Oriana said as she hugged back, tears starting to form in her eyes.

That was the first of many goodbyes. Everyone who had formed any kind of bond with Oriana came over to see her off. Even Robin swallowed her pride and gave her a heartfelt farewell. As Oriana gave them all hugs, Azure was awed by how quickly the little girl had adapted to life in a strange new world. She didn't know if she would have handled everything so well at Oriana's age. Oriana had gone from a frightened little kid, to a marauder in no time at all. Azure admired the shit out of her resiliency.

When the goodbyes were said, and the hugs hugged, Azure, Elijah, and Oriana walked out to a flat section of the rocky beach.

"Well, are you ready?" Azure asked, after taking a knee.

Oriana hesitated. "Yes."

"Alright. But first, I just want to say how great it was to meet you. You are truly the bravest little girl I have ever met."

"I bet you were braver. You're a pirate captain."

"Yes, but not much of that is due to bravery, really."

"What was it, then?"

Azure had to think. She still wondered why they had chosen her as captain over some of the others who were much more experienced and qualified than she was. She started to say that maybe it was kindness, but stopped herself short. Every marauder, to a person, was kind. It was sort of a requirement. So that wasn't it, either. There was the whole thing with Captain Roberts, of course. She had handled herself pretty good then, but that was only one time. It was probably somewhat due to the fact that none of the other marauders wanted to be the captain themselves.

"I don't know, to tell you the truth."

"I'm going to miss you," Oriana said, trying her best to hold back tears.

"I'm going to miss you, too. You'll always be an honorary marauder."

Now the tears broke through.

Azure and Elijah both embraced her and let her sob.

When she was done, and the only sounds on the beach were sniffles and the crashing of the waves on the rocks, Azure stood. She turned away from the others, said, "Earth," and slashed the portal knife through the air.

The sky opened in front of her, like a sail that had been slit vertically. On the other side of the opening was the inside of a strange building, filled with strange, unnatural light.

"Is this your ho—"

Azure's question was interrupted as a child-sized flying creature flew out into the Undering. It startled her, causing her to stumble back a few steps. As she regained her balance, she recognized what it was: a gargoyle, much like the one that Captain Roberts had conjured.

Oriana shrieked and hid behind Elijah's leg, gripping it hard with both arms.

"It's about time you opened up a portal back to Earth," the gargoyle said, it's voice gruff and cruel. "I've been getting tired of waiting."

The Gargoyle

Hovering in the air, the gargoyle scanned the area.

"Is there a big red dragon around here?" it asked.

Elijah looked like he was about to say something, but Azure stopped him with a subtle look. Her instinct was to let this play out a bit before offering any information. She was sure that this gargoyle must have been the reason Zoth-Avarex had been acting so strange, but she didn't have enough information, yet.

"Speak up!" the gargoyle bellowed, startling everyone. "Where is the dragon called Zoth-Avarex?"

No one spoke. Up the beach, Azure noticed several orcs, including the marauders, running toward them.

"You can either tell me where he is, or I can start killing you one by one, starting with her." The gargoyle pointed to Oriana as she hid.

"Do you mean the dragon that comes from the volcano?" The words spilled from Azure's mouth as an extremely vague plan began to form in her mind.

"What volcano?"

Azure pointed to the constant stream of black smoke to the southwest, barely visible from the Torsals.

"A red dragon resides there?"

"Yes. A fiery red dragon."

"You've seen this with your own eyes?"

"Yes. He comes out of that volcano from time to time, demanding virgin sacrifices."

"Fucking dragons." The gargoyle shook its head.

"I believe he's due to take another virgin very soon. At least that's what the locals have told me." Again, Azure pointed to the smoke. "That's where you'll find him." Her plan, although solidifying in her mind, wasn't quite tangible yet. But this could buy them time to think.

Nargol, Orok, and the others arrived at Azure's side. Nargol held a pistol, aiming it up at the gargoyle.

"You're going to need a bigger army than that to deal with me, I promise you."

"I wouldn't underestimate us," Nargol replied. "I heard you threaten our friends, and I would not recommend that."

"You see, the thing is, I can fly, and I'm very fast. Much too fast for you. I mean, sure, if one of you got a hold of me, I'd be dead, but I could snatch that little girl up and have her twenty feet in the air before you knew it. So, back off and put that primitive gun down before I demonstrate my abilities."

After getting a nod from Azure, Nargol did as the gargoyle said.

"Do you know where this girl's parents are?" Azure asked.

"Yes. I do." The gargoyle made a slashing gesture across its own throat, then tilted its head to the side and stuck its tongue out. Azure's head shot to Oriana, but her face was buried in Elijah's leg and she hadn't seen the gesture. "They had very simple instructions, too. All they had to do was divulge to me what they'd found in their research, and to lead me to the dragon. But they got all panicky and made a run for it." The gargoyle shook its head. "When I caught them, they had sent their daughter through to this world using an inter-dimensional blade. They were trying to go through themselves but I snatched them up before they could make it. And when they refused to give me anything else…" The gargoyle shrugged, a disgusting smirk on its face. "If you don't believe me, take a look for yourself."

Azure took two tentative steps forward and peered into the portal. Laying just on the other side were two bodies, a man and a woman, half-covered in dried blood. Azure looked for breathing, or any signs of life, but there were none.

"So, don't end up like them. Let me know what I want to know, and I'll move on."

Azure's chest felt empty. A profound sadness flooded over her as she remembered the pain of losing her mom at such a young age. Her heart absolutely ached for the little girl.

"I've got a job to do, for someone I'd rather not displease, and they were in the way of it," the gargoyle continued. "And trust me, that's not a place where any of you want to be."

Azure glared up at the gargoyle, wheels turning, but finding no realistic means by which to take it down.

"I'm going to the volcano to corroborate your story, but I'll be back. I have a feeling that you're holding something from me. I've noted your ship, and escape is not an option. If I find that you've lied to me, I will come back in a vengeful fury. Either way, expect me back sooner than later."

The gargoyle zipped away, vanishing on the horizon.

Oriana peeked out from Elijah's leg, and Azure could barely look her in the eye.

The Gargoyle's Investigation

Kxa, the gargoyle, sped over the expanse of calm sea, looking down at his reflection as he flew. This world was far from what he had expected. He knew that the dragon had gone off to a world on the edge of the known multiverse in order to escape, but he had expected worlds on the edge of the known multiverse to be different; shittier than this one. He wasn't sure why he believed this, or what he even meant by it. Everything on this plane of existence was shitty, if he was being honest. The beings on this plane disgusted him.

But these kinds of thoughts were pointless at the moment. He had a job to do, and his life depended on it. All he had to do was locate the world in which Zoth-Avarex was hiding and he'd be free from his...employer.

And so far, so good, really. The story about the dragon demanding virgin sacrifices checked out. Kxa would never understand the bizarre motivations of dragons. How could they possibly give a shit about humans? Or their sexual status? The idea was unfathomable.

The smoke on the horizon was growing, and the island was now in view.

Kxa was about to make his approach when another ship lurking nearby caught his eye. On that ship was the vaguest outline of another gargoyle. Some asshole human had most likely conjured the unlucky gargoyle to this plane. Kxa hated the fact that this could happen more than anything. How or when humans had figured out how to do this, he didn't know, but he would love to find out who started it and tear them limb from limb. The humiliation of it was almost too much to bear.

Once closer to the ship, he confirmed that it was, in fact, another one of his kind. Preferring information from a gargoyle much more than from an idiot human, Kxa changed course.

When he landed on the port rail, several men stopped what they were doing and aimed pistols at him.

"Calm down," Kxa said, unbothered. "I'm only here to have a quick chat with your gargoyle, there."

The other gargoyle, who stood on the ship's wheel while the rough-looking captain turned it, seemed to ask the captain for permission to speak with Kxa.

"How fucking pathetic," Kxa muttered to himself, shaking his head.

When permission was granted, the other gargoyle flew down to greet Kxa, something resembling a smile on his face.

"I don't get to see too many of us in this world," the other gargoyle said. "Where are you from?"

"The seventh plane."

"Really? I'm from the seventh, too. My name's Zra."

"I'm Kxa."

"Who conjured you here?"

"No one." His face scrunched up in disgust at the idea. "I'm working a job for this demi-god from another world."

"Oh. Well, at least you've got a little bit of freedom to move around in this world."

"Yeah. I guess. I just find everything in the lower planes so devoid of meaning. Anyway, I was wondering if you could help me out."

"Sure."

"Do you know anything about a red dragon that supposedly comes out of that volcano from time to time?" Kxa pointed a thumb toward Amenaza Island.

"Yeah. Actually, my mast—uh, the captain of this ship has brought us here because we keep hearing about this dragon and he wanted to check it out for himself."

"So, it's true, then?"

"Yeah. I mean, it's pretty common knowledge that there's a red dragon in this world, now. We had a run-in with it a while back, and the captain is eager to see it die."

"Was its name Zoth-Avarex?"

"That I couldn't tell you. I mean, who gives a shit about the names of beings on lower planes, right?"

"I agree. But this time, I need to know a name."

"Well, the captain is pretty convinced that the dragon is going to be here soon. And he figured that wherever that dragon was, the marauders and their new captain would likely be close by, too. He's still scared shitless of the dragon, but his dander is up worse than I've ever seen it. He is determined to find that woman captain of theirs and—"

"I couldn't possibly care less," Kxa said.

"Yeah. You're right. Sorry."

Kxa's initial suspicions were confirmed. That human had been holding something back. He made a mental note to keep the marauders, or whatever they called themselves, close until this whole ordeal was resolved.

"Okay. Thank you for the information. As a show of gratitude, would you like me to kill the human who conjured you so you can be released?" Kxa eyed the pirate captain.

Zra seemed to contemplate the question for a long moment. "The nature of my binding doesn't allow me to answer that question."

"Well just give me a nod, then."

"I can't do that, either."

"Blink once for no, and twice for yes."

Zra's eyelids stayed open.

"Alright. I appreciate the information, but I can't sit here all day trying to get around your binding. Maybe I'll see you on the seventh plane of existence some day." He wanted to kill the human, but wanted to get this job done and get out of this place as quick as possible even more.

Kxa took wing and headed for the volcano, again. He made for a small village along the coast and landed in its square. The villagers seemed very reluctant to approach him.

"I simply need information from you," the gargoyle called.

He picked at one of his claws while waiting for someone to speak. He wasn't going to wait long.

Every passing moment he waited felt like a direct insult from a group of far-inferior beings. The injustice of having to be here and wait on humans to speak to him caused his muscles to tense, and the buzz of anger to fill his chest. Just as his rage had built up enough for him to want to seek out and torture the information out of the closest human, a man stepped out into the square holding his palms up.

"Do you come from the volcano?" the man asked.

"No. Are you expecting a gargoyle from the volcano?"

"We have come to expect a fiery red dragon, like the one that circled our island several days ago."

"A red dragon? Do you happen to know its name?"

"We know not the name that Mordo has given it. Such names are unknowable to mortals."

"Who is Mordo?"

"You know not of Mordo? God of Doom and Volcanos? Mordo the Vengeful? The Bringer of Fire? The Bringer of Death?"

"Haven't heard of him."

The man seemed scandalized.

"Listen, I'm sure this god of yours is very important and powerful, but I just need more information about this dragon."

"It demands a virgin sacrifice. This is the only way to forestall the island's doom."

"When do you expect him to take this virgin sacrifice?"

"Very soon." He pointed up to the column of smoke. "Mordo's ire is near its peak. Soon the offering will be made, and we will pray that Mordo's servant finds it satisfactory."

"Soon is too vague for me," the gargoyle said. "Give me an exact time."

The man studied the smoke, then kneeled and put an ear to the ground, closing his eyes.

"In two days, we will make our offering."

"And you're convinced a red dragon is going to be here to take that offering?"

"Of course! We can only hope that—"

"Okay, that's enough of this bullshit for me. See you in two days."

Kxa shot up into the sky and headed for the volcano. Once over it, he peered inside, wondering if a dragon could really live in such a place. But he couldn't see a thing through the constant thick black smoke.

"Oh well," he said to himself. "I can wait a few days if I have to." He changed course toward the place where he had come through to this world. "But I do need to know what those marauders are hiding from me."

Consoling

Robin landed on Azure's shoulder. "What the fuck was that?" she said.

"A gargoyle." Azure noticed that the portal had vanished.

"Why was there a gargoyle here?"

"Oh." Azure sighed. "It came through the portal." Her gaze drifted toward the ground as she pictured the bodies on the floor of that strange place.

"Where did it go?"

Azure watched the waves smash against the rocks, only vaguely aware Robin had said something.

"Do you know where it went?" Robin said, louder.

"Amenaza Island, to corroborate a story I just made up on the spot."

"About what?"

"It wants Zoth-Avarex. I had to tell it something." Azure kept her head still, but moved her eyes to look at Oriana. The little girl had come out from behind Elijah and looked from adult to adult with a confused look on her face. Azure had to look away.

"What?" Robin said, incredulous.

"Yeah." She hesitated. "I knew Zoth was acting strange for a reason." Another idea formed in Azure's mind as she continued to watch the churning sea. "Maybe you could fly to Dragon Island and ask him? I told the gargoyle Zoth-Avarex would come out of that volcano because I needed to buy time. I need all the information I can get on this strangeness."

"How would I get through the Eternal Fog?"

"Maybe you can ask Syl if he can help you with that. He could make a directional will-o'-the-wisp for you, I think." Azure narrowed her eyes, deep in thought. "I think it's pretty important that we speak to the dragon right away." Azure went on to tell Robin everything that had happened, and the tentative plan she had began to enact, careful to not let Oriana overhear.

"Yeah." Robin took a deep breath, then stretched her wings and popped her neck by turning her head to the side. "I'm on it. Love ya, Az."

"I love you, too."

Robin took off for the *Adventure Ship* to find Syl.

Focus returned to Oriana, Azure's eyes started to water, but she shook it off and took a knee in front of her.

"Did you...understand any of that?" Azure asked, nodding to where the portal had been.

"No," Oriana said, shaking her head. But her bottom eyelids began to fill with tears. She knew something was wrong on an intuitive level.

"Well, I..." Azure had no idea how to continue. How did you tell a seven-year-old girl that her parents had been murdered? "I...think we should get back to the ship."

"What about the...portal back to Earth?" Oriana blinked away the tears as best she could.

"We can't do that right now. Let's get back to the ship and..." Azure felt like a coward, but she couldn't talk with Oriana at the moment. She took the little girl's hand. "Come on."

Reluctantly, Oriana followed.

Little Morgak approached Oriana, and, sensing she needed one, gave her another smothering embrace. Then she went with her parents to join the other orcs.

"What has happened?" Blunderbuss said as they boarded the ship.

Azure asked Elijah to take the little girl to the other side of the ship, then told Blunderbuss everything as quickly as possible.

"Dead?" he said in a low voice. "Are you sure?"

"Yes." Azure struggled to keep herself together.

"Oh, I'm so sorry." Blunderbuss hung his head. Two tiddly dragons dove down from the sails; one landed on his head, the other on his shoulder.

"What do I do?" Azure asked the older man, who had seen his share of death in the war between humans and Ciguapa. "Do I..."

Blunderbuss looked her in the eye, solemn sincerity and warmth written on his face. "You have to tell her, plainly and clear. She needs to hear it from you, and maybe Elijah, but that's it." He put a hand on Azure's shoulder. "You have to say the word *died*. Leave no doubt or wiggle room in her mind. That's important."

"But, then what do I say?"

"You'll know, Captain. You'll know how to be there for her, I promise."

Azure thought about the promise she'd made to Oriana and she couldn't hold it together any longer. She broke down, burying her head into Blunderbuss's free shoulder.

Blunderbuss wrapped her in a strong embrace. "I wouldn't want anyone else in the world to break bad news to me, Captain. You can help her grieve and heal starting right here in this moment. You've got this." He held her until the sobs had passed. When she pulled away, his eyes were red and wet, too.

"Okay." Azure took in a huge breath and blew it out slowly. She wiped her eyes and approached Oriana. She gave Elijah a look, but he shook his head, obviously ashamed about doing so. But Azure didn't blame him. He was still working on his confidence, and he wasn't ready for something like this, yet. Azure wasn't ready, either, but she refused to pass this off.

She sat on the deck, took Oriana's hand, and told her the truth.

The little girl pleaded, and negotiated, but Azure remained both firm and empathetic. It took a long time for Oriana's emotion to come out, but when it did, it burst out in a torrent of absolute heartbreak. She fell onto the deck in a heap, striking the boards repeatedly with her open palm. Her words were incomprehensible, the pain in her voice unbearable.

Azure steeled herself, then. With someone else pouring out raw emotion, Azure often took on the role of the strong one, offering what she could with a sort of detached numbness. She had done this ever since she was a kid.

Azure rubbed Oriana's back as a sign that she was still there with her but said nothing.

As she consoled the little girl, her mind returned to the problem of the gargoyle.

If it was here just to find out if Zoth-Avarex was here, what did that really mean? She had no doubt that the dragon could annihilate it in a fight, but the gargoyle seemed to be here at the behest of someone else. Whoever that could be—someone who could employ a murderous gargoyle to do their dirty work across multiple worlds—made Azure shiver.

As Oriana's sobs became quieter and less frequent, and as Azure stroked her hair and made a gentle shushing sound, a plan took full, tangible shape in her mind.

The Dragon and the Bird

Robin's wings burned as she flew through the Eternal Fog, following Syl's directional will-o'-the-wisp. As she gasped for the air that never seemed to fill her lungs enough, she reminisced about the old days—simpler times, before Azure had gone off to chase her dad across the Mirror Sea.

Sure, she had packed on some extra ounces back then, but she had the extra curves in all the right places. And sure, she was proud of her new toned physique. But this long-distance flight shit was decidedly not her thing. Ever since joining the marauders and their never-ending run of adventures, these long flights were becoming all-too regular.

Of course, she wouldn't trade it for the world. She would, however, be more than happy to take her frustrations out on this chicken-shit dragon as soon as she found him.

As Dragon Island became visible through the fog, she breathed a sigh of relief and dove down to land on the treasure beach. Panting, she scanned the relatively small island for the dragon, not seeing him anywhere.

"Shit," she said between breaths.

She lay on her side, thankful for the cool breeze swirling around the island.

As she recovered, she caught a slight movement out the corner of her eye. She jumped up and focused to find the blur of a shape ducking behind the dragon-shaped mountain in the middle of the island.

Before she could decide whether to call out to it or fly away, Zoth-Avarex stuck his head back out. "It's just you?" he said, emerging from behind the mountain.

"What are you doing? Hiding? On your own island? I mean you, a fucking dragon, hiding? Really?"

Zoth-Avarex hung his head. "You don't get it."

"You're gods-damned right I don't get it. I had to literally fly my ass off to get here, all because you were too scared to stick around when Az opened that portal."

"So, you flew all the way here to mock me? Alright, then. Mission accomplished. Now why don't you get the fuck out of here before I roast you?"

"We both know you aren't going to roast shit." Robin puffed up and stared him down. "Now, are you going to tell me what the hells is going on?"

"I can't," the dragon said. "And what does it matter, anyway?"

"Well, for one thing, a murderous gargoyle came out from the portal we cut, after having killed that little girl's parents, and the first thing it asks about is you."

"Could it have followed you here?" the dragon's eyes searched the fog above.

"No, it flew off to Amenaza Island, you big baby."

"Did anyone tell it about me?" Zoth-Avarex looked the most scared Robin had ever seen him.

"Gods no. You know Az isn't going to roll over on one of her own. Don't ask me why you're in that category, but that's how she sees you."

The dragon straightened up a bit. "What did she tell it?"

"She made up something on the fly. I'm not sure where she's going with it, but I think she's going to try to trick it into thinking you're going to come out of that volcano and eat a virgin or something."

Zoth-Avarex's eyes lit up, almost imperceptibly.

"So," Robin said, "are you going to come help us with this shit? Seeing as how it seems to be pretty you-centric?"

"I can't."

"Why not?" Robin's eyes had narrowed to angry slits.

"I..."

"Spit it out!"

"If it finds out I'm here, I'm done. All it has to do is verify that I'm in this world, and then..."

"Then what?"

Zoth-Avarex said nothing.

"You know, that gargoyle already threatened all of our lives, even that little girl's."

The dragon started to turn away. "The bottom line is that I can't help this time. Tell Azure I'm sorry, and that I appreciate her plan and hope it works, but I can't show my face on this one."

Robin turned away, too pissed to speak or take the rest she so dearly wanted, and took off back into the fog.

The Gargoyle Returns

Oriana had cried herself to sleep. As gently as possible, Azure stood, the little girl's head resting on her shoulder. The weight of her resonated with something inside Azure, but it was beyond her what that something was. She crept to the Captain's Quarters and lay Oriana down on the bed.

When she came back out, most of the crew was there waiting for her.

"I'm so sorry, Captain," Syl said.

She nodded to him, to all of them.

"As some of you already know, I've sent Robin to talk with the dragon. Hopefully whatever she finds will shed light on what we should do next." She sighed. "I expect that the gargoyle will be back soon, as well, and I want us to all be on the same page when it does. If it asks you about Zoth-Avarex, I want you to pretend to not know that name. I'd like you to be very vague about our interactions with an unnamed red dragon. I'd also like you to direct the conversation toward Amenaza Island, and the sacrifices at the volcano. For all we know, that same red dragon is the one who demands virgin sacrifices, there."

The crew nodded their assent.

"Thank you." Azure clutched the ship's wheel necklace in her palm. "I've got an idea of how we can be rid of the gargoyle, but I'm still working out the edges in my mind. If anyone has any ideas, I'd be glad to hear them."

The wind blew in the sails, and seagulls squawked overhead.

"Just let us know what you need, Captain," Nargol said, getting overzealous nods of agreement from the crew.

Azure took time to look at every crew member before continuing. "So, while we wait, I think we should divvy up our cut of Mr. Carlyle's treasure."

227

The crew gave a half-hearted cheer. "The gods must have designed it this way, because we've ended up with exactly one gold piece for each member of the crew, with a few left over for maintenance, supplies, and the like." At that, the crew cheered louder.

"You deserve it. Every one of you. Every job is important, whether you're going on these all-too-common off-ship adventures, making crucial repairs, or—"

Azure spotted the gargoyle on the horizon, and within a minute, he had landed among the rigging.

"Did you miss me?" he said.

When he didn't get a response, he continued. "You seem to be telling the truth about the perverted dragon demanding virgin sacrifices, but I have a strong feeling that you're leaving something out."

Again, no one said a word.

"We're going to Amenaza Island," the gargoyle said. "Set a course immediately."

No one moved.

"We?" Azure asked.

"Yes. Until I know what you're holding back, I am going to stay right here with you."

Azure considered the gargoyle's order. He gave her little choice, but her plan also involved going to Amenaza Island, so maybe she could play this to her advantage.

"What if we don't want to go?"

"You know what I'm capable of. You have about ten seconds to set sail or I'll snatch up one of your crew members and drop them out at sea."

Several of the closest marauders took instinctual steps back.

Azure showed a pained expression while counting down from ten in her head.

"Set sail for Amenaza Island," she called with only a second to spare.

Mr. Threepbrush barked out more specific orders, and the crew went to work.

Unwanted Guest

Once the *Adventure Ship* was at sea, the gargoyle retreated up to the crow's nest, seemingly happy to let them sail in relative peace.

But when Robin came back, completely out of breath, he came down from the rigging with a scowl.

"Where have you been, little bird?" Kxa said.

"None of your business, gargoyle."

The scowl grew meaner as he turned to Azure. "Where was the bird?"

"Hell if I know. She kind of does her own thing. She was probably back on some island cavorting with a seagull or something."

Robin shot her a scowl to rival the gargoyle's.

"You give me more and more reasons not to trust you," Kxa said, staring into Azure's eyes

"I don't know what to tell you. We do have lives that don't involve you. I guess it doesn't matter much whether or not you trust us."

The gargoyle shook his head. "I don't even know why I bother with you. If it wasn't for this job, you wouldn't be worth a second of my time."

"We're not exactly thrilled to be hanging out with you either," Robin retorted.

"You lower plane creatures have lives so devoid of meaning. How could I possibly care what you're thrilled about?"

"Our lives are devoid of meaning? Shit!"

"Yes. Everything you have here." He waved his hands, indicating the entire crew, the ship, and the Ring above. "All absolutely meaningless."

"Almost nothing, in the entire multiverse, has real meaning," Robin said, her dander rising. "Nothing but meaningless shit as far as the eye can see in

all directions, including whatever pompous plane of existence you're from."
Robin hopped closer to Kxa, but not within striking distance. "But there are
a few things that matter, and those few things are absolutely beautiful."

"What?" The gargoyle scoffed.

"Family." She looked to Azure. "Friends." She spread her wings, indicating the marauders around her. "And..." She paused, head tilted. "...fun. Those
are the only three F's I have to give. They're the things that have meaning in
this life, and that's about it."

"You have no idea how pathetic you are, do you?"

"Eat ass."

In a blur, Kxa darted for Robin, but she had been ready, and narrowly
avoided his grasp. She flew up and around the main mast, with the gargoyle
close behind.

Kxa was preternaturally fast, but he couldn't match Robin's size, quickness, and ingenuity. She ducked and darted through the rigging, always staying clear of the gargoyle's claws, before coming to land on Orok's shoulder.
Kxa made an impressive mid-air stop and backed slowly away. He had almost
gone within arm's reach of the eagerly waiting orc.

"And here I am, doing the very thing I was just admonishing myself for,"
Kxa said, more to himself than anyone. "Getting caught up in your trifling,
pathetic lives." Again, he turned to Azure. "Hurry up and get us to the volcano, before your bird's mouth gets someone killed."

"It'd be hard to kill anyone with those eyes pecked out," Robin shouted.

Azure held up her hands, shushing and narrowing her eyes at her friend.

"Idiots." Kxa flew up just beyond Orok's reach and sat on the lowest yard.
Robin puffed herself up, but remained quiet atop the orc's shoulder.

"You know, you are such a good fit for the marauders that it's scary," Syl
said to Robin, shaking his head and laughing. "I mean, you're a little feisty at
times, but you're like the Marauder King in so many ways. We actually have a
song that's a lot like what you were just talking about—about what's important in life and all that. MK made it up one night after coming back from a
pub in Whetstone. Would you like to hear it?"

"Of course. Anything to drown out this asshole." Robin aimed her beak
at the sulking gargoyle above.

"Alright." Syl paused and thought a moment. "This is a bit of a deep cut. There are only a handful of us on this ship who would remember it. MK didn't like it that much because it copied the melody of Marauder's Green too closely, so it just kind of faded away over time. But I never forgot it. I thought it was quite possibly his best work. It has a very faun-like philosophical flavor to it. MK says he got that from hanging around with me." Syl tried, but couldn't hide his pride in this.

"Let's hear it," said Azure, excited to hear a marauder song she hadn't heard yet.

Mr. Threepbrush handed Syl his ukulele, and he tuned it by ear before walking up to the makeshift stage, the only sounds were his hooves on the deck and the gentle breeze.

"Alright. Here it goes." Syl began to strum.

One night I was sitting in a pub with an ale,
Listening to an old man tell a melancholy tale.
He was down and defeated, and felt he'd been cheated.
His search for meaning in life had been destined to fail.
'All that we do is for nothing,' he said.
'We work and we eat and we shit till we're dead.
There's no greater purpose, and all this is worthless.
I don't even know why I get out of bed.'

Syl played the chords with a few skillful embellishments.

I sat there feeling so bad for him.
I wanted to help, but I didn't know how.
Then it just hit me that sure, life's a mystery.
But what matters most is living it now.
It was hard to sit and listen intently,
When the idea to me was quite plain.
'What you've got is today, don't piss it away!'
I said before I sang this refrain:
I laugh in the face of life's lack of meaning.
I guffaw at existential woes.
I chuckle, I chortle, I cackle, and roar!
Life may be pointless, but please give me more!

He sang the chorus much louder than the verses, swinging the ukulele back and forth as he played.

I don't have the answers, but to me it seems,
That it doesn't really matter what any of this means.
So, laugh and have fun, and love your loved ones.
Instead of pulling apart at all of life's seams.

With Syl's encouragement, the Marauders who knew the song began to sing along.

WE LAUGH IN THE FACE OF LIFE'S LACK OF MEANING.
WE GUFFAW AT EXISTENTIAL WOES.
WE CHUCKLE, WE CHORTLE, WE CACKLE AND ROAR!
LIFE MAY BE POINTESS, BUT PLEASE GIVE US MORE!

The crew tore through the chorus twice, getting louder and more rousing each time.

When they were done, Syl played the chords softer and slower, then sang the last verses at half speed.

He told me I didn't understand him.
And that the darkness was simply too strong.
So, I lent him my ear and my shoulder.
Because, who knows? I might well be wrong.
The truth is there isn't one answer.
What works for you may not work for me.
There's only one thing that I'm sure of,
We have to learn to live with empathy...

The crew gave a smattering of applause as Syl nodded to them, then jumped down from the stage.

"That song made me want to dance and drink one moment, then cry the next," Azure said to Syl.

"I told you," the faun said. "Some of the Marauder King's best work right there."

Azure considered her reasons for living, and came up more or less on the same page as Robin, Syl, and MK. But she also had to admit that she found meaning in the gods, and getting to the Ring, even though she still wasn't sure she truly believed in any of that.

As thoughts swirled, Robin swooped down and landed on a nearby rope.

"Hey, Az."

"Hey, Robin." Azure had a sudden urge to get something out in the air. "I think what you said to that gargoyle was pretty spot-on."

"Of course it was." Robin tilted her head.

"It got me thinking about Oriana."

Robin didn't respond.

"What if...there were no other options, and Oriana had no place to go? Would you..."

Azure wasn't exactly sure what she wanted to ask.

"Would I give you my blessing if you wanted to take Oriana forever?" Robin's voice betrayed no emotion, either way.

"Well...yeah."

Robin fidgeted.

"Do you really think I would say *no* to something like that?" Now her head tilt was almost vertical.

"I didn't think you would, but I still wanted to give you the chance to say it. I wanted you to know that nothing could ever come between me and you."

Robin flew into Azure's hand.

"I know I can be a cranky bitch sometimes, but I would never deny you anything based on my own feelings. And I'd be pretty horrible to try and keep you all to myself when you have so much love to give. I mean, I already *allowed* you to get involved with Elijah romantically." She gave a somehow sarcastic head tilt. "When I caught you two kissing on the docks that night, I was nothing but happy for you. I'll be even happier when you're married and you can finally..." Now her head tilt was unmistakably lewd. "So yes, you *would* have my blessing, a million blessings. And you'd be the best mom in this, or any other, world. I can state that as fact."

Azure was relieved Robin thought this way, but the word *mom* associated with herself was terrifying. She was already having mild doubts about getting married, but becoming a mother figure for a young girl was quite possibly too much.

"But even if I, er, we took her.... I have no idea how to be a parent."

"No one does. You give your love, and you do your best. You'd do great. Trust me."

"I don't even know if it will happen. She probably has family on her home world that she could live with. I can't imagine going to live on some strange world that wasn't my own."

"I did it, gladly."

"True..." Azure stared at a spot on the deck.

"Yeah...taking that parental responsibility is tough, though. I mean, I had my little brood for two weeks before they were ready to fledge and take wing, and then another two whole weeks after that before they flew off to make their ways in the world." Robin sighed. "Parenting isn't easy."

A smile tugged at the corner of Azure's mouth.

"Shit," she said, shaking her head. "Thank you, Robin, but I gotta focus on that gargoyle. Did you make it to...the place you were going?" Azure glanced up at the gargoyle, but its attention was elsewhere.

Robin nodded.

"Did you...meet up with that seagull?" She knew Robin would understand the coded question.

After shaking her head, Robin said, "Yes, I met with the seagull. And it was extremely unfulfilling."

"Did the seagull say anything, or was it a purely sexual encounter?" Azure tried to suppress a smile, but found it difficult. Once again, Robin had lifted Azure's spirits when she was feeling down.

"There was no sexual encounter to speak of, thank you very much. The lazy ass seagull wasn't interested in doing a damn thing."

"So, the seagull is staying in his nest?"

"Yeah. The lazy ass seagull is staying in his fancy nest."

"Did he give a reason?"

"Only that he was afraid to," Robin shot a look up at the gargoyle, then lowered her voice, "be seen by anyone."

"Hmm." Azure decided this poorly-disguised conversation was probably unwise to continue with the gargoyle so close by.

She intended to deal with the gargoyle, but found that her mind lingered on Oriana's future.

The ideal scenario was probably getting Oriana back to relatives in her home world. If that wasn't possible, Azure and Elijah could theoretically take her in, but was that really in the little girl's best interest? A life at sea might not be a good life for a kid. How would she get an education? Would she be in danger? The gods knew that trouble seemed to find the marauders, and if they took her in, Oriana would be in the path of that trouble.

Azure had heard of a well-regarded place on Paradise Island called the Found Family Orphanage. Maybe Oriana would do better there? Maybe she could find parents more suited to taking care of her. Even the thought of dropping her off at an orphanage gave her a sick feeling in her gut, but it was something she'd have to consider if and when the time came.

But it was best to take one thing at a time. The first priority was to get free of the gargoyle, then they could move on to the little girl's future.

Maybe because it felt like defiance of the gargoyle, or maybe because Syl's song had simply put them in the mood, the marauders began to sign up to sing songs, with Blunderbuss keeping the list.

As they burned through the old classics, the Ring glowing above, Azure made her way around the ship, carefully disseminating her plan to the crew under the gargoyle's nose.

Captain's Log: Meridian 2nd, 137

Nothing to see, here.

Just a routine Captain's Log entry.

We're heading to Amenaza Island in hopes to see a red dragon come out of a volcano so this gargoyle from the "seventh plane of existence" will leave us alone.

Gods! My life is strange, now...

Back on Amenaza Island

Some time during the night, Oriana had snuggled up next to Azure. Now, as the first rays of sunlight poured in from the windows at the ship's stern, both Azure and the little girl awoke.

"Good morning." Azure pushed a few wild strands of Oriana's hair behind her ear.

She didn't reply.

Having no idea what to say, Azure lay and stroked Oriana's hair. For several minutes, Azure contemplated what words to use. Should she go right into talking about what happened? Or was it better to make a little small talk first? Maybe she should praise the little girl's strength, or something like that?

Azure took a deep breath, then said, "You are just the sweetest girl I have ever met, Oriana. You know that?"

"You wouldn't say that if you knew me better." She didn't look at Azure as she spoke.

"Why do you say that?"

"The last time I talked to Daddy, I yelled at him and threw a fit."

"That doesn't make you less sweet. Everyone has arguments and throws fits from time to time, even adults."

Oriana sobbed into the blanket.

"Do you want to talk about it?" Azure wished she had a clue about how to talk to kids. "I mean, what happened?"

"I tried to get him to play a game with me, and he told me he was busy with work. So, I screamed, 'You're always busy!' like a little brat." She buried her head in the blanket.

"You are not a little brat. You're so kind, and strong, and your parents loved you very much, I'm sure of it."

"You don't know."

Azure continued to stroke her hair. "I suppose I don't, but—"

An idea alighted in Azure's head. "You know, my mom...died when I was very young." She began to untie her necklace. "She gave me this ship's wheel necklace because of an argument I had with my dad. This necklace is the object I treasure most in the world."

Oriana looked up, eyes bloodshot and wet.

"And I want you to have it." Azure showed her the ship's wheel. "I can't think of a more deserving person in the world."

Oriana was taken aback. Azure could see the gears turning in her head. The little girl started to speak but stopped herself. She wiped her cheeks with a corner of the blanket.

"You really want me to have it?"

"Absolutely. Can I put it on you?"

Oriana nodded, and Azure slipped the leather string over her head.

"Thank you." Her words came out as a whisper. She lifted the ship's wheel and studied it. "So, your mom—" She couldn't finish her question.

"Yes. She did."

"Were you really sad?"

"It was the saddest thing that ever happened to me. I wondered if I would ever feel happy again. But with time, I started to feel better. I started to heal."

Oriana sighed.

"In this world, we believe that people who pass on go up to another life on the Ring." Azure still struggled with whether or not she actually believed this, but it felt helpful in the moment. "Do you have anything like that in your world?"

"Yes. But my parents don't believe in that."

"Do you?"

"I don't know." Oriana stared at the wall.

"I like to think that my mom is up there somewhere and that she's happy."

"Do you know she is?"

"No. Not for sure. But I like to think it."

There was a knock on the door.

"Yes?" Azure called.

"Sorry to bother you," Elijah said. "But we're nearing Amenaza Island."

"Okay, I'll be right out."

Azure turned to Oriana. "Do you think you're ready to be around other people?"

She shook her head, still holding the necklace with both hands.

"Alright. Would it be okay if I left the room for a little bit?"

As Oriana contemplated the question, her eyes began to well up with tears, again. "Can Elijah come in?"

"I'm sure he could, let me go ask him real quick."

Azure opened the door to find Elijah waiting just outside.

"How is she doing?" he asked.

"She's getting through it, but it's gonna take time."

"Yeah." Elijah closed his eyes.

"She wants to know if you can go in and stay with her a while."

"She does?"

"Yes. Is that alright with you?"

"Of course." He couldn't hide how honored he was that Oriana had asked.

"Thank you." Azure kissed him, then started away to meet Mr. Threepbrush at the wheel, when Elijah stopped her.

"What's going to happen with her?" he asked.

"I don't know."

"Do you think we..." He trailed off. "I mean, would you want to...take her in?"

"I've already considered it, but this isn't the world where she belongs. She probably has other family that would want to take her in. Someone better than random pirates from a strange world."

"I—" He cut himself off. "I think I would probably be a terrible father. I wouldn't know the first place to start with any of that. I can barely even take care of myself. But if it was something you wanted to do, I just want you to know that I'm willing to do anything to make you happy."

"First off, I don't think you'd be a terrible father, at all. And second, we're really going to have to discuss this later. I'm sorry, but I've got to go." She kissed him again and rushed to Mr. Threepbrush.

Out ahead, the column of smoke pouring from the volcano was thicker than ever. Above, the gargoyle looked down from his perch amongst the rigging.

Azure subtly scanned the horizon, but there was no sign of the dragon. That was good. Robin had said that Zoth-Avarex refused to help, and for once, Azure was happy about that. His showing up here now would ruin everything.

"Would you like us to dock now, Captain?" Mr. Threepbrush asked.

Before Azure could answer, the ship rounded a jetty and the bay came in-to view. Azure's heart dropped at the sight of another ship anchored near the dock.

"That's Captain Roberts' ship!" Mr. Threepbrush blurted. "What would you like me to do?"

Azure glanced up at the gargoyle, her throat suddenly dry.

"Go ahead and dock," she said.

THE TOWN OF LAVAVIEW was abuzz with activity. Seemingly all of the people on the island were gathered in the town square, every one of them wearing fancy clothes. Ladies in corsets and gowns, and men with their finest doublets, breeches, and ruff collars. Their clothing was nice but long out of style. Even Azure, a girl from the Nameless Isles, knew that.

Azure's plan called for Robin, Brisa, Blunderbuss, Mr. Threepbrush, Syl, and all four orc marauders to join her ashore. Unfortunately, the gargoyle, Kxa, followed close behind. Elijah had agreed to stay on the ship with Ori-ana, even though he wanted to come along and help. When Azure asked him to stay behind, he told her he felt somewhat emasculated. Azure was sorry for that but didn't see a better way around it. In the end, Elijah knew that his responsibility lied with the little girl.

"Welcome," a man said as he approached. Azure didn't recognize him at first, but quickly realized he was the leader of the small village they had run into. She remembered his name was James. Probably.

"You are lucky to have arrived here in time for the ceremony," James said, a wide grin on his face. "Mordo must smile upon you. It is a privilege most off-islanders don't get to experience."

The man, or the other people in the town, weren't shrieking in terror at the gargoyle's appearance. The people of this island were an enigma. They were progressive in their attitudes toward other races, but their fashion and religious practices were antiquated.

"So, you're about to go and sacrifice a virgin?" Azure asked.

"Yes. Would you like to meet him?"

"Not—"

"I won't be but a minute." The man rushed into the crowd and came back with a young man of about eighteen, as far as Azure could guess. The man was decked out in frills and lace and wore a crown of leaves on his head. He seemed much too happy for someone who was about to be thrown into an active volcano.

James made no formal introduction, instead, he stood and looked back and forth from the young man to Azure.

"So...you're the virgin?" Blunderbuss said, breaking the awkward tension.

"Yeah. I'm the virgin." He kicked at a small rock on the ground. "I mean, there was this one night with Susan when I got really close, but she had had a few too many drinks and I just didn't feel right about it. Then there was this time with Janet when we had a lot of mutual hand—"

"Alright, Joseph. I don't think they were asking for your life story," James cut in.

"Are you...happy about...being sacrificed?" Azure asked.

"Of course. It's a great honor to be chosen. My family will reap the benefits of the prestige I'm earning, and I get to be with Mordo, and all the other gods on the Ring. Plus, I'll get to...you know, with a maiden who is much more beautiful than any found in the Undering." Aside from a childish embarrassment about saying something like this to a woman, there was a hint of trepidation on his face and in his voice, but he hid it well.

"Oh." Azure forced a smile.

"It was nice meeting you. But I've got to get back to the procession, this being my time to shine and all." The young man waved and melted back into the crowd.

"May I ask why you are here today?" James said.

"Uh..." Azure realized for the first time that her plan was going to really mess with the islanders here. She mentally kicked herself for being so thoughtless. But maybe she could change this place while she was at it? Maybe make it better?

But people didn't always see needed change as better. She didn't want to play like she was one of the gods, but she didn't like seeing nice young virgins sacrificed either.

"We're here for the festivities," Kxa said, flying up next to Azure.

"Great!"

"And you're sure a red dragon will come out of that volcano," Kxa pointed, "and snatch up that virgin guy?"

"We have never actually seen it come out, to be honest. We, with our great sacrifices, have always forestalled our doom. In my lifetime anyway."

"But there will be a red dragon, right?"

"I would never dare to presume how Mordo will present himself, or what entity he will send to collect our tribute. But we think that the fiery red dragon that circled our islands was a portent of things to come. Without our tribute, many believe that very dragon will return and destroy the island."

"Yeah, that's what I heard, too." Azure squeezed her eyes shut, embarrassed about her inability to not blurt out unnecessary words.

The gargoyle looked to the smoking mountain. "It had better show up soon. I am sick and tired of being in this world."

James excused himself and returned to the procession. Once at the front, he grabbed a large mallet from a table and struck a giant, silvery bell three times. The crowd fell silent and began to organize into perfect rows. Joseph, the virgin, sat in a lavish, velveted chair that was hoisted onto the shoulders of four muscular men with connected bamboo poles. Even from a distance, Azure could see the trepidation showing through his smile.

Once everyone was in their proper places, James struck the bell one more time. In the silence, the resonance was almost eerie.

"For Mordo," Joseph called from his elevated throne, his voice cracking.

As a group, everyone began to march forward. They sang as they marched, a song that praised Joseph and his family, claiming that he would never be forgotten.

As the marauders watched the procession scale the volcano, Sir Terry zipped into view and landed in the dirt in front of them.

"M'lady." He made a deep bow in Robin's direction, then faced Azure. "Captain Roberts is here!" he squawked.

"We know," Azure replied. "But thank you."

"He's at the town's pub, right there." The raven raised a wing to point. He and a few men have taken over the place. His gargoyle, too. They're in there getting drunk and ranting about...you. Master Wakeman is in there with them. He's trying his best to placate them, but I fear their hearts are set upon revenge. He has sent me to warn you, as I saw your ship approaching from the roof."

Azure's eyes darted to Kxa, then the slow-moving procession. "Could he just wait until this whole other thing we have going on is resolved? That'd be really great."

"I don't know how I could accomplish such a task, but I shall try." The raven hopped toward the pub, about to take wing.

"Thank you, Sir Terry, but the question was rhetorical. I don't expect you to risk your life to make mine less complicated."

The raven bowed again. "I am at your service. Whatever I can do to help, you need only ask."

Kxa growled from behind them, staring up at the billowing black smoke.

Dragon Island

There was no pleasure for Zoth-Avarex as he rolled around in his treasure. His mind wouldn't allow him to let go and forget about the rest of the multiverse. Instead, it repeated annoying shit that gnawed at his newly developed conscience.

"Fucking consciences!" he roared.

For a moment, he was about to harden his resolve, as he had done many times before. He would retreat back into his singular goal of greed and forget everything else.

But once that gods-damned conscience had established itself, it was as stubborn as a team of delicious mules.

"But if I go to help," the dragon said to himself, "I'll risk..." He stopped himself short, unwilling to chance even saying the name aloud.

The truth was, that although Zoth-Avarex was a damn-near all-powerful being, there were others greater than him. And one of them had kept him, on and off, for millennia, as a pet.

The dragon spit, hating even to think that word.

His...master ruled over a realm universes away. He was a demi-god, with Old Magic powers Zoth-Avarex couldn't begin to comprehend. He was a jealous master, too, and he wanted his dragon back.

As soon as Zoth-Avarex had heard the word *Earth,* he knew what was happening. He could feel it from scales to bones. His master was trying to find him. He must have sent that gargoyle to try to track him down.

Fucking gargoyles.

Zoth-Avarex had jumped from world to world, trying to find somewhere so far away from his home realm that he could never be found. He had discovered an opening with that Pratt asshole. Hearing him try to summon dragons with his pathetic understanding of magic, Zoth-Avarex had whispered his own name into Pratt's mind from across realms. He hoped that this place, the Undering as they called it, was deep enough into the backwaters of the multiverse to possibly never be found.

But the gargoyle had done it. He had gone to Earth, the last place Zoth-Avarex had unsuccessfully escaped to, and somehow tracked him down. Now all he had to do was show his handsome face, and that gargoyle prick would report back to his master.

The gig would be up.

What was the alternative, though?

If he did nothing, hiding on his treasure pile, Azure and the marauders could be killed. And if what that smart-ass Robin said was true, they were currently risking their lives for him. Could he live with their deaths? Could he possibly enjoy his vast treasure as the knowledge of what he'd allowed to happen ate away at him? It was just a gargoyle after all. He could beat one of them with both arms tied behind his back.

There was a pang in his gut. And although he was really hungry—he hadn't eaten in about a month—the pang was more than hunger. It was telling him to go and do what he could to help his friends.

The Dragon Returns

"You know," Azure said to the gargoyle, "I can send one of my men to accompany you as you follow this sacrificial parade. I'm sure you'll want to get a closer look at this Zovarex you spoke of. To really make sure it's him."

"My vision is better by far than any lifeforms in this plane. I can see fine from right here."

Shit! Azure did her best to not appear flustered. How were they going to cast an illusion spell with that gods-damned gargoyle right near them? Her stupid plan was already beginning to unravel.

She turned her head and rubbed the back of her neck as she considered possible alternatives. A shape on the horizon made her let out an unintentional yelp.

Zoth-Avarex was flying toward the island.

Azure quickly looked to Kxa to see if he'd noticed anything. Fortunately, he was staring up at the ever-increasing smoke.

"Robin," Azure whispered.

"Yeah?" Robin said from Azure's shoulder.

"Go east as fast as you possibly can and intercept that dragon before he screws everything up, here."

Robin looked east, then said, "What an idiot," in a low voice. She looked to the gargoyle, who was still entranced by the smoke, then took off without another word.

Sir Terry watched her go for a moment, then jumped up and flew after her.

249

Azure held her breath, willing the gargoyle to not turn and see them flying away, or to see the dragon flying in.

ROBIN FLEW AS FAST as her little wings could take her. She gained in altitude and met the dragon just off the east coast of the island.

Zoth-Avarex slowed to a stop, a quizzical look on his face.

"Can you turn invisible?" Robin asked.

"Yeah."

"Then fucking do it!"

"I don't take orders from you."

"Do you want that gargoyle to see you?"

"No."

"Then do it, now!"

The dragon vanished.

"Alright...good. Now, uh, follow me into the jungle on the other side of this damned volcano."

As Robin took off, Sir Terry changed course and flew up beside her.

"Where are we going, M'lady?"

"We've gotta hide this invisible halfwit behind us."

"I can fire when cloaked, you know," Zoth-Avarex said.

"Yeah, yeah. Let's land in between those two big trees ahead."

Robin dove down through the jungle's canopy and landed on a branch near the ground. Sir Terry landed nearby as the ground shook with the impact of the dragon.

"Did he see us?" Zoth-Avarex's disembodied voice said. "Was he following you?"

"No. I think it worked out." At least Robin hoped it had.

The dragon materialized in front of them.

"I thought you needed me to come help," Zoth-Avarex said.

"We did, but then Azure came up with this plan to throw the gargoyle off your track. And the *only* thing we needed from you was for you to not be here."

"Oh."

In the silence that followed, a curious kindness of capybaras wandered into view.

"So, what are we going to do, then?"

"Just wait here until we get the all clear from Azure, I guess."

The dragon shook his massive head and mumbled to himself. "Gods! It's like I'm an idiot sometimes."

"No. I don't think so," Robin said.

"You don't?" His face scrunched up in confusion.

"No. I wouldn't say it's *like* you're an idiot. I would say that, by definition, you're objectively an idiot. I also take exception to the inclusion of the word *sometimes*."

"Fuck you," Zoth-Avarex said through a grin.

Robin chuckled. "You set me up too easy, there."

"Yeah, yeah."

The capybaras moved closer, apparently unafraid of a giant dragon. Sir Terry stood stoic as well, looking all majestic on his branch. Robin admired his shiny black feathers.

"Well I'm hungry, and those rodents of unusual size," Zoth-Avarex pointed at the capybaras, "or whatever you call them, look mighty tasty. I'm gonna roast 'em up and pop 'em like chicken nuggets."

"No, you're not!" Robin said.

"Why not?"

"Because Azure would kill me if she knew I let you do that."

"Oh, gods. Now you're telling me what I can and can't do? I gotta eat too, you know?"

"I know. And I'm not telling you what to do, I'm just asking, please, not right now."

The dragon's scaly eyebrows scrunched together.

"I can't believe I'm even considering listening to a stupid little bird. How the mighty have fallen."

"She is not stupid, sir!" Sir Terry said, puffing up his chest. "I must insist that you take back your hurtful words and apologize."

"Seriously?" The dragon looked to Robin. "Who the fuck is this guy?"

"This is just how we talk to each other," Robin said to her raven defender, ignoring the dragon's comment.

"Nevertheless," said Sir Terry, "I cannot stand by as someone blatantly mocks a lady I—uh, blatantly mocks a lady in my presence."

"What do you suggest then, little crow?" The dragon grinned. "A battle to the death?"

"You have me at too great a disadvantage in that regard, and you know it, sir. Perhaps we can find another way to settle my grievance?" Sir Terry re-puffed his chest. "And I am a raven, not a crow."

"How about a battle of wits, then? A battle of riddles?"

"I accept. And if I am the victor, you shall apologize to the lady and re-frain from speaking to her in this manner henceforth."

"Agreed. And if I win, I'll talk to the little shitbird however I want."

Very reluctantly, Sir Terry nodded his head.

"I guess there are worse ways to pass the time." Robin shrugged, then got comfortable in the Y of a branch.

"If you would like to go first," Sir Terry said, "I shall cede the floor to you."

"That is very gracious of you." Zoth-Avarex bowed, then cleared his throat, letting out an unintentional burp of fire. "Alright, there are three crows sitting on a fence. An angry farmer shoots one of them. How many are left on the fence?"

"Well I don't know about crows, but if someone shoots a fellow raven whilst I am sitting on a fence with them, I will take wing as fast as anything. So, the answer is none."

"You're smarter than you look," the dragon said.

"Now I shall have a go. What is it that if given one, you'll have either two or none?"

Zoth-Avarex made a show of yawning, then said, "A choice."

"Very well." The raven was obviously disappointed.

The dragon held a claw in the air. "If a rooster laid an egg on top of a north-facing barn, which way would the egg roll?"

"Roosters don't lay eggs," Sir Terry said, triumphantly.

The dragon shook his head.

"I have another one," Sir Terry said. "Name me, and so you shall break me."

Robin yawned, and the riddle competition faded away to silence as she fell into a dreamless sleep.

Hostage

Azure prayed to the gods on the Ring that Robin and Sir Terry would escape undetected, but apparently, they weren't listening.

"Where are they going?" the gargoyle asked, just as Sir Terry disappeared among the trees.

A swirl of wind picked up dust, spiraling it in the air.

"They probably flew off to do what birds do. Didn't you ever get the talk about the birds and the bees?" Azure hoped she wasn't agitating him further.

Kxa looked into Azure's eyes, then the jungle where the birds had flown.

"I don't trust a word you're saying."

With unnatural quickness, the gargoyle lunged at Blunderbuss, and before anyone could blink, had him held by the neck about a foot off the ground.

Blunderbuss's face turned red as he struggled for air.

"Put him down!" Azure cried.

Surprisingly, the gargoyle complied. "I don't want to kill him, yet. But I'm going to hold onto this one until I see this supposed dragon for myself." He kept one arm wrapped around Blunderbuss's throat while eyeing the orcs, who were tensed and ready to attack. "Stay back, or I'll kill him like the insect he is." The gargoyle backed up several meters.

Shit! Azure glanced up at the smoke, which poured out thicker and faster than before. The last person from the procession had been engulfed by the jungle, and James, who was leading, could now be seen on the steep trail along the volcano's rocky side. The birds and the dragon were completely out of sight, so that was good, but everything else was falling apart.

The ground rumbled beneath her feet.

254

An explosion of sparks coughed up out of the smoke and rained down on the procession like Ringfall. A glowing red ember landed on Brisa's shoulder and she brushed it off with a yelp of pain.

Azure's gaze turned toward the pub. Thankfully, the door was still closed.

How in seven hells was she going to perform a Zoth-Avarex illusion with the gargoyle's beady little eyes staring her down?

"There seems to be a lot going on in that tiny human mind of yours," Kxa said. "Don't think too hard, you might hurt yourself."

"The only thing I'm thinking about is the safety of my crew. I'd like to get off this island and as far away from this apocalyptic scene as possible."

"As soon as I see Zoth-Avarex, I'll be gone from this plane and couldn't possibly care less about what you do. But until then, you're staying right here with me."

A smoking rock plummeted out of the sky and smashed a nearby palm tree to splinters.

"Are you alright?" she asked Blunderbuss.

"I've been wrapped in the arms of better, but yeah, I'm fine." He forced a smile.

Azure nodded, her eyes darting from Blunderbuss, to the volcano, to the jungle, to the door of the pub, and back. She looked to Brisa, hoping she would have an idea of what to do. But the look on her face indicated that she was just as stuck as Azure was.

A loud bang sounded from the right. Azure turned to see the door of the pub open and hanging from its bottom hinge. Wakeman Carlyle lay bloodied on the ground. Captain Roberts stared right at her, sword drawn and gargoyle floating overhead.

Captain Roberts

The captain seemed taller, and meaner, than the last time Azure had seen him. The look on his face made her knees weak. She had never seen a person so confident that he was about to thoroughly destroy his enemy.

There were three men with him, all holding pistols, and his conjured gargoyle flying just behind.

Wakeman, apparently not dead, stumbled across the town to his home and ducked inside.

Azure fumbled with the wand in her pocket, finally getting it out. Her hand shook as she pointed it at Captain Roberts.

The captain continued, stopping just ten yards in front of her, head and chest held high. "I, Captain Roberts of the *Widow's Lament*, challenge Azure Brine to a duel."

All eyes were on Azure. She wondered if they could hear her heart pounding as well as she could.

Scenarios played out in her mind, none of them ending well. She found herself considering whether it would be better to die from a magical bolt, a sword, or a bullet. She pictured the training dummy, whose head she had taken off with a bolt back on Pratt's galleon, and figured a quick magical death might be the best way to go.

Her thoughts went to Robin, to Elijah, to Oriana. She wasn't ready to leave any of them yet.

"No thanks," she said with a half-shrug and half smile.

"I reckoned you might try that," Captain Roberts's voice boomed.

Before anyone could move, the other gargoyle shot across the gap between he and Brisa, and had her in a chokehold similar to the one Blunderbuss was already struggling under. Again, the orcs menaced forward, but were held in check as the gargoyle placed a sharpened claw across her throat.

"Shit!" Azure shouted in pure frustration.

Two of Azure's crew were now held captive, and the procession was likely only minutes away from reaching the top of the volcano. What a failure of a captain she had turned out to be. She reached for the ship's steering wheel around her neck, realizing it was no longer there.

She looked to Captain Roberts, her expression one of someone who had already been defeated. "I accept, then."

"I thought you might come around."

"Let me guess," Azure said, "you're going to circumvent the unwritten rules of dueling *again* and not allow me to choose which weapons we'll use?"

"You know me too well." Captain Roberts chuckled. "It's a shame, really. In another life we could have made an unstoppable team. But in this one, you have to die, simple as that. We will be using swords, even though my favorite sword, the sword handed down for generations, the sword Griffin the Unrivaled once wielded, has mysteriously vanished from its scabbard." Azure knew, because Zoth-Avarex had told her, that the captain's precious sword now lay on the bottom of the sea. "We will fight with cutlasses, and we will fight to the death."

"And if I win, your men will release Brisa and get the fuck out of here."

"I promise, it will be done." He turned and gave the gargoyle and his men stern looks and subtle nods.

Azure tucked her wand away and gulped.

The Duel, the Virgin, and the Dragon

One of Captain Roberts's men tucked away his pistol and presented Azure with a choice of two fantastic cutlasses. She couldn't tell if there were any differences between them, so she just grabbed one. The pirate sneered at her, then handed the other cutlass to his captain.

"I have to admit," the captain said as he removed his coat, "that you bested me all those months ago. Of course, if it wasn't for that dragon, things might have turned out differently, but that's neither here nor there." He searched the skies while folding the coat and handing it to one of his men. "Since that day, my hold over these islands has slipped more steadily than I could have imagined. There was a mutiny on my ship. *My* ship! And after crushing it, I was left with less than half the crew I once had." He raised his sword, his feet already forming the perfect base of a disciplined fighting stance. "I respect the hell out of you, Azure Brine, but the two of us simply cannot coexist upon the Mirror Sea. I am willing to risk the wrath of your red dragon because I have no choice in the matter. It's either you or me, right here and now."

Azure glanced at Kxa, hoping he hadn't heard that bit about the dragon. He was still staring at the volcano's top and looked incredibly bored.

Knees shaking, Azure raised her cutlass. She had trained in sword fighting with the marauders for months, now. But she was no match for Captain Roberts and she knew it.

A sort of numbness washed over her, an acceptance that this was the end. She thought of Robin, and how sad she would be. She would likely die in the avenging attempt to peck the captain's eye out, but she would be ready for death.

Elijah and Oriana would have each other. Maybe he would even raise her as his own. He would do great, and they could make happy lives for themselves. Maybe her dad would help raise the little girl. He would probably be a great grandpa.

One of the marauders would step up to the captaincy. Any number of them would do a wonderful job. The *Adventure Ship* would sail on. The idea of the marauders would persist. It had to.

Azure's jaw clenched as she tried to push these thoughts away and focus on the fight in front of her. Her doom would not likely be forestalled, but she would try her best to hold onto life, for as long as she could.

Azure's eyes were drawn back to the volcano, as if any of that mattered, now. The procession had arrived at the lip of the crater already.

"Let's get this over with," Captain Roberts called, a curious hint of regret in his voice.

The duelists approached each other in the middle of the town square as volcanic ash began to rain down on their heads.

ROBIN STARTLED FROM sleep as a flaming rock crashed into the ground only feet away. The smoke surging from the volcano had increased in volume and violence, but the raven and the dragon didn't seem to notice. Robin wondered how long she had been out, as the riddle contest was still going.

"I'm going on a picnic," Sir Terry said, "and I'm bringing an apple, a banana, a capybara, a duck, an egg, a...fish, a..."

Robin shook her head. That didn't sound like a riddle, but she couldn't possibly care less at the moment. Her mind was on Azure, and whether or not she was safe. She wanted to fly back to town and see what was happening, but she also didn't want to mess up Azure's plan in any way. And she didn't know if she could trust the stupid dragon to not do something stupid in her absence.

She hoped to see the Zoth-Avarex illusion coming out from the volcano very soon. Maybe then she could zip back and make sure everything was alright.

THE GIANT SILVER BELL could be heard from the top of the volcano.

The ceremony had begun.

Azure moved laterally, circling Captain Roberts while wondering what she should do. She didn't think she should attack first. He was too good, and probably waiting for her to make the first amateurish move so he could counter it and cut her down. On the other hand, if he came at her, she didn't trust her defensive skills either.

The captain feinted at her and she jumped back, eliciting guffaws from his crew.

"You tell your men to shut the hell up before I do it for them," Nargol said.

"Quiet, boys," he called with a smile. "This is a solemn affair between me and her. We don't need any clamor from the peanut gallery."

The crew members clammed up and took several steps away from Nargol.

Captain Roberts lunged forward, his sword cutting a wide arc through the air from Azure's left. She threw her sword arm across her body, smashing her blade into his with a hand-numbing clang.

He wasted no time, continuing forward with a stabbing motion that Azure barely dodged. Her movement had left her wrong-footed, though. She felt as if she might topple over and land on her butt, so she backpedaled several steps. The pirate crew members struggled to suppress their chuckles, eyes darting from the duel to Nargol.

"You're quick," said the captain with a grin. "But your footwork needs improvement."

Azure knew he was right. She widened her stance, heart bounding, and raised her sword.

ROBIN FLEW STRAIGHT up in an attempt to get any idea of what was going on.

On top of the volcano, the villagers were conducting their sacrifice ceremony. Black smoke continued to pour from its crater, with the occasional explosion of rock and molten lava. The virgin guy seemed to be getting a kiss on the cheek from every young girl on the island.

Robin tried her best to see the town, but the volcano blocked her vision.

They should have made that dragon illusion by now. Anxiety buzzed from Robin's head to the tips of her tail feathers.

She dove back down to where Sir Terry and Zoth-Avarex were still engaged in...whatever they were engaged in.

"Are you sentient?" Sir Terry asked.

"Yes."

"And you're food?"

"Yes."

"You're both sentient, and food?"

"Are you sure you want to use one of your twenty questions to ask something as redundant as that?"

"No, I just—"

"Shut the fuck up, you two," Robin said. She turned to Sir Terry. "Could I ask a favor of you?"

"Of course. Anything." The raven puffed up as if this moment was the culmination of his entire life.

"Could you sneak back to town and see what's going on there? I'm afraid if I go and that gargoyle sees me, it might make him suspicious and ruin Azure's plan."

"I shall leave immediately and return posthaste with news." He bowed, then leapt up and darted away.

CAPTAIN ROBERTS HAD pushed Azure back to a small copse of palm trees at the edge of town.

She could barely see the ceremony atop the volcano now, but it seemed as if the virgin was about to go in at any minute.

Azure's sword arm was tired and sore. She had difficulty gripping the hilt as the constant barrage of attacks were inexpertly parried away.

"Alright," Captain Roberts said between swings. "Time to get this over with."

He feigned a blow from the right, causing Azure to bring her sword up to block it. But then he brought his elbow up and whipped the sword around from the other direction.

Azure had no time to block as the blade sped toward her exposed neck.

As she tried to duck away from it, her foot slipped and she fell to her butt at the base of a palm tree.

Captain Roberts' sword bit into the tree with a loud thunk.

Azure glanced up to see the sword lodged into the tree's trunk. Captain Roberts grunted as he tried to pry it from the tree.

Without thinking, Azure kicked out, striking the captain in his knee. He cried out in pain and dropped to the ground in a heap.

Azure quickly regained her feet, circled around to Captain Roberts' head, and pressed her sword against his throat.

"Concede and I'll let you and your crew go."

"You'll have to kill me!" spat the captain.

"It doesn't have to come to that."

"Or…" The captain's grin rematerialized through obvious pain. "…are you even able to kill me?"

Azure made the best nonchalant face she could muster. "I'll kill you if I have to, but I'm giving you a chance to walk away." She hoped like hell he wouldn't call her bluff.

"You've never killed anyone, have you?" The captain scooped a handful of sand, not even trying to be slick about it.

Azure pushed the blade into the side of his neck, drawing blood. "Don't you—"

The air was forced from Azure's lungs as a blurry mass struck her from the side. She toppled to the ground, dropping her sword as she fell.

In a daze, she saw Captain Roberts' gargoyle floating over him, teeth bared.

"Ha!" came the voice of Kxa, who still held Blunderbuss hostage. "How pathetic! You've been on this miserable plane for far too long if you've grown to give a shit about your *master.*"

The other gargoyle appeared to be hurt by Kxa's words, but stayed in a defensive position over the captain.

Captain Roberts tried to stand, but his knee wouldn't support his weight. He collapsed back down, holding it with both hands.

The gargoyle approached Azure; claws outstretched.

Azure's sword was unreachable in the sand underneath the gargoyle, now. She reached for her wand, but apparently, it had fallen out during the duel at some point. She raised her hands and balled them into fists, hoping maybe she could get a good punch in before he tore her to shreds.

But the gargoyle stopped midair. Then, as if held by a giant invisible hand, he jerked to the side, flipped so he was parallel to the ground, then smashed down into the sand. He let out a guttural groan as he was lifted back into the air and smashed down again, even harder this time.

Brisa ran up next to the now barely-conscious gargoyle, hands out in front of her like she was holding an invisible capybara. She moved her arms up, and the gargoyle lifted from the ground, again. But when she realized that he was nearly out cold, she lay him back on the sand somewhat gently.

"Enough!" shouted Kxa. "How dare you treat a being of the seventh plane like that!"

In his frustration, Kxa raked a claw down the side of Blunderbuss's face, tearing through his ear and slicing a red line across his cheek.

Blunderbuss cried out and struggled to get away, but the gargoyle still held him tight.

"All you idiots are making this way harder than it needs to be," Kxa said, calmness restored. "I just need to see this supposed dragon so I can leave. I've had enough of all this petty drama. Now just shut up and—"

A flash of black and yellow streaked across the sky, almost too fast to see. There was a percussive sound, and Kxa let go of Blunderbuss, clasping his hands to his ears.

Another flash of black and yellow, and another. Before Azure could take a breath, the sky swam with tiddly dragons. They all seemed to have the same objective; attack Blunderbuss's captor.

Kxa fell from the air, claws still covering his ears. The tiddly dragons continued their relentless attack, and soon the gargoyle was brought to his knees. His eyes lost focus as the little creatures bombarded him from all sides.

Blunderbuss stumbled away, covering his ears, as well.

Azure looked to the volcano. She was sure the virgin was about to be tossed into it.

"Cover me," she said, as subtly as possible, to the marauders.

The four orcs formed a line between Kxa and Azure, trying their best to seem as if they weren't forming a line between Kxa and Azure.

She sprinted to her wand and scooped it up from the sand.

Brisa, Blunderbuss, and Syl surrounded Azure, each of them touching her shoulders or back.

She focused on the volcano's crater, aimed her wand, and imagined Zoth-Avarex. She could feel the marauders' magical power surging through her chest. She closed her eyes and visualized the big red dragon emerging from the smoking volcano.

When she opened her eyes, her illusion was manifesting. Her magic was far from perfect, but it was good enough, hopefully.

The great red dragon crawled out of the crater. It looked a lot like Zoth-Avarex but was covered in fiery sparks, much like the dragon that had circled the island days before. Azure figured it would be a good touch and a way to tie the two dragons together in everyone's minds.

The procession on top of the volcano all took frightened steps back. Azure could have sworn she heard the virgin scream from all the way down at the bottom of the mountain.

On a whim, Azure meddled in the island's affairs.

"No more virgin sacrifices," the dragon said, so loud she could hear it clearly from the beach.

Azure made the dragon wave to the procession, then sink back down into the volcano. In seconds the illusion had vanished back into the thick black smoke.

Azure stashed her wand in a pocket, then glanced at Kxa. He stared up at the volcano, claws still clasped over his ears and a look of utter frustration on his face.

Gargoyles

"That was the dragon?" Kxa said in disbelief.

"Yeah," said Azure. "Looked like a dragon to me."

"Shut up," he snapped. "I'm asking my fellow gargoyle."

Still dazed and on the ground, Zra said, "I didn't get a great look, but I'm sure that was him. Even sounded like him."

Blunderbuss extended his arms out to his sides, and within seconds they were covered in adorable tiddly dragons.

"Thank you for coming to my rescue," he said to them. "It's bacon for every one of you tonight."

Azure could have sworn they understood him.

Kxa looked as if he might rage on anyone nearby. Nargol and Orok stepped toward him, hands up and ready.

"That was obviously an illusion," he said. "Not even a very good one. Couldn't any of you see that?"

"I don't know," Azure said, cognizant that she shouldn't overact or say too much.

"Shit! It was probably some human on this island who created this whole myth around a dragon and a volcano in order to exert some kind of control over the people here."

"Why would anyone do that?"

"Why do humans do anything they do? I mean, they do that kind of shit all the time."

Azure kept her mouth shut.

"All I know is that wasn't Zoth-Avarex." Kxa shook his head.

"Oh...well, sorry. I thought that was who you were looking for."

267

"I should have known those idiots from Earth would lead me astray," the gargoyle said to himself. "Now I gotta start back at square one."

He turned and took wing, but didn't make it far before spinning back around.

"You!" he said, looking at Captain Roberts, who was still sitting in the sand. "Pathetic pirate guy."

Captain Roberts grunted.

"Release Zra from his bindings. I can't stand to see one of my own in such a pathetic state. He needs to get back home."

"I'm not going to do that," Captain Roberts said. "I'll need him now more than ever."

Kxa swooped over to the captain, grabbed him under his arms, and shot straight up into the air, at least thirty feet high.

At first, Captain Roberts tried to squirm away, but quickly must have realized what a poor choice of action that was.

"You have two options," Kxa said, "release the gargoyle you conjured from his bindings, or fall to your death, or, at the very least, an extremely painful maiming. You have five...whatever you idiots use to measure time as you experience it."

"Seconds?" offered a panicked Captain Roberts.

"Yes, seconds."

"I hereby release the bindings I have placed on the gargoyle called Zra!"

Kxa looked down to his fellow gargoyle. "Did it work?"

Zra rolled his shoulders and flexed his claws a few times. "Yeah, it did. I'm free."

Kxa shot up another thirty feet and dropped Captain Roberts, who screamed as he plummeted toward the ground. But the newly-freed Zra zipped under him and caught him as gently as he could. He floated to the ground and set Captain Roberts back down in the sand.

"Thank you," the captain said, a solemn and sincere look on his face.

"You're pathetic," called Kxa, shaking his head.

"Yeah, I very well might be." Zra shrugged. "Thank you for getting me unbound."

Zra whispered a word and vanished.

"Well," Kxa said, "On to the next lead, I guess. I hate all of you and hope the worst for each and every one of you." He made a gesture with his claws that had to be something lewd and insulting. "But I'm not wasting one more second in this world."

And just like his counterpart, Kxa disappeared from the Undering.

Collapse and Goodbye

Azure looked to the volcano, thinking their next move should probably be to get the hell off the island, but it had calmed considerably. There was still a steady stream of black smoke, and the occasional explosion of lava, but it no longer seemed to threaten un-forestalled doom for the island, and the sacrificial procession was making its way back down the mountain with the virgin in the lead.

Before Azure could utter a word, Sir Terry came shooting out of the jungle and landed on a nearby bush.

"Where's Robin?" Azure's heart dropped, as the appearance of Sir Terry without her felt like a portent of horrible news.

"She is well, I assure you."

Damned anxiety. Azure blew out her breath through pursed lips, eyes closed.

"I have been sent by the lovely Robin," Sir Terry continued, "to find out what was transpiring here in town."

"You missed a few things, but everyone is alright."

"The danger has passed? Can the dragon show himself, again?"

"Yes, he *could* show himself, but I think we should spare the people of this island from any more excitement for now."

"Shall I lead you to Robin, then?"

"That would be great. Thank you."

Sir Terry nodded, then took wing.

"Just a minute, though," Azure called. "We have to figure out what we're going to do with Captain Roberts, first."

At some time during all the commotion, Nargol and Orok had rounded up the pirate's crew.

Captain Roberts shot Azure a look, still sitting in the sand and holding his leg.

She wasn't sure what she wanted to do with him. But if she let him go free, he would likely come back for her in another attempt to get revenge. And he had even more motivation now.

Azure was fearful, but worried about her crew, too. If Captain Roberts did return to seek revenge someday, it would put the marauders at risk.

"Let's tie him up, take him to the nearest island with a League jail, and turn him in to the authorities, there," she said to the crew.

Captain Roberts cursed her name, but put up little resistance as the marauders secured him. The other members of his crew, with two orcs looming over them, scurried away without looking back.

"Alright, Sir Terry, lead the way."

Again, the raven took flight.

"You can all head back to the ship," Azure told the crew. "No use in hanging around an active volcano any longer than we need to. I'll round up Robin and we'll be on our way.

The marauders led Captain Roberts toward the *Adventure Ship*, but didn't get two steps before a particularly loud explosion sounded from the volcano.

Azure looked up in time to see a half-molten rock the size of a house falling right for them. Everyone scattered as the rock smashed into the ground next to Wakeman's house. It pushed up soil in a violent burst, immediately toppling the building into a pile of debris.

A baby's scream pierced the air.

"Shit!" Wakeman and his entire family were in that house.

As the baby continued to wail, the marauders rushed over to the collapsed structure. Nargol and Orok ran to one side, Kogar and Borug to the other. They began lifting the roof from the top of the pile, but it must have been extremely heavy, as they couldn't lift the entire roof at once.

Syl dove to the ground and belly-crawled under the lifted section of the roof. There was some muffled conversation, then Syl called, "You need to lift it a little higher."

The orcs strained to elevate the roof another forearm's length; their faces scrunched up with concentration.

"Good," Syl shouted.

Azure dropped to her hands and knees and peered under the roof. Syl had crawled into a tight space between two splintered wall support boards. Only his hooves were visible.

"Do you need help?" she called to him.

"Just a second." The muffled conversation continued, barely audible over the baby's cries.

Syl disappeared completely into the rubble.

The only sounds were the strained grunts from the orcs and the continuing rumble of the volcano.

Syl's head emerged from the darkness. He was laying on his back and sliding himself out with his legs. On his chest was a red-faced little baby girl, extremely unhappy, but unhurt.

"Wakeman's leg is trapped under part of a wall," Syl said as he scooted toward daylight. "I don't think I can budge it by myself."

Once out from under the roof, Syl passed the baby to Brisa, who tried to comfort her.

Although she was already weak from the duel and performing magic, Azure took a deep breath and shimmied into the space that Syl had come from. After getting past the debris, a relatively large space opened up in front of her. There was faint light pouring in from her left; just enough to see the forms of Wakeman and his wife, Hester.

"Is she out?" Wakeman said, voice shaky. "Is our little Anna safe?"

"Yes, she's out, and my crew is taking care of her."

"Thank the gods. Can you take my wife out next? She's unconscious, but still breathing."

"Move up a bit," came Syl's voice from behind.

Azure climbed awkwardly over Wakeman, taking a cramped place at his wife's head.

"We can't hold this much longer, Captain," Orok said from above.

"We're almost done," she shouted, hoping he could hear her.

Syl gripped the part of the wall that pinned Wakeman's leg. "Help me lift this off his leg."

"Just get my wife out," Wakeman said.

From her position, Azure couldn't get an effective leverage point. Ignoring Wakeman's pleas, she tried for several crucial seconds before leaning back and drawing her wand.

Head woozy, she did her best to focus her attention on the wall.

"Ready?" she said.

"Yes," Syl replied.

"Lift!"

Azure imagined the wall moving upward. Syl grunted as he lifted up on the boards. Wakeman, seeing that they weren't listening to him, did his best to lift the wall from his position.

Azure's head wobbled. Her vision began to go even darker. But she shook her head and refocused her energy.

The wall budged. It wasn't much, but Wakeman was able to pull his leg free before it came crashing back down.

Syl grabbed Hester's feet, and Wakeman thrust his hands under her armpits. Together, they made their way for the small opening.

Azure must have lost consciousness, because the next thing she knew, everyone was gone. The orcs outside were shouting at her to get out from the rubble.

She slapped herself in the face, dropped to her stomach, and began to slide through the exit.

The roof dropped, but stopped just before smashing into the back of her head.

"Sorry, Captain," came an orc's voice. "It's slipping. You need to get out now!"

The space was so tight now that she could barely move. Claustrophobia began to take hold of her, turning rational thoughts into pure panic. Azure thrashed wildly, pushing as hard as she could with her feet, but not getting very far.

The roof slipped, again. It was touching her back, now.

Her vision darkened around the edges. She fought to keep her head up and continued struggling in vain to move forward.

A beautiful face appeared out ahead, like an angel coming down to take her to the Ring.

Someone gripped both of Azure's wrists and pulled her out from the rubble.

The roof crashed down just as her feet had cleared its edge.

Brisa rolled Azure to her back. She put her fingers to Azure's temples and whispered a word. The world became immediately much clearer.

"It's never easy, is it?" Brisa said, a warm smile across her face.

Azure blinked at her, then turned her head. Wakeman was holding Anna with one hand, and running his fingers through his wife's hair with the other. Hester's eyes were open, and there was the tiniest hint of a smile on her face. They seemed as if they'd be alright, and with the gold from his chest that Azure still needed to hand over, they could afford a new and improved house, maybe even out of the immediate eruption zone.

Azure pushed herself up to a sitting position and tried to catch her breath.

"Captain Roberts got away, didn't he?" Azure said.

Brisa looked around. "Yes. I'm afraid he did."

Azure nodded.

Behind her, the sounds of the congregation grew louder and louder. Eventually, she swung around to see them emerge from the jungle.

James walked right over to her. "Did you see that?" he said, as if searching for confirmation.

"Yes."

"We're not as crazy as everyone thinks we are, are we?"

"I suppose not."

"But I guess next time we'll have to sacrifice someone who isn't a virgin anymore."

"Uh," Azure said, "I don't think that's what the dragon meant."

"Of course it did." James' smile was manic. "Mordo no longer wants virgins, so we'll give him a more...experienced sacrifice from now on."

Azure shook her head.

"IT SHOULD BE JUST A little further," said Sir Terry as he flew through the jungle.

He had been leading Azure and Syl for at least half an hour. Much of Azure's energy had returned, but she was still exhausted and soaked with sweat. Syl had taken the lead and hacked his way through the dense underbrush. It would have been much faster, and easier, to simply send Sir Terry to fetch Robin and Zoth-Avarex, but Azure didn't want to cause any additional panic with another red dragon appearance.

"We're here." Sir Terry alighted on a high branch just ahead.

After a few more swings of the machete, Syl and Azure found themselves in a clearing. Zoth-Avarex was laying on his back among ferns. He turned his head, eyes half closed and nodded.

Robin zipped in and landed on Azure's shoulder.

"You're okay!" Robin said.

"Yeah. It was quite a day. But we're all okay."

"What happened?"

Azure went on to tell the entire story. Zoth-Avarex rolled over and stood, paying very close attention to her words. When she finished, she could see the tension release from the dragon's body. He closed his eyes and let out a big sigh.

"You guys did all that, and all I did is sit here like a bump on a log." Robin shook her head.

"Your job was very important, too."

"My entire job was to keep this big idiot hidden. Not quite as heroic as what you did."

"But every bit as important."

"Thank you." Zoth-Avarex's booming voice startled everyone in the clearing. "Thank you, Azure. Thank you, Syl. And yes, even a thank you to Robin."

Robin tilted her head, quizzically.

"Sir Terry, I would have beaten you had our contest continued, but I thank you, as well."

The raven puffed with pride.

The dragon turned to Azure. "You did more than save my life today. You gave me so much more than you probably even realize. You've given me a chance to live without the constant fear of returning to captivity. I still don't fully understand why someone would risk their life to do that for someone else, but I'll never forget it."

"But you *do* know," Azure said. "You were on your way here to do just that, weren't you?"

"Well...yeah, but—"

"And you almost fucked up the entire plan by growing a conscious at the exact wrong time," Robin added, playfully.

"But everything worked out in the end," Azure said, trying to head off a fight before it started.

In the silence that followed, Zoth-Avarex scratched an itch between his eyes.

"You're welcome," Azure said. "You're a marauder, after all."

The itch apparently became more intense.

"Do you want me to roast Captain Roberts?" the dragon said, the itch now gone.

Azure considered for the span of a heartbeat, then said, "No." Although he was going to be a liability, and a danger to her and the crew as long as he lived, she wasn't capable of ordering anyone's death like that. He would have to be dealt with whenever the time came, as anxiety-inducing as that was.

"Alright, well...thanks again. I can only handle so much of this sentimental shit in one sitting, so I'm gonna head back to the old treasure pile if it's all the same to you."

"See you later." Azure waved.

"See ya, stupid." Robin nodded.

"Goodbye, shitbird."

Sir Terry tried to protest, but the dragon leapt into the air and flew away in a gale force rush of wind.

The Crossbow

Zoth-Avarex gazed up at the Ring as he flew leisurely toward his treasure. "So, this is home now," he said to himself, failing to suppress a smile.

This world, what they called the Undering, was the only place in the multiverse where he could be sure to stay safe from his master's view. It seemed too good to be true. A beautiful planet with an awe-inspiring ring overhead and a completely isolated island covered in treasure. And, he supposed, a group of beings who he truly considered to be his friends, as strange as that was.

He didn't deserve to fall into a place this perfect. The gods knew he had caused enough death and destruction in his life to earn a place in whichever hell humans could imagine. But guilt was a useless emotion, not that he felt any. And in a cruel, uncaring multiverse, concepts like *deserving* were meaningless. He had seen enough people who deserved the world get absolutely nothing, and enough people who deserved shit sandwiches get the world. What he deserved didn't matter. He was here, and it was damn near perfect.

The sound of waves crashing against the rocks below and the wonderful smell of laze filled the air. It reminded him of the place he was born. Volcanos as big as—

An incredible pain shot through the right side of his neck. Bright red blood sprayed into the clear blue sky. The great dragon tumbled down and to the left as he tried to regain his bearings. A palm tree-sized shaft of polished wood protruded from his neck, and a monstrous metal point stuck out the other side.

As he fell, he momentarily locked on to the source of the attack. Captain Roberts's ship was anchored not more than a hundred feet below. Pirates aboard gave an almost-inaudible cheer. They were gathered around some kind of giant crossbow.

Nearing the water, Zoth-Avarex strained to right himself, flapping his wings with every ounce of strength he could muster. He slowed his decent, but couldn't stop himself from crashing into the sea.

The blood was easier to see underwater. It gushed out at a disturbing pace, clouding the water with red all around him. He raised a claw to the crossbow bolt, gripped the sharp metal point, and pulled the entire length of the shaft through his neck. He roared in unbearable pain as the fletching passed through the wound. Bubbles mingled with blood as they raced to the surface in an effervescent rush. Zoth-Avarex pressed a claw on either side of the wound and used his wings to push himself into the air above. When his head was finally out of the water, he gulped a lungful while trying to orient himself to the closest piece of land, feeling dangerously weak already.

How the fuck could this have happened? He had been so wrapped up in celebrating his fortuitous new lot in life that he had paid absolutely zero attention to the world around him. It would have taken the bare minimum of awareness to notice that crossbow bolt and dodge it. At the very least he could have activated his magical shield protection, because even though he liked to brag about his impenetrable scales, the truth, obviously, was that they weren't.

And how the fuck did they even make that shot, anyway? That had to be about a one in a million chance. They should have never reached him with that thing. The whole idea was idiotic. Anyone with half a bird's brain should have known it wouldn't work.

But it did work.

What a ridiculous and humiliating way to be taken down. He shouldn't have tempted fate with all those thoughts of finally being happy and free.

With every move excruciating, the dragon made his way toward the shore. His vision darkened with each passing moment. Barely able to keep his head above water, he pushed on.

Mercifully, he felt the rocky shore scraping underneath him. He dragged himself up out of the water as relentless waves crashed over his head. Once on dry land, he turned to his back and focused all the energy he had left on his wound. The blood loss had slowed, but not enough to sustain life for much longer. His vision was getting darker, his body weaker. Exsanguination had robbed him of conscious thought and the ability to make meaningful movements.

Gasping for air—the Ring above not more than a silvery blur across the blue sky—Zoth-Avarex closed his eyes and sunk into darkness.

Oriana

There was much to celebrate, but Azure didn't partake with the rest of the crew. Instead, she and Elijah took Oriana to the bow of the ship to talk. The night air was calm, and they could see the orange glow of the volcano behind them. The Ring shone bright overhead, and a small fleet of ciguapa ships lit the horizon to the east.

Azure gulped. She was absolutely not ready for this, but there was no way she could turn away from it.

"Oriana..." Azure found she didn't know how to start. She looked to Elijah, but he deferred back to her.

Azure took the portal knife out from a makeshift case that Blunderbuss had made.

"Would you like to go back to your home world, now? We know your parents are...gone. But do you have other relations you could live with?"

Oriana looked hurt. "No. I don't have anybody like that."

"No aunts or uncles? Or grandparents?"

"I only know one grandpa, and he's mean."

A feeling of relief washed over Azure. When the time came, she didn't know if dread or relief would win out, but now she had her answer. This was the right thing. Not only from a moral perspective, but a simple feeling, as well. The fire in her chest had been pointing her in this direction all along. Fear and anxiety had tried to dampen the fire and redirect her, but she had overcome both. She closed her eyes and tried to keep a straight face.

"Well...I'm sorry about that, but I'm also kinda glad to hear it."

A glimmer of hope shone on Oriana's little face, but she pushed it away quickly. "Why?" she asked.

"Do you remember when we first met, in the jungle, when you had all those capybaras protecting you?"

"Yes."

"Do you remember the first time you held my hand?"

"Yeah. I couldn't understand you."

Azure smiled. "And I couldn't understand you, either. But when you rushed out of your hiding place and took my hand, I felt something I had never felt before."

"What?"

"It's hard to explain, but I just knew that you were special. There was a fire in my chest, like Brisa talks about, and something like the thrum of energy I get when I do magic."

"But why were you glad to hear that I don't have any relatives?" Oriana was clearly trying to draw a more straightforward answer from her.

Azure gulped again. "Because, Little Treasure...Elijah and I were wondering if you would like to stay here with us. And we could maybe be a...family...together."

Tears began to pool in Oriana's eyes.

"I know it won't be—"

Oriana rushed forward and hugged Azure's thighs.

Azure knelt on the deck and wrapped the little girl in her arms. Elijah did the same, enveloping both of them in a strong embrace.

So many things raced through Azure's mind. Was it right to take her from the world she was born into? Would Azure be a good parent? Was a life at sea fit for a child? But none of that really mattered in this moment. She knew she had made the right decision by the warmness in her chest and the smile on Oriana's lips.

The crew erupted in excitement. At first, Azure figured they had been watching her and Elijah with Oriana, but when she looked up, the marauders all had their heads tilted back, ogling the sky.

Azure turned and faced the most brilliant show of Ringfall she'd ever seen. Showers of bright sparks cascaded over the sea like a fiery waterfall, like a fireworks display made for the gods themselves.

The three of them stood, Elijah and Azure on either side of the little girl, watching the sparks dance across the night sky.

If this wasn't a sign that they'd made the right choice, then nothing would be. Azure's belief in the gods, which had been waning since her childhood, moved in the opposite direction.

Eventually, the Ringfall faded away and the new family turned to the crew.

"Marauders," Azure called, immediately capturing their attention. "We have an announcement to make."

A gentle hubbub spread through the crew.

"Elijah and I have decided to...adopt Oriana." She held up the little girl's hand. "Welcome the newest marauder!"

The crew gave a raucous cheer as Oriana looked up to Azure. Her eyes were red and wet, but her face shone with pure joy.

Robin flew over and landed on the rail next to Oriana. "Welcome to the crew," she said, sounding only slightly forced. "And welcome to the family." Robin flew to Oriana's shoulder and nuzzled her cheek for a fraction of a second, then she was off into the sails with Sir Terry, who had come along with them for the night.

Azure had a feeling that this moment might be the best she had ever experienced, and likely would ever experience. It was almost too perfect, which sent an anxious chill through her chest.

Shaking off the unbidden thought, Azure called, "I need to borrow a knife," to the crew.

Nargol stepped forward and handed Azure something that looked much closer to a sword.

"Oriana, could you put your back against the mizzenmast, please?" Azure pointed to the nearby mast.

Oriana did as she was asked.

"Stand up nice and straight."

Again, the little girl complied.

Azure gently placed the flat part of the sword knife on top of Oriana's head with the sharp edge touching the wood of the mast.

"Alright, you can move out, now."

As Oriana stepped away, Azure began to carve a horizontal line into the mast. When the line was nice and visible, she carved Oriana's name and the date.

As she worked, Azure's eyes filled with tears.

She was taken back to her childhood, at the inn, when her parents used to mark her height along the door frame. Her mom used to act like every inch Azure grew was an accomplishment to be commended and celebrated, like she had grown through mere force of will. Her mom had always strived to make her feel special, to make her sure she knew that she was loved. The woman was flawed as a person, but she did nothing short of her best at being a good mother.

Azure would do her best with Oriana, and she hoped it would be good enough. She knew she was flawed, too, but she would try, with everything she had, to emulate all the best parts of her mother. She would make Oriana feel special, and loved above all else. She would give her a good life. She had to.

"Do me next!" Nargol said, backing up to the mast. "And then Morgak."

"Hold on," Azure said, wiping her face with her sleeve. "Let me get a barrel to stand on."

The crew laughed, then some broke into song while others took turns congratulating Oriana. The line stretched halfway around the ship, but Morgak didn't let that stop her from cutting to the front.

"You're staying?" She said. "Forever?"

"Yes." The two of them clasped hands and began jumping up and down.

"So, does that mean we're gonna be best friends?" the little orc asked.

"Of course it does!"

Forgetting about the line of well-wishers, the two friends ran off together, hand in hand, chattering at a manic pace. They stopped to engage in a quick sword fight using chicken legs that had been left at the bar, then settled down next to the Covingtons to pet their heads.

Azure felt strong hands pulling her into an embrace, turned, and rested her head on Nargol's chest.

"You're going to do great," Nargol said. "And when you have questions, you can come to Aunty Nargol, anytime."

"Thank you." Azure closed her eyes, a contended smile on her lips.

Her worries melted away as Nargol stroked her back with a giant, but gentle hand. Maybe a life at sea wasn't a normal way for a child to grow up, but she couldn't see being raised by the marauders as anything other than good. They would show her kindness and patience at every turn, they would do everything in their power to help in the hard times, and they would fill her life with song and joy. And even if it didn't work out, and they determined that Oriana should go to a proper school on land, they would always have a place in Barren to fall back on.

Azure gasped when her feet left the floor, opening her eyes to find that Nargol had picked her up by the waist.

"Alright, mark my height, would ya?" Nargol said with a chuckle.

Captain's Log: Meridian 13th, 137

D o we have any idea what we're doing?
     Absolutely not.
But are we going ahead full sails?
You can call *hoard* on it!

Epilogue

The wedding was perfect.

It happened on a gorgeous, calm day next to The Red Dragon Inn, overlooking the Mirror Sea and the back-to-normal stream of smoke coming from Amenaza Island.

Everyone she cared about had made it out, except for the Marauder King, who was busy with his play, and Zoth-Avarex, who she hadn't spoken to since the whole volcano virgin sacrifice thing. She felt a slight tinge of guilt for not using her summoning spell to invite the dragon but didn't think it would be his thing, anyway.

Azure's dress was a work of art, and even she had to admit she looked damned good in it, although the corset was starting to get annoying.

Elijah was the most handsome man she'd ever seen in his dark blue suit with a bare minimum of ruffles at the sleeves and collar. Oriana and Morgak did wonderful jobs as the flower girls, and everyone loved when Robin flew up and dropped the rings into the lucky couples' hands.

When her dad handed her over to Elijah, he had talked to her all the way down the aisle. "I made so many mistakes with you, and yet look how wonderful you turned out," he said, tearing up. "You're everything to me, and I look forward to seeing what crazy adventure you'll get up to next. As long as you're safe, that is."

Azure had blinked away the tears, not wanting to mess up Brisa's makeup job quite yet.

Now, as Azure watched Elijah do his awkward best to work the reception crowd, she couldn't wait to get him back to the captain's quarters. But there was a party to attend to, and a whole lot of already toasty people looking to sing, dance, and get toastier.

"We've really missed you, Az," said Kevan, one of her best friends from childhood, as he approached with Andrew, her other best friend from childhood.

"Yeah," said Andrew, "it's hard to keep up with a badass pirate captain."

"We prefer *marauders*," Azure said with a smile. "I miss you guys, too."

"Oh, sorry." Andrew threw his hands up, playfully mocking her.

"Did you know we're moving to Whetstone soon?" Kevan said.

"No! Why?"

"I'll give you one guess."

"Oh, of course." Azure shook her head. Bigotry had many different forms in Barren, and she understood their urge to get away from it.

"Anyway," Andrew said, "we'll catch up with you in a bit. We know you have rounds to make." He flashed her an easy smile, as if they hadn't been apart for all but a few days of the last year.

"I'll come find you two. I'm not done with you yet."

Her friends nodded, then headed for the open bar.

"Congrats, Captain!"

Azure swung around to see Mr. Threepbrush and Orok, arm-in-arm, with drinks in their hands.

"Thank you, guys."

"Yeah, congratulations, Azure," Syl said, holding the hand of a faun woman. "And allow me to introduce you to Ceda. I didn't get a chance to do it earlier, and you were so busy getting ready."

"It's no problem at all, Syl." Azure smiled at his date. "It's very nice to meet you, Ceda."

The two exchanged handshakes and pleasantries.

"And since you're meeting dates," Brisa said as she strolled up from another direction, "I'd like you to meet Mari."

Azure shook Mari's hand while staring, wide-eyed, at her. Azure would have thought it impossible for there to be someone more stunning than Brisa in the entire Undering, but now she was face to face with a woman who left her speechless.

As Nargol, Borug, Kogar, and Blunderbuss approached, a black blur dove down from above. At first, Azure figured it was a tiddly dragon, but as the blur landed, she saw that it was Nova with a note tied to his leg, again.

"I have another message from MK," said Nova, out of breath.

He untied the note with his beak. Azure picked it up and began to read.

Dearest Marauders,

I'm afraid I have nothing but bad news, but first let me offer my congratulations to young Azure and Elijah, and my deepest regrets that I was unable to attend your wedding, which was no doubt a wonderful occasion.

The news I send concerns Reginald Pratt. He has been broken out of jail with the help of Captain Roberts and some rich casino owner from Mirth Island. Many followers have flocked to him, and things are getting pretty bad here in Whetstone.

My play has been shut down due to ongoing violence and threats. Tis a sad, sad day for our islands...

I'm sorry to be the bearer of such dreadful news, especially so close to the happiness of the wedding, but I wanted you all to be aware of what was going on across the sea. And don't worry about me! I've got my dear Chastity, and we are being both smart and careful. I absolutely DO NOT need a rescue mission or some such thing (I know you're already thinking about it). It would be absolutely disastrous if you were to show up here right now.

Enjoy this joyful time in your lives, but I pray that you stay cautious, as well.

As always, I send you my love, and again, my congratulations.

Yours Forever,

MK

"Well shit," Azure said, tucking the rolled-up note into her corset.

Robin came in for a landing on Azure's shoulder. "What's going on?"

After Azure gave a brief synopsis of the letter, Nova began his dance. He glided back and forth across the ground in a way that was both impressive and ridiculous.

Robin let out a sound that was something like, "Mmmm," and began to fidget.

Just when it seemed that Robin was going to leap from Azure's shoulder, Sir Terry landed nearby, balancing a tiny plate of cake in his beak. He set the plate down, then looked back and forth between Robin and Nova.

For a moment, Azure thought the two male birds were going to launch themselves at each other and fight, but they simply continued looking at each other.

"Are you two...together?" Nova asked Robin.

Robin paused, but only for a second. "Yes. Yes, we are."

Nova nodded. "Does he treat you good?"

"He treats me like an actual queen."

Nova turned to Sir Terry. "Good luck to you, then, my friend."

"Thank you, sir," said Sir Terry in an even more grandiose voice than usual. "I too wish you good fortune in whichever endeavors lay ahead of you."

Nova nodded at both birds. "I'll see you two around."

"Bye," Robin said as Nova flew away, the slightest hint of wistfulness in her voice.

Azure smiled at the pleasant little exchange, but her thoughts were immediately drawn back to the letter. What was it going to mean for the marauders? Was there going to be some kind of war on the islands, now?

She shook her head. She wasn't going to let this ruin her moment. Elijah was looking too damned good in his suit for her to be thinking about Reginald Pratt. How much damage could a disgraced prison escapee do, anyway?

Azure looked around at forlorn faces. "Is this a celebration?" she asked.

When she received affirmations from everyone, she grabbed a bottle of wine from a nearby table, raised it in the air, and said, "Then let's celebrate!"

The marauders cheered, and a jovial feeling returned to the party as if it had never gone.

GETTING OUT OF THE stupid corset could have been a real mood killer, but Elijah made it fun with silly jokes and his awkwardness, which had never been so prominent.

Once the corset was off, Elijah tossed it to the floor next to the bed in the captain's quarters, then stood still as if he had no idea what to do next.

Azure stepped to him, pushed herself up on tippy-toes, and began to kiss him. Their bodies pressed together as Elijah took her in his arms, and right away, Azure could tell that he was into it. The two of them lowered themselves to the bed, never breaking the kiss, and only smashing their teeth together once.

Azure fumbled with the buckle on Elijah's belt, but eventually unclasped it. She pushed his pants down over his perfectly-shaped ass and ran the tip of her tongue across the side of his neck, eliciting shivers of pleasure.

They rolled, and Elijah took a position over the top of Azure. As she looked up at him in the candlelight, there was no doubt that she had made the right decision.

She closed her eyes and drew in a deep breath through her nose. She was so ready for this that it almost hurt.

Eyes still closed, she turned her head to the side, waiting.

"Shit," said Elijah.

Azure noticed that the warm, comfortable feel of his hand on her shoulder had turned cold and hard.

Slowly, Azure turned her head back toward Elijah's face and opened her eyes.

Elijah's head had become a skull, again.

He pushed himself up onto skeletal knees and said, "I'm sorry, Az."

Acknowledgments

Thank you to everyone I thanked in the first book x2!

This time, I wanted to take a moment to thank whomever it is that is holding this book. I really appreciate you. Being an "Indie" author is tough sometimes. It's hard to get the word out about your books when there are so many good books out there. So, thank you for landing on this one, somehow!

If you enjoyed this book, please give it a quick review. They are so incredibly important for indie authors, especially on that site that stole their name from a beautiful river and rainforest.

Thank you!!

Krrlockhaven.com
Twitter- @Kyles137
TikTok- @krrlock
Facebook- KRR Lockhaven

About the Author

K.R.R (Kyle Robert Redundant) Lockhaven writes humorous, fun fantasy books with ever-increasing infusions of heart. He lives in Washington State with his wife and two sons. When not writing or raising kids, he works as a firefighter/paramedic.

He can be found on twitter @Kyles137 or on his website, www.krrlock-haven.com